Austin Dobson, William Davenport Adams

Latter-day Lyrics

Being Poems of Sentiment and Reflection by Living Writers

Austin Dobson, William Davenport Adams

Latter-day Lyrics
Being Poems of Sentiment and Reflection by Living Writers

ISBN/EAN: 9783744787932

Printed in Europe, USA, Canada, Australia, Japan

Cover: Foto ©Andreas Hilbeck / pixelio.de

More available books at **www.hansebooks.com**

Austin Dobson, William Davenport Adams

Latter-day Lyrics
Being Poems of Sentiment and Reflection by Living Writers

ISBN/EAN: 9783744787932

Printed in Europe, USA, Canada, Australia, Japan

Cover: Foto ©Andreas Hilbeck / pixelio.de

More available books at **www.hansebooks.com**

LATTER-DAY LYRICS.

LATTER-DAY LYRICS

BEING

Poems of Sentiment and Reflection
By Living Writers

Selected and Arranged with Notes

By W. DAVENPORT ADAMS

WITH A NOTE ON SOME FOREIGN FORMS OF VERSE
BY AUSTIN DOBSON

London
CHATTO AND WINDUS, PICCADILLY
1878

𝕭𝖆𝖑𝖑𝖆𝖓𝖙𝖞𝖓𝖊 𝕻𝖗𝖊𝖘𝖘.
BALLANTYNE, HANSON AND CO.
EDINBURGH AND LONDON

To my Wife.

O thou most dear,—before thy feet
I strew these flow'rets fair and sweet;
  These blossoms, latest from the tree
  Of Britain's gold-branch'd poesy,
Now lie where all the virtues meet.

Nor will they wither: neither heat
Nor chill of passing Time can cheat
  The world of their rare fragrancy,
              O thou most dear.

Nor will Time banish Love, or greet
Thy charms with shadow of defeat:
  They bud and bloom, and still with me
  Their scent and loveliness will be;
Yes, Love will stay, though Time be fleet,
              O thou most dear.

                          W. D. A.

PREFACE.

SO far as the Editor is aware, this is the first attempt that has been made to bring together in one volume specimens of the serious poetry of living writers only. Other collections have been partially indebted to the aid of contemporary authors. The Editor was himself largely assisted by them in the arrangement of his " Lyrics of Love," and was wholly obliged to them in his " Comic Poets of the Nineteenth Century." But whereas the latter work was confined to the poetry of wit and humour, the present is devoted to the poetry of sentiment and reflection. It is therefore unique in aim and character, and will, it is hoped, receive a proportionately hearty welcome.

The collection does not profess to be representative of living poets in the sense of illustrating exhaustively their peculiar powers. The Editor's desire has been rather to avoid the poems which are generally adduced as specimens of the writers' style of thought and of expression, in favour of those which, whilst still characteristic of their authors, have the merit of being at least comparatively fresh and novel. To the best of his belief, this volume does not contain more than half a dozen poems which have appeared in any previous collection. Some favourite pieces may consequently be found absent from it, but, on the other hand, the book is full of lyrics which, if not familiar to the general reader, ought to be so, and need only to be read to be admired.

In pursuance of this effort towards novelty and freshness, the Editor has gone not only to the recent works of our more celebrated poets, but to the publications of several writers who have only of late years made their reputations. In consequence, many names appear in this volume which have not hitherto figured in such works, and the result, it is believed, will be agreeable to the reader.

Another feature of the present work is the attention paid, for the first time, to the late re-introduction into English poetry of old French measures. Some English specimens of these have been selected, and form the third book of the "Lyrics." Mr. Austin Dobson—in whose "Proverbs in Porcelain" they first attracted notice—has, at the Editor's request, kindly contributed a short "Note" in illustration and description of them, which will be found (the Editor believes) both valuable and interesting, even by those who may not altogether approve of the nationalisation in this country of the forms in question.

The arrangement of the poems is as follows. In the first place, the songs and other lyrics have been separated from the sonnets, which cannot strictly be described as lyrical in character; whilst the foreign forms have been gathered together in Book III., according to an order which enables them to be read in easy connection with Mr. Dobson's "Note." Further, in placing the poems in Books I. and II., care has been exercised in bringing together pieces which illustrate one another, either in the way of similarity or contrast in idea or form.

A few Notes have been added, and will be found, it is hoped, useful and suggestive; they have obviously no pretensions to the character of exhaustive criticisms.

The Editor has, in conclusion, to express his gratitude to the poets who have so generously placed their poems at his disposal, notably to those who have permitted him to publish several hitherto unprinted pieces (Nos. 182, 183, 206, 208, 210, 211, 213, 217, 219, 222). He has also to thank those publishers who have in like manner courteously waived their copyright in regard to certain of the poems quoted.

W. DAVENPORT ADAMS.

CONTENTS.

		PAGE
DEDICATION . . .	.	iii
PREFACE	.	v

𝔅𝔬𝔬𝔨 𝔘.

SONGS AND OTHER LYRICS.

NO.			
1.	Love, the Pilgrim	. Hamilton Aïdè -. .	3
2.	The Guest . .	. Thomas Ashe . .	5
3.	" Love is come ".	. Alfred Tennyson . .	6
4.	Love gives all Away	. Hon. J. Leicester Warren	7
5.	Sweet love is dead	. Alfred Austin . .	10
6.	Love's Votary . .	. George Augustus Simcox	11
7.	Destiny . .	. Edwin Arnold . .	12
8.	Rococo . .	. Thomas Bailey Aldrich .	13
9.	Dorus to Lycoris	. E. Clarence Stedman .	14
10.	A Chain to Wear	. Robert, Lord Lytton .	16
11.	" Hapless doom of woman "	. Alfred Tennyson .	18
12.	Before Parting .	. A. C. Swinburne .	19
13.	Parting at Morning	. Robert Browning .	21
14.	A Farewell . .	. Coventry Patmore	22
15.	" The Pity of It "	. Hon. Roden Noel .	24
16.	Auf Wiedersehen	. James Russell Lowell .	26
17.	Sudden Light . .	. Dante Gabriel Rossetti .	28
18.	" I made another garden "	. Arthur O'Shaughnessy .	29

NO.			PAGE
19.	"Oh, were I rich and mighty"	Lewis Morris	31
20.	Misconceptions	Robert Browning	32
21.	Ilicet	Edmund W. Gosse	33
22.	Gathered Roses	F. W. Bourdillon	35
23.	A Worm within the Rose	Alfred Tennyson	36
24.	Love	Robert Browning	37
25.	"Stay me no more"	Ernest Myers	38
26.	"A sigh in the morning gray"	Aubrey de Vere	39
27.	"Oh, love is like the rose"	Philip James Bailey	40
28.	"Along the shore"	Dinah Maria Craik	41
29.	She Came and Went	James Russell Lowell	43
30.	Never Again	Augusta Webster	45
31.	"What matter, O friend"	Alfred Domett	46
32.	Love and Friendship	Sir Noel Paton	47
33.	Dallying	Thomas Ashe	48
34.	Charmian	Robert Buchanan	49
35.	Not Love	Augusta Webster	52
36.	Somewhere or other	Christina Rossetti	54
37.	Outcry	Arthur O'Shaughnessy	55
38.	If	Christina Rossetti	58
39.	A Smile and a Sigh	Christina Rossetti	60
40.	"If ever, dear"	Lewis Morris	61
41.	A Love-Thought	Richard, Lord Houghton	63
42.	Nocturne	Thomas Bailey Aldrich	64
43.	"Shame upon you, Robin"	Alfred Tennyson	65
44.	Pansie	Thomas Ashe	66
45.	Evey	William Allingham	67
46.	Serenade	Alfred Austin	69
47.	At Her Window	Frederick Locher	71
48.	Love-Lily	Dante Gabriel Rossetti	73
49.	"Give her but the least excuse"	Robert Browning	75
50.	The Oblation	A. C. Swinburne	76
51.	"The bee to the heather"	Sir Henry Taylor	77
52.	A Daisy Chain	H. Cholmondeley-Pennell	78
53.	A Wild-wood Spell	Earl of Southesk	80
54.	Reine d'Amour	Francis Turner Palgrave	82
55.	"I thank thee, dear"	Frederick Myers	84

NO.				PAGE
56.	My Neighbour	. . .	Gerald Massey . .	85
57.	Blanche . . .	James Hedderwick .	87
58.	No and Yes . .	Thomas Ashe . .	89
59.	" Love within " . .	George Meredith . .	90
60.	"Like an island " .	Philip James Bailey .	91
61.	The Treasure-Ship .	Richard, Lord Houghton	92
62.	" Seek not the tree " .	Aubrey de Vere . .	94
63.	"In long enchanted weather"	Arthur O'Shaughnessy .	96
64.	A Song of the Four Seasons	Austin Dobson . .	99
65.	Wild Rose . . .	Thomas Woolner . .	101
66.	Daisy's Dimples . .	J. Ashby-Sterry . .	103
67.	Gertrude's Glove .	Frederick Locker . .	104
68.	Angelica . . .	William Sawyer . .	105
69.	A Garden Idyll . .	Frederick Locker . .	107
70.	November Snow . .	Earl of Southesk . .	109
71.	Dawn	Thomas Woolner . .	110
72.	The Tryst . . .	E. Clarence Stedman .	111
73.	In a Gondola . .	Robert Browning . .	112
74.	The Dial . . .	Edwin Arnold . .	113
75.	A Kiss . . .	Alfred Domett . .	114
76.	The Mountain Fir .	Earl of Southesk . .	116
77.	The Letter . . .	Alfred Tennyson . .	118
78.	Marriage Morning .	Alfred Tennyson . .	119
79.	" One so fair—none so fair "	Gerald Massey . .	121
80.	John Anderson's Answer	Hon. J. Leicester Warren	123
81.	Renunciation . .	W. W. Story . .	125
82.	Windle-straws . .	Edward Dowden . .	127
83.	Bagatelles . . .	Theophile Marzials .	129
84.	Tragedies . . .	Theophile Marzials .	130
85.	Majolica and Rococo .	Theophile Marzials .	132
86.	Baby	George Macdonald .	133
87.	To a Child . . .	Francis Turner Palgrave	135
88.	Paris à Maçon . .	Frederick Myers . .	136
89.	Unreflecting Childhood	Frederick Locker . .	138
90.	Naturæ Reparatrici .	Francis Turner Palgrave	140
91.	Flowers without Fruit .	John Henry Newman .	142
92.	Pleasure and Pain .	Richard, Lord Houghton	143

NO.				PAGE
93.	The Hidden Self	*Lewis Morris*		145
94.	"A genial moment".	*Richard Chenevix Trench*		147
95.	The Toys .	*Coventry Patmore*		148
96.	Loss and Gain .	*Richard, Lord Houghton*		150
97.	February .	*William Morris*		152
98.	March	*William Morris*		154
99.	April	*William Morris* .		156
100.	Spring is Coming	*F. W. Bourdillon* .		158
101.	A Spring Evening	*F. W. Bourdillon* .		159
102.	In Spring .	*Francis Turner Palgrave*		160
103.	"The year's at the spring"	*Robert Browning* .		162
104.	"It was in the prime"	*George Eliot* .		163
105.	A Glee for Winter	*Alfred Domett*		164
106.	My Star .	*Robert Browning* .		166
107.	"I would thou might'st not"	*Lewis Morris*		167
108.	The Unrealized Ideal	*Frederick Locker* .		168
109.	"Warm whispering"	*George Eliot* .		170
110.	After-Thought .	*Jean Ingelow*		171
111.	Isolation .	*Matthew Arnold* .		172
112.	The Solitude of Life .	*Richard, Lord Houghton*		174
113.	Not to Be .	*Augusta Webster* .		177
114.	"Too soon"	*Augusta Webster* .		178
115.	Nothing Lost .	*Lewis Morris*		180
116.	"Life knows no dead"	*Joaquin Miller* .		182
117.	Changed .	*H. W. Longfellow*		183
118.	"Like to the moan".	*Sir. F. H. Doyle* .		184
119.	Leafless Hours .	*Robert, Lord Lytton*		186
120.	"Oh roses"	*Christina Rossetti* .		187
121.	"For me no roseate garlands twine".	*Aubrey de Vere and Sir Henry Taylor*		188
122.	"I bring a garland" .	*Edmund W. Gosse*		189
123.	The Falling Rose	*William Cox Bennett*		190
124.	The Rose in October .	*Mary Townley* .		191
125.	Dover Beach	*Matthew Arnold* .		192
126.	Burdens	*Edward Dowden* .		194
127.	On the Shore .	*Augusta Webster* .		195
128.	"The waters are rising"	*George Macdonald*		196

NO.   PAGE

129. "O life, O death " . . *Richard Chenevix Trench*   197
130. Oasis   .   .   .   *Edward Dowden* .   198
131. The Epicurean .   .   *Sir F. H. Doyle* .   .   199
132. Departure.   .   .   *Coventry Patmore*   .   201
133. Before Sedan .   .   *Austin Dobson*   .   203
134. "O bairn, when I am dead" *Robert Buchanan*   .   205
135. "Girls, when I am gone ". *Edward Dowden* .   .   207
136. "Passing away"   .   .   *Christina Rossetti*   .   209
137. "Push off the boat ".   *George Eliot* .   .   .   211
138. The Undiscovered Country *E. C. Stedman* .   .   212
139. Not Yet .   .   .   *Beatrix Tollemache*   .   213
140. By-and-By   .   .   *Augusta Webster* .   .   214
141. After   .   .   .   *Philip Bourke Marston* .   215
142. The Sick Man and the Birds *Austin Dobson*   .   .   217
143. Rest .   .   .   .   *James Rhoades*   .   .   220
144. A Voice from Afar .   *John Henry Newman* .   221
145. "The world is great" . *George Eliot* .   .   223
146. "If but thy heart" .   *Ernest Myers*   .   .   224
147. The Sea-Limits .   .   *Dante Gabriel Rossetti* .   226
148. Violets .   .   .   *George Meredith* .   .   228
149. The Apology   .   .   *Ralph Waldo Emerson* .   229
150. L'Envoi .   .   .   *Dora Greenwell* .   .   231

Book II.

SONNETS.

151. The Singer's Plea .   *Edward Dowden* .   .   235
152. Shakspeare   .   .   *Matthew Arnold* .   .   236
153. Letty's Globe .   .   *C. Tennyson Turner* .   237
154. Love the Musician .   *Edmund W. Gosse*   .   238
155. Love Passing .   .   *J. W. Inchbold* .   .   239
156. Love's Quest .   .   *Philip Bourke Marston* .   240
157. Love's Answer .   .   *Philip Bourke Marston* .   241
158. Winged Hours .   .   *Dante Gabriel Rossetti* .   242

NO.			PAGE
159.	Broken Music . .	. *Dante Gabriel Rossetti* .	243
160.	Nightingales . .	. *C. Tennyson Turner* .	244
161.	Lilith . . .	. *Dante Gabriel Rossetti* .	245
162.	Love-Sweetness .	. *Dante Gabriel Rossetti* .	246
163.	The Bridesmaid .	. *Alfred Tennyson* .	247
164.	Spring Love . .	. *William Bell Scott* .	248
165.	Why ? . . .	. *John Godfrey Saxe* .	249
166.	Remembrance . .	. *John Godfrey Saxe* .	250
167.	"Let not our lips" .	. *James Hedderwick* .	251
168.	"I would not have " .	. *James Russell Lowell* .	252
169.	"Our love is not " .	. *James Russell Lowell* .	253
170.	After Death . .	. *Christina Rossetti* .	254
171.	Love, Time, and Death	. *Frederick Locker* .	255
172.	Hoardèd Joy . .	. *Dante Gabriel Rossetti* .	256
173.	Rural Nature . .	. *William Barnes* .	257
174.	"When man alone" .	. *James Hedderwick* .	258
175.	"There never yet" .	. *James Russell Lowell* .	259
176.	"It may be" . .	. *Richard Chenevix Trench*	260
177.	"I saw in dream" .	. *James Rhoades* .	261
178.	Below the Old House	. *William Bell Scott* .	262
179.	Projected Shadows .	. *John Payne* . .	264
180.	"Count each affliction "	. *Aubrey de Vere* .	265
181.	"Blessed is he " .	. *Aubrey de Vere* .	266
182.	Now or When ? .	. *Richard Wilton* . .	267
183.	Hawthorn and Wild Rose	. *Richard Wilton* .	268
184.	The Sound of the Sea	. *H. W. Longfellow* .	269
185.	"I ask not" . .	. *James Russell Lowell* .	270
186.	"I grieve not" . .	. *James Russell Lowell* .	271
187.	To Helen . . .	. *Sir F. Hastings Doyle* .	272
188.	Autumn . . .	. *William Allingham* .	273
189.	October . . .	. *William Cullen Bryant*	274
190.	Worldly Place . .	. *Matthew Arnold* . .	275
191.	Good Shepherd with the Kid	*Matthew Arnold* .	276
192.	East London . .	. *Matthew Arnold* .	277
193.	The Better Part .	. *Matthew Arnold* . .	278
194.	Immortality . .	. *Matthew Arnold* . .	279
195.	Development in Nature	. *William Bell Scott* .	280

NO.			PAGE
196.	Science Abortive	*William Bell Scott*	281
197.	Self-Deception	*William Bell Scott*	282
198.	Past and Future	*Emily Pfeiffer*	283
199.	Faith	*William Bell Scott*	284
200.	The Footprints	*Robert Buchanan*	285

Book III.

ENGLISH EXAMPLES OF FRENCH FORMS OF VERSE.

TRIOLETS.

201.	"When first we met"	*Robert Bridges*	289
202.	A Kiss	*Austin Dobson*	290

RONDEL.

| 203. | "Kiss me, sweetheart" | *John Payne* | 291 |

RONDEAUX.

204.	"His poisoned shafts"	*Robert Bridges*	292
205.	"With pipe and flute"	*Austin Dobson*	293
206.	"If love should faint"	*Edmund W. Gosse*	294
207.	"Life lapses by"	*John Payne*	295
208.	The Coquette	*Samuel Waddington*	296
209.	Carpe Diem	*Theophile Marzials*	297

RONDEAUX REDOUBLÉS.

210.	"My day and night"	*John Payne*	298
211.	"My soul is sick"	*W. Cosmo Monkhouse*	300

KYRIELLE.

| 212. | "A lark in the mesh" | *John Payne* | 302 |

xvi   *CONTENTS.*

NO.			PAGE

VIRELAI.

213. Spring Sadness . . . *John Payne* . . . 304

VILLANELLES.

214. "When I saw you last, Rose" *Austin Dobson* . . 308
215. "O summer time " . . *Emily Pfeiffer* . . 310
216. " Wouldst thou not " . *Edmund W. Gosse* . 312
217. "The air is white " . . *John Payne* . . . 314

BALLADES.

218. The Prodigals . . . *Austin Dobson* . . 316
219. " What do we here " . *John Payne* . . . 318

BALLADE À DOUBLE REFRAIN.

220. Prose and Rhyme . . *Austin Dobson* . . 320

CHANTS ROYAL.

221. The God of Wine . . *Edmund W. Gosse* . 322
222. The God of Love . . *John Payne* . . . 326

A NOTE ON SOME FOREIGN FORMS OF VERSE.—By
   Austin Dobson 331

NOTES TO THE POEMS.—By the Editor 351

INDEX OF WRITERS 380
INDEX OF FIRST LINES 383

BOOK I.

Songs and other Lyrics.

1.

LOVE, THE PILGRIM.

EVERY day a Pilgrim, blindfold,
　　When the night and morning meet,
　　Entereth the slumbering city,
　　　　Stealeth down the silent street ;
Lingereth round some battered doorway,
　　Leaves unblest some portal grand,
And the walls, where sleep the children,
　　Toucheth, with his warm young hand.
　　　　Love is passing ! Love is passing !—
　　　　Passing while ye lie asleep :
　　　　In your blessed dreams, O children,
　　　　Give him all your hearts to keep !

Blindfold is this Pilgrim, Maiden ;
　　Though to-day he touch'd thy door,
He may pass it by to-morrow—
　　Pass it—to return no more.
Let us then with prayers entreat him,—
　　Youth ! her heart, whose coldness grieves,

May one morn by Love be softened ;
 Prize the treasure that he leaves.
  Love is passing ! Love is passing !
   All, with hearts to hope and pray,
  Bid this pilgrim touch the lintels
  Of your doorways every day.

        HAMILTON AÏDÉ.

II.

THE GUEST.

LIGHTS Love, the timorous bird, to dwell,
 While summer smiles, a guest with you ?
Be wise betimes, and use him well,
 And he will stay in winter, too :
For you can have no sweeter thing
Within the heart's warm nest to sing.

The blue-plumed swallows fly away,
 Ere autumn gilds a leaf ; and then
Have wit to find, another day,
 The little clay-built house again :
He will not know, a second spring,
His last year's nest, if Love take wing.

THOMAS ASHE.

III.

LOVE is come with a song and a smile,
Welcome Love with a smile and a song :
Love can stay but a little while.
Why cannot he stay ?   They call him away :
Ye do him wrong, ye do him wrong ;
Love will stay for a whole life long.

ALFRED TENNYSON.

LOVE GIVES ALL AWAY.

" AND what is Love by nature ? "
  My pretty true-love sighs ;
  And I reply, In feature
   A child with pensive eyes ;

An infant, forehead shaded
  With many ringlet rings,
And pearly shoulders faded
  In the colour of his wings.

His ways are those of children
  Who come to be caressed ;
Or, as a little wild wren
  Who fears to leave her nest.

He is shy ; if one shall beckon,
  He hides, will not obey ;
He spends, and will not reckon,
  For Love gives all away.

He hoards to lavish only,
  And lives in miser way,

Now hermit-like is lonely,
   Now gallant-like is gay.

Slay Love, he is not broken ;
   Wound him, his hurt will heal.
More than his lips have spoken
   His cunning eyes reveal.

His sighs the still air sweeten,
   As primrose woods do May ;
His locks are pale, as wheaten
   Fields in the wan moon-ray.

His palm is always tender,
   His eyes are rainy grey ;
His wage-return is slender,
   For Love gives all away.

His aspect, as he muses,
   Is paler than the dead ;
He weeps more when he loses,
   Than he laughs when he is fed.

Love at a touch will falter,
   Love at a nod will stay ;
But armies cannot alter
   One hairbreadth of his way.

He trembles at a rose-leaf,
   And rushes on a spear ;
A thorn-prick and he shows grief,
   But Death he cannot fear.

The tyrant may not quench him,
    He laughs at prison bars;
The water-floods may drench him,
    The fire may give him scars.

Though thou lay chain and fetter
    On ankle, wrist, and hands,
He will not serve thee better,
    But soar to unknown lands.

He follows shadow faces
    Into graveyards unawares;
He reaps in sterile places,
    And brings home sheaves of tares.

One tear will heal his anger;
    He will wait and watch all day;
He scoffs at toil and danger,
    His last crust gives away.

He will strip off his raiment
    To make his dear one gay;
And will laugh at any payment,
    Having given all away.

When care his heart engages,
    And his rose-leaf gathers grey,
He will claim a kiss for wages,
    And demand a smile for pay.

HON. JOHN LEICESTER WARREN.

SWEET LOVE IS DEAD.

SWEET Love is dead :
    Where shall we bury him ?
        In a green bed,
        With no stone at his head,
        And no tears nor prayers to worry him.

Do you think he will sleep
Dreamless and quiet ?
    Yes, if we keep
    Silence, nor weep
O'er the grave where the ground-worms riot.

    By his tomb let us part ;
But hark ! he is waking ;
    He hath winged a dart,
    And the mock-cold heart
With the woe of want is aching.

    Feign we no more
Sweet Love lies breathless ;
    All we forswore
    Be as before !
Death may die, but Love is deathless.

ALFRED AUSTIN.

LOVE'S VOTARY.

·THERS have pleasantness and praise,
    And wealth; and hand and glove
They walk with worship all their days,
    But I have only Love.

And therefore if Love be a fire,
    Then he shall burn me up;
If Love be water out of mire,
    Then I will be the cup.

If Love come worn with wayfaring,
    My breast shall be his bed;
If he come faint and hungering,
    My heart shall be his bread.

If Love delight in vassalage,
    Then I will be his thrall,
Till, when I end my pilgrimage,
    Love give me all for all.

GEORGE AUGUSTUS SIMCOX.

VII.

DESTINY.

SOMEWHERE there waiteth in this world of
    ours
    For one lone soul another lonely soul,
      Each chasing each through all the weary
        hours,
   And meeting strangely at one sudden goal.
Then blend they, like green.leaves with golden flowers,
   Into one beautiful and perfect whole ;
And life's long night is ended, and the way
Lies open onward to eternal day.

EDWIN ARNOLD.

ROCOCO.

B Y studying my lady's eyes
    I've grown so learnéd day by day,
So Machiavelian in this wise,
    That when I send her flowers, I say

To each small flower (no matter what;
  Geranium, pink, or tuberose,
Syringa, or forget-me-not,
  Or violet) before it goes:

" Be not triumphant, little flower,
  When on her haughty heart you lie,
But modestly enjoy your hour:
  She'll weary of you by and by."

THOMAS BAILEY ALDRICH.

DORUS TO LYCORIS,

WHO REPROVED HIM FOR INCONSTANCY.

WHY should I constant be?
　　The bird in yonder tree,
　　　　This leafy summer,
　　　Hath not his last year's mate,
Nor dreads to venture fate
　　　With a new-comer.

Why should I fear to sip
The sweets of each red lip?
　　　In every bower
The roving bee may taste
(Lest aught should run to waste)
　　　Each fresh-blown flower.

The trickling rain doth fall
Upon us one and all;
　　　The south wind kisses
The saucy milkmaid's cheek,
The nun's, demure and meek,
　　　Nor any misses.

Then ask no more of me
That I should constant be,
     Nor eke desire it;
Take not such idle pains
To hold our love in chains,
     Nor coax, nor hire it.

Rather, like some bright elf,
Be all things in thyself
     For ever changing,
So that thy latest mood
May ever bring new food
     To fancy ranging.

Forget what thou wast first,
And, as I loved thee erst
     In soul and feature,
I'll love thee out of mind
When each new morn shall find
     Thee a new creature.

        EDMUND CLARENCE STEDMAN.

A CHAIN TO WEAR.

I.

AWAY! away! The dream was vain;
  We meet too soon, or meet too late:
Still wear, as best you may, the chain
  Your own hands forged about your fate,
        Who could not wait!

II.

What!—you had given your life away
  Before you found what most life misses?
Forsworn the bridal dream, you say,
  Of that ideal love, whose kisses
        Are vain as this is!

III.

Well, I have left upon your mouth
  The seal I know must burn there yet;
My claim is set upon your youth;
  My sign upon your soul is set;—
        Dare you forget?

IV.

And you'll haunt, I know, where music plays,
    Yet find a pain in music's tone ;
You'll blush, of course, when others praise
    That beauty scarcely now your own.
                    What's done, is done !

V.

For me, you say, the world is wide—
    Too wide to find the grave I seek !
Enough ! whatever now betide,
    No greater pang can blanch my cheek.
                    Hush !—do not speak.

ROBERT, LORD LYTTON.

XI.

HAPLESS doom of woman happy in betrothing!
    Beauty passes in a breath and love is lost
      in loathing :
        Low, my lute ; speak low, my lute, but say
          the world is nothing—
            Low, lute, low !

Love will hover round the flowers when they first
    awaken ; ·
Love will fly the fallen leaf, and not be overtaken ;
Low, my lute ! Oh, low my lute ! we fade and are
    forsaken—
        Low, dear lute, low !

                ALFRED TENNYSON.

BEFORE PARTING.

MONTH or twain to live on honeycomb
 Is pleasant ; but one tires of scented time,
 Cold sweet recurrence of accepted rhyme,
 And that strong purple under juice and foam
Where the wine's heart has burst ;
Nor feel the latter kisses like the first.

Once yet, this poor one time, I will not pray
Even to change the bitterness of it,
The bitter taste ensuing on the sweet,
To make your tears fall where your soft hair lay,
All blurred and heavy in some perfumed wise
Over my face and eyes.

And yet who knows what end the scythèd wheat
Makes of its foolish poppies' mouths of red ?
These were not sown, these are not harvested,
They grow a month and are cast under feet,
And none has care thereof,
As none has care of a divided love.

I know each shadow of your lips by rote,
Each change of love in eyelids and eyebrows,
The fashion of fair temples tremulous
With tender blood, and colour of your throat ;
I know not how Love is gone out of this,
Seeing that all was his.

Love's likeness there endures upon all these,
But out of these one shall not gather love.
Day hath not strength, nor the night shade enough
To make Love whole, and fill his lips with ease,
As some bee-builded cell
Feels at filled lips the heavy honey swell.

I know not how this last month leaves your hair
Less full of purple colour and hid spice,
And that luxurious tremble of closed eyes
Is mixed with meaner shadow and waste care :
And love, kissed out by pleasure, seems not yet
Worth patience to regret.

ALGERNON CHARLES SWINBURNE.

PARTING AT MORNING.

ROUND the cape of a sudden came the sea,
And the sun looked over the mountain's rim :
And straight was a path of gold for him,
And the need of a world of men for me.

ROBERT BROWNING.

A FAREWELL.

WITH all my will, but much against my
     heart,
  We two now part.
   My Very Dear,
Our solace is, the sad road lies so clear.
  It needs no art,
With faint, averted feet
And many a tear,
In our opposèd paths to persevere.
Go thou to East, I West.
  We will not say
There's any hope, it is so far away.
  But, O my Best,
When the one darling of our widowhood,
  The nursling Grief,
  Is dead,
And no dews blur our eyes
To see the peach-bloom come in evening skies,
  Perchance we may,
Where now this night is day,

And even through faith of still averted feet,
Making full circle of our banishment,
Amazèd meet ;
The bitter journey to the bourne so sweet
Seasoning the termless feast of our content
With tears of recognition never dry.

COVENTRY PATMORE.

XV.

" THE PITY OF IT."

OF OUR love may fail, Lily,
    If our love may fail,
    What will mere life avail, Lily,
    Mere life avail !

Seed that promised blossom,
Withered in the mould,
Pale petals overblowing,
Failing from the gold !

When the fervent fingers
Listlessly unclose,
May the life that lingers
Find repose, Lily,
Find repose !

Who may dream of all the music
Only a lover hears,
Hearken to hearts triumphant
Bearing down the years ?
Ah ! may eternal anthems dwindle
To a low sound of tears ?

Room in all the ages
For our love to grow—
Prayers of both demanded
A little while ago :

And now a few poor moments,
Between life and death,
May be proven all too ample
For love's breath !

Seed that promised blossom,
Withered in the mould,
Pale petals overblowing,
Failing from the gold !

I well believe the fault lay
More with me than you,
But I feel the shadow closing
Cold about us two.

An hour may yet be yielded us,
Or a very little more ;
Then a few tears, and silence
For evermore, Lily,
For evermore !

HON. RODEN NOEL.

XVI.

AUF WIEDERSEHEN!

THE little gate was reached at last,
    Half hid in lilacs down the lane;
She pushed it wide, and, as she past,
A watchful look she backward cast,
    And said—"*Auf Wiedersehen!*"

With hand on latch, a vision white
    Lingered reluctant, and again
Half doubting if she did aright,
Soft as the dews that fell that night,
    She said—"*Auf Wiedersehen!*"

The lamp's dear gleam flits up the stair;
    I linger in delicious pain;
Ah, in that chamber, whose rich air
To breathe in thought I scarcely dare,
    Thinks she—"*Auf Wiedersehen!*"

'Tis thirteen years; once more I press
    The turf that silences the lane;

I hear the rustle of her dress,
I smell the lilacs, and—ah, yes,
   I hear—"*Auf Wiedersehen!*"

Sweet piece of bashful maiden art!
   The English words had seemed too fain,
But these—they drew us heart to heart,
Yet held us tenderly apart;
   She said—"*Auf Wiedersehen!*"

JAMES RUSSELL LOWELL.

XVII.

SUDDEN LIGHT.

I HAVE been here before,
   But when or how I cannot tell :
I know the grass beyond the door,
   The sweet keen smell,
The sighing sound, the lights around the
      shore.

You have been mine before,—
   How long ago I may not know :
But just when at that swallow's soar
   Your neck turned so,
Some veil did fall,—I knew it all of yore.

Has this been thus before ?
   And shall not thus time's eddying flight
Still with our lives our love restore
   In death's despite,
And day and night yield one delight once more ?

DANTE GABRIEL ROSSETTI.

XVIII.

I MADE another garden, yea,
　　For my new love :
I left the dead rose where it lay
　　And set the new above.
Why did the summer not begin ?
　　Why did my heart not haste ?
My old love came and walked therein,
　　And laid the garden waste.

She entered with her weary smile,
　　Just as of old ;
She looked around a little while,
　　And shivered at the cold.
Her passing touch was death to all,
　　Her passing look a blight ;
She made the white rose-petals fall,
　　And turned the red rose white.

Her pale robe, clinging to the grass,
    Seemed like a snake
That bit the grass and ground, alas !
    And a sad trail did make.
She went up slowly to 'the gate ;
    And there, just as of yore,
She turned back at the last to wait,
    And say farewell once more.

ARTHUR O'SHAUGHNESSY.

XIX.

OH ! were I rich and mighty,
  With store of gems and gold,
  And you, a beggar at my gate,
  Lay starving in the cold ;
I wonder, could I bear
To leave you pining there ?

Or, if I were an angel,
And you an earth-born thing,
Beseeching me to touch you
In rising with my wing ;
I wonder should I soar
Aloft, nor heed you more ?

Or, dear, if I were only
A maiden cold and sweet,
And you, a humble lover,
Sighed vainly at my feet ;
I wonder if my heart
Would know no pain or smart ?

LEWIS MORRIS.

XX.

MISCONCEPTIONS.

I.

THIS is a spray the Bird clung to,
    Making it blossom with pleasure,
Ere the high tree-top she sprung to,
    Fit for her nest and her treasure.
    Oh, what a hope beyond measure
Was the poor spray's, which the flying feet hung to,—
So to be singled out, built in, and sung to!

II.

This is the heart the Queen leant on,
    Thrilled in a minute erratic,
Ere the true bosom she bent on,
    Meet for love's regal dalmatic,
    Oh what a fancy ecstatic
Was the poor heart's, ere the wanderer went on,—
Love to be saved for it, proffered to, spent on!

ROBERT BROWNING.

XXI.

ILICET.

WHEN first the rose-light creeps into my room
    And stirs the liquid gloom,
      My heart awakes, and sighs with its old pain,
      Its ringing pulses jar with their old strain,
     And Love, my lord and bane,
    Renews that wild desire that is my doom.

To free myself from him, I rise and go,
Down terrace-paths below,
    Whence watered gardens lead by winding ways
    To that green haunt and bay-environed maze,
    Where, in these summer days,
She early walks whose soul attracts me so.

Fool and forgetful ! Shall I cool desire
    By looking at those lovely eyes of hers,
    That passionate Love prefers
To his own brand for setting hearts on fire ?

O fool! to dream that what began with pain
   Could end it! Rather, noiseless, let me fly
   Out of her world, and die,
Where hopeless longing knows that all is vain.

                EDMUND W. GOSSE.

XXII.

GATHERED ROSES.

ONLY a bee made prisoner,
    Caught in a gathered rose !
Was he not 'ware, a flower so fair
    For the first gatherer grows ?

Only a heart made prisoner,
    Going out free no more !
Was he not 'ware, a face so fair
    Must have been gathered before ?

F. W. BOURDILLON.

XXIII.

A WORM WITHIN THE ROSE.

ROSE, but one, none other rose had I,
    A rose, one rose, and this was wondrous fair,
    One rose, a rose that gladdened earth and
        sky,
One rose, my rose, that sweetened all my air—
I cared not for the thorns ; the thorns were there.

One rose, a rose to gather by and by,
One rose, one rose, to gather and to wear,
No rose but one—what other rose had I ?
One rose, my rose ; a rose that will not die,—
He dies who loves it,—if the worm be there.

ALFRED TENNYSON.

XXIV.

L O V E.

O, the year's done with !
    (*Love me for ever !*)
All March begun with,
    April's endeavour ;
May-wreaths that bound me
June needs must sever ;
Now snows fall round me,
    Quenching June's fever—
    (*Love me for ever !*)

ROBERT BROWNING.

XXV.

STAY me no more; the flowers have ceased to
  blow,
        The frost begun;
Stay me no more; I will arise and go,
        My dream is done.

My feet are set upon a sterner way,
        And I must on;
Love, thou hast dwelt with me a summer day,
        Now, Love, begone.

ERNEST MYERS.

XXVI.

A SIGH in the morning gray!
And a solitary tear,
Slow to gather, slow to fall;
And a painful blush of shame
At the mention of thy name—
This is little, this is all,
False one, that remains to say,
That thy love of old was here—
That thy love hath passed away!

AUBREY DE VERE.

XXVII.

OH ! love is like the rose,
    And a month it may not see,
    Ere it withers where it grows—
    Rosalie !
I loved thee from afar ;
Oh ! my heart was lift to thee
Like a glass up to a star—
Rosalie !

Thine eye was glassed in mine
As the moon is in the sea,
And its shine was on the brine—
Rosalie !
The rose hath lost its red,
And the star is in the sea,
And the briny tear is shed—
Rosalie !

PHILIP JAMES BAILEY.

XXVIII.

ALONG the shore, along the shore
    I see the wavelets meeting ;
But thee I see—ah, never more,
    For all my wild heart's beating.
The little wavelets come and go,
The tide of life ebbs to and fro,
    Advancing and retreating :
But from the shore, the steadfast shore,
    The sea is parted never :
And mute I hold thee evermore,
    For ever and for ever.

Along the shore, along the shore,
    I hear the waves resounding,
But thou will cross them never more
    For all my wild heart's bounding :
The moon comes out above the tide,
And quiets all the waters wide,
    Her pathway bright surrounding :

While on the shore, the dreary shore,
  I walk with weak endeavour,
I have thy love's light evermore,
  For ever and for ever.

DINAH MARIA CRAIK.

XXIX

SHE CAME AND WENT.

AS a twig trembles which a bird
    Lights on to sing, then leaves unbent,
So is my memory thrilled and stirred ;—
    I only know she came and went.

As clasps some lake, by gusts unriven,
    The blue dome's measureless content,
So my soul held that moment's heaven ;—
    I only know she came and went.

As, at one bound, our swift Spring heaps
    The orchards full of bloom and scent,
So clove her May my wintry sleeps ;—
    I only know she came and went.

An angel stood and met my gaze,
    Through the low doorway of my tent ;
The tent is struck, the vision stays ;—
    I only know she came and went.

Oh, when the room grows slowly dim,
And life's last oil is nearly spent,
One gush of light these eyes will brim,
Only to think she came and went.

JAMES RUSSELL LOWELL.

XXX.

NEVER AGAIN.

NEVER again.   This shivering rose, that sees
      Its dwindled blossoms droop and fall to earth
      Before the chillness of the autumn rain,
Will bud next summer with more fair than these—
But when have love's waned smiles a second birth?
            Never again, never again.

Never again.   Oh, dearest, do you know
All the long mournfulness of such a word?
And even you who smile now on my pain
May seek some day for love lost long ago,
And sigh to the long echo faintly heard—
            Never again, never again.

Never again.   The love we break to-day
May linger in my heart unto the last;
And even with you some memory must remain,
But ah! no more.   The sunlight died away
Will wake again, but never wakes the past—
            Never again, never again.

AUGUSTA WEBSTER.

XXXI.

I.

HAT matter—what matter—O friend, though
    the Sea
    In lines of silvery fire may slide
    O'er the sands so tawny and tender and wide,
        Murmuring soft as a bee ?—

"No matter, no matter, in sooth," said he :
    " But the sunlit sand and the silvery play,
    Are a trustful smile long past away :
        —No more to me ! "

II.

What matter—what matter—dear friend, can it be,
    If a long blue stripe, dim-swelling and dark,
    Beneath the lighter blue headland, may mark
        All of the town we can see ?—

"No matter, no matter, in truth," said he :
    " But the streak that fades and fades as we part,
    Is a broken voice and a breaking heart :
        —No more to me ! "

ALFRED-DOMETT.

XXXII.

LOVE AND FRIENDSHIP.

SWEET ! in the flow'ry garland of our love,
Where fancy, folly, frenzy, interwove
Our diverse destinies, not all unkind,
A secret strand of purest gold entwined.

While bloomed the magic flowers we scarcely knew
The gold was there.   But now their petals strew
Life's pathway ; and instead, with scarce a sigh,
We see the cold but fadeless circlet lie.

With scarce a sigh !—and yet the flowers were fair,
Fed by youth's dew and love's enchanted air.
Ay, fair as youth and love ; but doomed, alas !
Like these and all things beautiful, to pass.

But this bright thread of unadulterate ore—
Friendship—will last though Love exist no more ;
And though it lack the fragrance of the wreath,—
Unlike the flowers, it hides no thorn beneath.

SIR NOEL PATON.

DALLYING.

DEAR love, I have not ask'd you yet;
   Nor heard you, murmuring low
As wood-doves by a rivulet,
   Say if it shall be so.

The colour on your cheek, which plays
   Like an imprison'd bliss,
To its unworded language, says,
   "Speak, and I'll answer 'Yes.'"

See, pluck this flower of wood-sorrel,
   And twine it in your hair;
Its woodland grace becomes you well,
   And makes my rose more fair.

Oft you sit 'mid the daisies here,
   And I lie at your feet;
Yet day by day goes by;—I fear
   To break a trance so sweet.

As some first autumn tint looks strange,
   And wakes a strange regret,
Would your soft "yes" our loving change?—
   Love, I'll not ask you yet.

THOMAS ASHE.

CHARMIAN.

ON the time when water-lilies shake
    Their green and gold on river and lake,
    When the cuckoo calls in the heart o' the
        heat,
When the Dog-star foams and the shade is sweet;
Where cool and fresh the River ran,
I sat by the side of Charmian,
And heard no sound from the world of man.

All was so sweet and still that day!
The rustling shade, the rippling stream,
All life, all breath, dissolved away
Into a golden dream;
Warm and sweet the scented shade
Drowsily caught the breeze and stirred,
Faint and low through the green glade
Came hum of bee and song of bird.
Our hearts were full of drowsy bliss,
And yet we did not clasp nor kiss,
Nor did we break the happy spell
With tender tone or syllable.

But to ease our hearts and set thought free
We pluckt the flowers of a red Rose-tree,
And leaf by leaf, we threw them, Sweet,
Into the river at our feet,
And in an indolent delight,
Watched them glide onward, out of sight.

Sweet, had I boldly spoken then,
How might my love have garner'd thee !
But I had left the paths of men,
And sitting yonder dreamily,
Was happiness enough for me !
Seeking no gift of word or kiss,
But looking in thy face, was bliss !
Plucking the Rose-leaves in a dream,
Watching them glimmer down the stream,
Knowing that Eastern heart of thine
Shared the dim ecstasy of mine !

Then, while we linger'd, cold and gray
Came twilight, chilling soul and sense ;
And you arose to go away,
Full of a sweet indifference !
I missed the spell—I watch'd it break,—
And such come never twice to man :
In a less golden hour I spoke,
And did *not* win thee, Charmian !

For wearily we turned away
Into the world of everyday,

And from thy heart the fancy fled
Like the Rose-leaves on the river shed ;
But to me that hour is sweeter far
Than the world and all its treasures are :
Still to sit on so close to thee,
Were happiness enough for me !
Still to sit on in a green nook,
Nor break the spell by word or look !
To reach out happy hands for ever,
To pluck the Rose-leaves, Charmian !
To watch them fade on the gleaming River,
And hear no sound from the world of man !

ROBERT BUCHANAN.

XXXV.

NOT LOVE.

I HAVE not, yet I would have loved thee, sweet ;
   Nor know I wherefore, thou being all thou
     art,
  The engrafted thought in me throve incomplete,

And grew to summer strength in every part
  Of root and leaf, but hath not borne the flower : .
Love hath refrained his fulness from my heart.

I know no better beauty, none with power
  To hold mine eyes through change and change as
     thine,
Like southern skies that alter with each hour

And yet are changeless, and their calm divine
  From light to light hath motionlessly passed
With only different loveliness for sign.

I know no fairer nature, nor where, cast
  On the clear mirror of thine own young truth,
The imaged things of heaven lie plainer glassed ;

Nor where more fit alike show tender ruth,
   And anger for the right, and hopes aglow,
And joys and sighs of April-hearted youth.

But some day I, so wont to praise thee so,
   With unabashed warm words for all to hear,
Shall scarcely name another, speaking low.

Some day, methinks, and who can tell how near,
   I may, to thee unchanged, be praising thee
With one not worthier but a world more dear ;

With one I know not yet, who shall, may be,
   Be not so fair, be not in aught thy peer ;
Who shall be all that thou art not to me.

                        AUGUSTA WEBSTER.

XXXVI.

SOMEWHERE OR OTHER.

OMEWHERE or other there must surely be
   The face not seen, the voice not heard,
   The heart that not yet—never yet—ah me !
   Made answer to my word.

Somewhere or other, may be near or far ;
   Past land and sea, clean out of sight ;
Beyond the wandering moon, beyond the star
   That tracks her night by night.

Somewhere or other, may be far or near ;
   With just a wall, a hedge between ;
With just the last leaves of the dying year
   Fallen on a turf grown green.

CHRISTINA ROSSETTI.

XXXVII

OUTCRY.

IN all my singing and speaking,
  I send my soul forth seeking ;
  O soul of my soul's dreaming ;
    When wilt thou hear and speak ?
Lovely and lonely seeming,
Thou art there in my dreaming,
Hast thou no sorrow for speaking ?
  Hast thou no dream to seek ?

In all my thinking and sighing,
  In all my desolate crying,
I send my heart forth yearning,
  O heart that may'st be nigh !
Like a bird weary of flying,
My heavy heart, returning,
Bringeth me no replying,
  Of word, or thought, or sigh.

In all my joying and grieving,
  Living, hoping, believing,
I send my love forth flowing,
  To find my unknown love.

O world, that I am leaving,
O heaven, where I am going,
Is there no finding and knowing,
    Around, within, or above?

O soul of my soul's seeing,
    O heart of my heart's being,
O love of dreaming and waking
    And living and dying for—
Out of my soul's last aching,
Out of my heart just breaking—
Doubting, falling, forsaking,
    I call on you this once more.

Are you too high or too lowly
    To come at length unto me?
Are you too sweet or too holy
    For me to have and to see?
Wherever you are, I call you,
Ere the falseness of life enthral you,
Ere the hollow of death appal you,
    While yet your spirit is free.

Have you not seen, in sleeping,
    A lover that might not stay,
And remembered again with weeping,
    And thought of him through the day?—
Ah! thought of him long and dearly,
Till you seemed to behold him clearly,

And could follow the dull time merely
   With heart and love far away ?

Have you not known him kneeling
   To a deathless vision of you,
Whom only an earth was concealing,
   Whom all that was heaven proved true ?
Oh surely some wind gave motion
To his words like a wave of the ocean ;
Ay ! so that you felt his devotion,
   And smiled, and wondered, and knew.

And what are you thinking and saying,
   In the land where you are delaying ?
Have you a chain to sever ?
   Have you a prison to break ?
O love ! there is one love for ever,
And never another love—never ;
And hath it not reached you, my praying
   And singing these years for your sake ?

We two, made one, should have power
   To grow to a beautiful flower,
A tree for men to sit under
   Beside life's flowerless stream ;
But I without you am only
A dreamer fruitless and lonely ;
And you without me, a wonder
   In my most beautiful dream.

ARTHUR O'SHAUGHNESSY.

XXXVIII.

IF.

IF he would come to-day, to-day, to-day,
  Oh, what a day to-day would be!
  But now he's away, miles and miles away
  From me across the sea.

O little bird, flying, flying, flying,
  To your nest in the warm west,
Tell him as you pass that I am dying,
  As you pass home to your nest.

I have a sister, I have a brother,
  A faithful hound, a tame white dove;
But I had another, once I had another,
  And I miss him, my love, my love!

In this weary world it is so cold, so cold,
  While I sit here all alone;
I would not like to wait and to grow old,
  But just to be dead and gone.

Make me fair when I lie dead on my bed,
   Fair where I am lying;
Perhaps he may come and look upon me dead—
   He for whom I am dying.

Dig my grave for two, with a stone to show it,
   And on the stone write my name;
If he never comes, I shall never know it,
   But sleep on all the same.

CHRISTINA ROSSETTI.

A SMILE AND A SIGH.

SMILE because the nights are short !
    And every morning brings such pleasure
Of sweet love-making, harmless sport :
    Love that makes and finds its treasure,
    Love, treasure without measure.

A sigh because the days are long!
    Long, long these days that pass in sighing,
A burden saddens every song :
    While time lags which should be flying,
    We live who would be dying.

CHRISTINA ROSSETTI.

XI.

IF ever, dear,
    I might at last the barren victory gain,
    After long struggle and laborious pain,
      And many a secret tear,
To think, since think I must of thee,
Not otherwise than thou of me.

    Haply I might
Thy chilling coldness, thy disdain, thy pride,
Which draw me half reluctant to thy side,
    With a like meed requite,
And I my too fond self despise,
Seeing with disenchanted eyes.

    But now, alas,
So fast a prisoner am I to thy love,
No power there is that can my chains remove,
    So sweet the caged hours pass,
That if it parted me from thee,
I would not willingly grow free.

    Nor would I dare
To ask for recompense of love again,
Who love thee for the height of thy disdain.
    Thou wouldst not show so fair
If we should burn with equal fire,
Instinct with emulous desire.

    Full well I know
That what I worship is not wholly thee,
But a fair dream, a pious fantasy,
    Such as at times doth grow
On yearnings of the cloistered mind,
Or the rapt vision of the blind.

    Scorn me then, sweet,
I would not thou shouldst leave thy lofty place;
Thy lover should not see thee face to face,
    But prostrate at thy feet.
No recompense, no equal part I seek,
Only that thou be strong and I be weak.

LEWIS MORRIS.

XLI.

A LOVE-THOUGHT.

ALL down the linden-alley's morning shade
Thy form with childly raptures I pursue ;
No hazel-bowered brook can seek the glade
With steps more joyous or with course
more true.

But when all haste and hope I reach my goal,
And Thou at once thy full and earnest eyes
Turnest upon me, my encumbered soul
Bows down in shame and trembles with surprise.

I rise exalted on thy moving grace,
Peace and goodwill in all thy voice I hear ;
Yet if the sudden wonders of thy face
Fall on me, joy is weak and turns to fear.

RICHARD, LORD HOUGHTON.

XLII.

NOCTURNE.

ITALY.

UP to her chamber window
    A slight wire trellis goes,
  And up this Romeo's ladder
    Clambers a bold white rose.

I lounge in the ilex shadows,
  I see the lady lean,
Unclasping her silken girdle,
  The curtain's folds between.

She smiles on her white-rose lover,
  She reaches out her hand
And helps him at the window—
  I see it where I stand !

To her scarlet lip she holds him,
  And kisses him many a time—
Ah, me ! it was he that won her,
  Because he dared to climb !

THOMAS BAILEY ALDRICH.

XLIII.

SHAME upon you, Robin,
   Shame upon you now!
  Kiss me would you? with my hands
    Milking the cow?
 Daisies grow again,
 Kingcups blow again,
And you came and kiss'd me milking the cow.

Robin came behind me,
  Kissed me well, I vow;
Cuff him could I? with my hands
  Milking the cow?
  Swallows fly again,
  Cuckoos cry again,
And you came and kiss'd me milking the cow.

Come, Robin, Robin,
  Come and kiss me now;
Help it can I? with my hands
  Milking the cow?
  Ringdoves coo again,
  All things woo again.
Come behind and kiss me milking the cow.

ALFRED TENNYSON.

E

PANSIE.

CAME, on a Sabbath noon, my sweet,
   In white, to find her lover.
The grass grew proud beneath her feet,
   The green elm leaves above her—
     Meet we no angels, Pansie?

She said, " We meet no angels now,"
   And soft lights streamed upon her;
And with white hand she touched a bough,
   She did it that great honour—
     What, meet no angels, Pansie?

Oh sweet brown hat, brown hair, brown eyes,
   Down-dropp'd brown eyes so tender;
Then what, said I? gallant replies
   Seem flattery and offend her;
     But—meet no angels, Pansie?

THOMAS ASHE.

E V E Y.

BUD and leaflet, opening slowly,
    Woo'd with tears by winds of Spring,
Now, of June persuaded wholly,
    Perfumes, flow'rs, and shadows bring.

Evey, in the linden-alley,
    All alone I met to-day,
Tripping to the sunny valley
    Spread across with new-mown hay.

Brown her soft curls, sunbeam-sainted,
    Golden, in the wavering flush ;
Darker brown her eyes are, painted
    Eye and fringe with one soft brush.

Through the leaves a careless comer,
    Never nymph of fount or tree
Could have press'd the floor of summer
    With a lighter foot than she.

Can this broad hat, fasten'd under
  With a bright blue ribbon's flow,
Change my pet so much, I wonder,
  Of a month or two ago?

Half too changed to speak I thought her,
  Till the pictured silence broke,
Sweet and clear as dropping water,
  Into words she sung or spoke.

Few her words; yet, like a sister,
  Trustfully she look'd and smiled;
'Twas but in my soul I kiss'd her
  As I used to kiss the child.

Shadows, which are not of sadness,
  Touch her eyes, and brow above.
As pale wild roses dream of redness,
  Dreams her innocent heart of love.

                              WILLIAM ALLINGHAM.

SERENADE.

I.

SLEEP, lady fair !
 Oh but thy couch should be
The fleeciest cloudlet of the summer air,
 The softest billow of the summer sea ;—
  Or that unforsaken rest
  I keep warm in my true breast,
 For thee, for thee !

II.

Dream, lady sweet !
 The moon and planets bright
Now thread thy slumbers with unsounding feet,
 Now drench thy fancies with unshaped delight :
  As my spirit fain would steep
  Thine, when only half asleep,
 This night, this night !

III.

Wake, lady mine !
  See ! are awake the flowers,
Their opening cusps bright tipped with dewy wine,
  And, buoyed on song, the moist lark trills and towers.
    Wake !   If thou must be away
    Nightly, let at least the day
  Be ours, be ours !

ALFRED AUSTIN.

AT HER WINDOW.

BEATING heart! we come again
    Where my Love reposes :
This is Mabel's window-pane ;
    These are Mabel's roses.

Is she nested?   Does she kneel
    In the twilight stilly;
Lily clad from throat to heel,
    She, my virgin lily?

Soon the wan, the wistful stars,
    Fading, will forsake her;
Elves of light, on beamy bars,
    Whisper then, and wake her.

Let this friendly pebble plead
    At her flowery grating,
If she hear me will she heed?
    Mabel, I am waiting!

Mabel will be deck'd anon,
   Zoned in bride's apparel ;
Happy zone !—oh hark to yon
   Passion-shaken carol !

Sing thy song, thou trancèd thrush,
   Pipe thy best, thy clearest ;—
Hush, her lattice moves, oh hush—
   Dearest Mabel !—dearest . . .

FREDERICK LOCKER.

XLVIII.

LOVE-LILY.

ETWEEN the hands, between the brows,
  Between the lips of Love-Lily,
    A spirit is born whose birth endows
      My blood with fire to burn through me;
Who breathes upon my gazing eyes,
  Who laughs and murmurs in mine ear,
At whose least touch my colour flies,
  And whom my life grows faint to hear.

Within the voice, within the heart,
  Within the mind of Love-Lily,
A spirit is born who lifts apart
  His tremulous wings and looks at me;
Who on my mouth his finger lays,
  And shows, while whispering lutes confer,
That Eden of Love's watered ways
  Whose winds and spirits worship her.

Brows, hands, and lips, heart, mind, and voice,
　　Kisses and words of Love-Lily,—
Oh ! bid me with your joy rejoice,
　　Till riotous longing rest in me!
Ah ! let not hope be still distraught,
　　But find in her its gracious goal,
Whose speech Truth knows not from her thought
　　Nor Love her body from her soul.

DANTE GABRIEL ROSSETTI.

XLIX.

I.

GIVE her but a least excuse to love me !
    When—where—
    How—can this arm establish her above me,
    If fortune fixed her as my lady there,
There already, to eternally reprove me ?
    (" Hist !"—said Kate the queen ;
But " Oh," cried the maiden, binding her tresses,
    "'Tis only a page that carols unseen,
Crumbling your hounds their messes !")

II.

Is she wronged ?—To the rescue of her honour,
    My heart !
Is she poor ?—What costs it to become a donor ?
    Merely an earth to cleave, a sea to part.
But that fortune should have thrust all this upon her !
    (" Nay, list !"—bade Kate the queen ;
And still cried the maiden, binding her tresses,
    "'Tis only a page that carols unseen,
Fitting your hawks their jesses !")

ROBERT BROWNING.

THE OBLATION.

ASK nothing more of me, sweet ;
   All I can give you I give.
      Heart of my heart, were it more,
     More would be laid at your feet :
. Love that should help you to live,
   Song that should spur you to soar.

All things were nothing to give
   Once to have sense of you more,
     Touch you and taste of you sweet,
Think you and breathe you and live,
   Swept of your wings as they soar,
     Trodden by chance of your feet.

I that have love and no more,
   Give you but love of you, sweet :
     He that hath more, let him give ;
He that hath wings, let him soar ;
   Mine is the heart at your feet
     Here, that must love you to live.

ALGERNON CHARLES SWINBURNE.

THE bee to the heather,
  The lark to the sky,
The roe to the greenwood,
  And whither shall I?

Oh, Alice! ah, Alice!
  So sweet to the bee
Are the moorland and heather
  By Cannock and Leigh!

Oh, Alice! ah, Alice!
  O'er Teddesley Park
The sunny sky scatters
  The notes of the lark!

Oh, Alice! ah, Alice!
  In Beaudesert glade
The roes toss their antlers
  For joy of the shade!—

But Alice, dear Alice!
  Glade, moorland, nor sky
Without you can content me,
  And whither shall I?

SIR HENRY TAYLOR.

A DAISY CHAIN.

HE white rose decks the breast of May,
  The red rose smiles in June,
   Yet autumn chills and winter kills
   And leaves their stems alone ;
Ah,. swiftly dies the garden's pride
 Whose sleep no waking knows;—
But my love she is the daisy
 That all the long year grows.

The early woods are gay with green,
 The fields are prankt with gold;
But fair must fade and green be greyed
 Before the year is old ;
The blue-bell hangs her shining head,
 No more the oxslip blows,—
But my love she is the daisy
 That all the long year grows.

Still deck, wild woods, your mantle green,
　All meads bright jewels wear,
Let showers of spring fresh violets bring .
　And sweetness load the air ;
Whilst summer boasts her roses red
　And March her scented snows,—
My love be still the daisy,
　And my heart whereon she grows.

H. CHOLMONDELEY-PENNELL.

LIII.

A WILD-WOOD SPELL.

COME to the woods, Medora,
   Come to the woods with me;
   The leaves are green, the summer sheen
Is on the linden tree.

Up in the woods, Medora,
The thrushes warble free;
Around, above, they sing of love,
So let me sing to thee!

On the low thorn, Medora,
The finch is fair to see,
A jewel bright, a heart's delight—
Ah! so art thou to me.

From the dark pines, Medora,
There flows a balmy sea;
The air's soft kiss is heavenly bliss—
How sweet art thou to me!

Through the wood-moss, Medora,
The emerald lizards flee,
Away, away,—they will not stay ;
Oh, flee not thus from me !

Come to the woods, Medora,
Come to the shade with me ;
The roses bloom in that sweet gloom—
So bloom, dear rose, for me !

EARL OF SOUTHESK.

REINE D'AMOUR.

CLOSE as the stars along the sky,
    The flowers were in the mead,
    The purple heart, and golden eye,
       And crimson-flaming weed :—
And each one sigh'd as I went by,
   And touch'd my garment green,
And bade me wear her on my heart
   And take her for my Queen
      Of Love,—
   And take her for my Queen.

And one in virgin white was drest
   With lowly gracious head ;
And one unveil'd a burning breast
   With Love's own ardour red ;
All rainbow bright, with laughter light,
   They flicker'd o'er the green,
Each whispering I should pluck her there
   And take her for my Queen
      Of Love,—
   And take her for my Queen.

But sudden at my feet look'd up
  A little star-like thing,
Pure odour in pure perfect cup,
  That made my bosom sing.
'Twas not for size, nor gorgeous dyes,
  But her own self, I ween,
Her own sweet self, that bade me stoop
  And take her for my Queen
      Of Love,—
  And take her for my Queen.

Now all day long and every day
  Her beauty on me grows,
And holds with stronger sweeter sway
  Than lily or than rose ;
And this one star-outshines by far
  All in the meadow green ;—
And so I wear her on my heart
  And take her for my Queen
      Of Love,—
  And take her for my Queen.

          FRANCIS TURNER PALGRAVE.

LV.

I THANK thee, dear, for words that fleet,
    For looks that long endure,
For all caresses simply sweet
    And passionately pure ;

For blushes mutely understood,
    For silence and for sighs,
For all the yearning womanhood
    Of grey love-laden eyes.

Oh how in words to tell the rest ?
    My bird, my child, my dove !
Behold I render best for best,
    I bring thee love for love.

Oh give to God the love again
    Which had from Him its birth,—
Oh bless Him, for He sent the twain
    Together on the earth.

FREDERICK MYERS.

MY NEIGHBOUR.

" OVE thou thy Neighbour," we are told,
    " Even as thyself." That creed I hold ;
    But love her more, a thousand-fold !

My lovely Neighbour ; oft we meet
In lonely lane, or crowded street ;
I know the music of her feet.

She little thinks how, on a day,
She must have missed her usual way,
And walked into my heart for aye :

Or how the rustle of her dress
Thrills thro' me like a soft caress,
With trembles of deliciousness.

Wee woman, with her smiling mien,
And soul celestially serene,
She passes me, unconscious Queen !

Her face most innocently good,
Where shyly peeps the sweet red blood :
Her form a nest of Womanhood !

Like Raleigh—for her dainty tread,
When ways are miry—I could spread
My cloak, but, there's my heart instead.

Ah, Neighbour, you will never know
Why 'tis my step is quickened so ;
Nor what the prayer I murmur low.

I see you 'mid your flowers at morn,
Fresh as the rosebud newly born ;
I marvel, can *you* have a thorn ?

If so, 'twere sweet to lean one's breast
Against it, and, the more it prest,
Sing like the Bird that sorrow hath blest.

I hear you sing !   And thro' me Spring
Doth musically ripple and ring ;
Little you think I'm listening !

You know not, dear, how dear you be ;
All dearer for the secrecy :
Nothing, and yet a world to me.

So near, too ! you could hear me sigh,
Or see my case with half an eye ;
But must not.   There are reasons why.

GERALD MASSEY.

BLANCHE.

WERE I a breath of summer air,
　　I'd wander over bank and lea,
And bring, from every wild-flower there,
　　Sweet messages of love to thee.

Were I a stream, with low soft song,
　　I'd woo thee to some green retreat,
And linger as I pass'd along,
　　In bliss to murmur at thy feet.

Were I a bird with mellow throat,
　　I would forsake the pleasant grove,
And tune for thee the softest note
　　That music dedicates to love.

For thee my daily wishes burn;
　　In dreams thy angel face I see;
I bid my thoughts to others turn,
　　My thoughts unbidden turn to thee.

Such love thyself mayst live to prove ;
 Yet thine will be unmixed with pain,
For never, surely, canst thou love,
 But thou wilt be beloved again.

JAMES HEDDERWICK.

LVIII.

NO AND YES.

F I could choose my paradise,
    And please myself with choice of bliss,
    Then I would have your soft blue eyes
    And rosy little mouth to kiss ;
Your lips, as smooth and tender, child,
As rose-leaves in a coppice wild.

If fate bade choose some sweet unrest,
    To weave my troubled life a snare,
Then I would say " her maiden breast,
    And golden ripple of her hair ; "
And weep amid those tresses, child,
Contented to be thus beguiled.

THOMAS ASHE.

LIX.

LOVE within the lover's breast
    Burns like Hesper in the West,
    O'er the ashes of the sun,
    Till the day and night are done ;
Then when dawn drives up his car—
Lo ! it is the morning star.

Love ! thy love pours down on mine
As the sunlight on the vine,
As the snow rill on the vale,
As the salt breeze on the sail ;
As the song unto the bird
On my lips thy name is heard.

As a dewdrop on the rose
In thy heart my passion glows ;
As a skylark to the sky,
Up into thy breast I fly ;
As a sea-shell of the sea
Ever shall I sing of thee.

GEORGE MEREDITH.

LX.

IKE an island in a river,
　　Art thou, my love, to me ;
　　And I journey by thee ever
　　　With a gentle ecstasie.
I arise to fall before thee,
　I come to kiss thy feet ;
To adorn thee and adore thee,
　Mine only one ! my sweet !

And thy love hath power upon me,
　Like a dream upon a brain ;
For the loveliness which won me,
　With the love, too, doth remain.
And my life it beautifieth
　Though love be but a shade,
Known of only ere it dieth,
　By the darkness it hath made.

PHILIP JAMES BAILEY.

THE TREASURE-SHIP.

M Y heart is freighted full of love,
  As full as any argosy,
  With gems below and gems above,
  And ready for the open sea;
For the wind is blowing summerly.

Full strings of nature's beaded pearl,
Sweet tears! composed in amorous ties
And turkis-lockets, that no churl
Hath fashioned out mechanic-wise,
But all made up of thy blue eyes.

And girdles wove of subtle sound,
And thoughts not trusted to the air,
Of antique mould,—the same as bound,
In Paradise, the primal pair,
Before Love's art and niceness were.

And carcanets of living sighs;
Gems that have dropped from Love's own stem,
And one small jewel that I prize—

The darling gaud of all of them —
I wot, so rare and fine a gem
Ne'er glowed on Eastern anadem.

I've cased the rubies of thy smiles,
In rich and triply-plated gold ;
But *this* no other wealth defiles,
Itself, itself can only hold—
The stealthy kiss on Maple-wold.

RICHARD, LORD HOUGHTON.

LXII.

I.

SEEK not the tree of silkiest bark
    And balmiest bud,
  To carve her name while yet 'tis dark
    Upon the wood.
The world is full of noble tasks,
  And wreaths hard won :
Each work demands strong hearts, strong hands,
  Till day is done.

II.

Sing not that violet-veinèd skin,
  That cheek's pale roses,
The lily of that form wherein
  Her soul reposes :
Forth to the fight, true man, true knight ;
  The clash of arms
Shall more prevail than whispered tale
  To win her charms.

III.

The warrior for the True, the Right,
   Fight's in Love's name :
The love that lures thee from that fight
   Lures thee to shame :
The love which lifts the heart, yet leaves
   The spirit free,
That love, or none, is fit for one
   Man-shaped, like thee.

AUBREY DE VERE.

LXIII.

ON the long enchanted weather,
  When lovers came together,
    And fields were bright with blossoming,
      And hearts were light with song;

When the poet lay for hours,
In a dream among the flowers,
And heard a soft voice murmuring.
  His love's name all day long;

Or for hours stood beholding
The summer time unfolding
Its casket of rich jewelries,
  And boundless wealth outpoured;

Saw the precious-looking roses
Its glowing hand uncloses,
The pearls of dew and emeralds
  Spread over grass and sward;

When he heard besides the singing,
Mysterious voices ringing
With clear unearthly ecstasies
   Through earth and sky and air;

Then he wondered for whose pleasure
Some king made all that treasure—
That bauble of the universe,
   At whose feet it was laid :

Yea, for what celestial leman,
Bright saint or crownèd demon,
Chimed all the tender harmonies
   Of that rich serenade.

But his heart constrained him, sinking
Back to its sweetest thinking,
His lady all to celebrate,
   And tell her beauty's worth.

And he sought at length what tender
Love-verses he should send her :
Oh, the love within him overflowed,
   And seemed to fill the earth !

So he took, in his emotion,
A murmur from the ocean ;
He took a plaintive whispering
   Of sadness from the wind;

G

And a piteous way of sighing
From the leaves when they were dying,
And the music of the nightingales
  With all his own combined ;.

Yea, he stole indeed some phrasès
Of mystic hymns of praises,
The heaven itself is perfecting
  Out of the earthly things ;

And with these he did so fashion
The poem of his passion,
The lady still is listening,
  And still the poet sings !

ARTHUR O'SHAUGHNESSY.

A SONG OF THE FOUR SEASONS.

WHEN Spring comes laughing
    By vale and hill,
    By wind-flower walking
      And daffodil,—
Sing stars of morning,
    Sing morning skies,
Sing blue of speedwell,
    And my Love's eyes.

When comes the Summer,
    Full-leaved and strong,
And gay birds gossip
    The orchard long,—
Sing hid, sweet honey
    That no bee sips;
Sing red, red roses,
    And my Love's lips.

When Autumn scatters
　The leaves again,
And piled sheaves bury
　The broad-wheeled wain,—
Sing flutes of harvest
　Where men rejoice ;
Sing rounds of reapers,
　And my Love's voice.

But when comes Winter
　With hail and storm,
And red'fire roaring
　And ingle warm,—
Sing first sad going
　Of friends that part ;
Then sing glad meeting
　And my Love's heart.

AUSTIN DOBSON.

WILD ROSE.

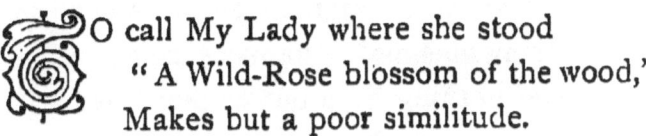O call My Lady where she stood
    "A Wild-Rose blossom of the wood,"
    Makes but a poor similitude.

For who by such a slight would reach
An aim, consumes the worth in speech,
And sets a crimson rose to bleach.

My Love, whose store of household sense
Gives duty golden recompense,
And arms her goodness with defence :

The sweet reliance of whose gaze
Originates in gracious ways,
And wins that trust the trust repays :

Whose stately figure's varying grace
Is never seen unless her face
Turn beaming toward another place ;

For such a halo round it glows,
Surprised attention only knows
A lively wonder in repose.

Can flowers that breathe one little day
In odorous sweetness life away,
And wavering to the earth decay,

Have any claim to rank with her,
Warmed in whose soul impulses stir
Then bloom to goodness; and aver

Her worth through spheral joys shall move
When suns and systems cease above,
And nothing lives but perfect Love?

THOMAS WOOLNER.

LXVI.

DAISY'S DIMPLES.

I.

LITTLE dimples so sweet and soft,
    Love the cheek of my love;
The mark of Cupid's dainty hand,
    Before he wore a glove.

II.

Laughing dimples of tender love,
    Smile on my darling's cheek;
Sweet hallowed spots where kisses lurk,
    And play at hide and seek.

III.

Fain would I hide my kisses there
    At morning's rosy light,
To come and seek them back again
    In silver hush of night.

J. ASHBY-STERRY.

GERTRUDE'S GLOVE.

LIPS of a kid-skin deftly sewn,
  A scent as through her garden blown,
  The tender hue that clothes her dove,
  All these, and this is Gerty's glove.

A glove but lately dofft, for look—
It keeps the happy shape it took
Warm from her touch!   What gave the glow?
And where's the mould that shaped it so?

It clasp'd the hand, so pure, so sleek,
Where Gerty rests a pensive cheek,
The hand that when the light wind stirs,
Reproves those laughing locks of hers.

Your fingers four, you little thumb!
Were I but you, in days to come
I'd clasp, and kiss,—I'd keep her—go!
And tell her that I told you so.

FREDERICK LOCKER.

LXVIII.

ANGELICA.

FAIR is my Love, so fair,
   I shudder with the sense
Of what a light the world would lose
   Could she go hence.

Sweet is my Love, so sweet,
   The leaves that, fold on fold,
Swathe up the odours of the rose,
   Less sweetness hold.

True is my Love, so true,
   Her heart is mine alone,
The music of its rhythmic beat
   Throbs through my own.

Dear is my Love, so dear,
   If I but hear her name,
My eyes with tears of rapture swim,
   My cheek is flame.

Spáre her, immortals, spare,
  Till all our days are done—
Your heaven is full of angel forms,
  Mine holds but one.

WILLIAM SAWYER.

A GARDEN IDYLL.

E have loiter'd and laugh'd in the flowery
croft,
    We have met under wintry skies ;
    Her voice is the dearest voice, and soft
    Is the light in her wistful eyes ;
It is sweet in the silent woods, among
  Gay crowds, or in any place
To hear her voice, to gaze on her young
    Confiding face.

For ever may roses divinely blow,
  And wine-dark pansies charm
By the prim box-path where I felt the glow
  Of her dimpled, trusting arm ;
And the sweep of her silk as she turn'd and smil'd,
  A smile as fair as her pearls ;
The breeze was in love with the darling child,
    As it moved her curls.

She show'd me her ferns and woodbine sprays,
    Foxglove and jasmine stars,
A mist of blue in the beds, a blaze
    Of red in the celadon jars:
And velvety bees in convolvulus bells,
    And roses of bountiful June—
Oh, who would think that summer spells
        Could die so soon!

For a glad song came from the milking-shed,
    On a wind of that summer south,
And the green was golden above her head,
    And a sunbeam kiss'd her mouth;
Sweet were the lips where that sunbeam dwelt—
    And the wings of Time were fleet
As I gazed; and neither spoke, for we felt
        Life was so sweet!

And the odorous limes were dim above
    As we leant on a drooping bough;
And the darkling air was a breath of love,
    And a witching thrush sang "Now!"
For the sun dropt low, and the twilight grew
    As we listen'd, and sigh'd, and leant—
That day was the sweetest day—and we knew
        What the sweetness meant.

FREDERICK LOCKER.

LXX.

NOVEMBER SNOW.

THE snow upon the rose-flow'r sits,
  And whitens all the spray ;
  Sweet Robin Redbreast o'er it flits,
  And shakes the snow away.

The snow upon my life-bloom sits,
And sheds a dreary blight :
Thy spirit o'er my spirit flits,
And crimson comes for white.

EARL OF SOUTHESK.

LXXI.

DAWN.

LILY, with the sun of heaven's
   Prime splendour on thy breast !
My scattered passions toward thee run,
   Poising to awful rest.

The darkness of our universe
   Smothered my soul in night;
Thy glory shone; whereat the curse
   Passed molten into light.

Raised over envy; freed from pain;
   Beyond the storms of chance :
Blessed king of my own world I reign,
   Controlling circumstance.

THOMAS WOOLNER.

LXXII.

THE TRYST.

SLEEPING, I dreamed that thou wast mine,
   In some ambrosial lover's shrine.
   My lips against thy lips were pressed,
   And all our passion was confessed ;
So near and dear my darling seemed,
I knew not that I only dreamed.

Waking, this mid and moonlight night,
I clasp thee close by lover's right.
Thou fearest not my warm embrace,
And yet, so like the dream thy face
And kisses, I but half partake
The joy, and know not if I wake.

EDMUND CLARENCE STEDMAN.

IN A GONDOLA.

SHE SINGS.

I.

THE moth's kiss, first!
    Kiss me as if you made believe
    You were not sure, this eve,
    How my face, your flower, had pursed
Its petals up; so, here and there
You brush it, till I grow aware
Who wants me, and wide ope I burst.

II.

The bee's kiss, now!
Kiss me as if you entered gay
My heart at some noonday,
A bud that dares not disallow
The claim, so all is rendered up,
And passively its shattered cup
Over your head to sleep I bow.

ROBERT BROWNING.

LXXIV.

THE DIAL.

NLY when Summer's sun is high,
  And the blue is broad in the summer sky,
The shadows on the dial face
    Tell of day's race.

Only when so we sit together,
And loving eyes make pleasant weather,
Live I—my soul in sunny blisses
      Counts life by kisses.

EDWIN ARNOLD.

LXXV.

A KISS.

I.

SWEET mouth ! Oh let me take
One draught from that delicious cup !
The hot Sahara-thirst to slake
That burns me up !

II.

Sweet breath ! all flowers that are,
Within that darling frame must bloom ;
My heart revives so at the rare
Divine perfume !

III.

Nay, 'tis a dear deceit,
A drunkard's cup that mouth of thine ;
Sure poison-flowers are breathing, sweet,
That fragrance fine !

IV.

I drank—the drink betrayed me
Into a madder, fiercer fever ;
The scent of those love-blossoms made me
          More faint than ever.

V.

Yet though quick death it were
That rich heart-vintage I must drain,
And quaff that hidden garden's air,
          Again—again !

ALFRED DOMETT.

THE MOUNTAIN FIR.

THEY sat beneath the mountain fir,
    Beneath the evening sun;
With all his soul he looked at her—
    And so was love begun.

The tit-mice blue in fluttering flocks
    Caressed the fir-tree spray;
And far below, through rifted rocks,
    The river went its way.

As stars in heavenly waters swim,
    Her eyes of azure shone;
With all her soul she looked at him—
    And so was love led on.

The squirrel sported on the bough,
    And chuckled in his play;
Above the distant mountain's brow
    A golden glory lay.

The fir-tree breathed its balsam balm,
  With heather scents united ;
The happy skies were hushed in calm—
  And so the troth was plighted.

EARL OF SOUTHESK.

LXXVII.

THE LETTER.

WHERE is another sweet as my sweet,
　　Fine of the fine, and shy of the shy?
Fine little hands, fine little feet—
　　Dewy blue eye.
Shall I write to her? shall I go?
　　Ask her to marry me by and by?
Somebody said that she'd say No;
　　Somebody knows that she'll say Ay!

Ay or no, if ask'd to her face?
　　Ay or no, from shy of the shy?
Go, little letter, apace, apace,
　　　　Fly;
Fly to the light in the valley below—
　　Tell my wish to her dewy blue eye:
Somebody said that she'd say No;
　　Somebody knows that she'll say Ay!

ALFRED TENNYSON.

MARRIAGE MORNING.

LIGHT, so low upon earth,
    You send a flash to the sun.
    Here is the golden close of love,
    All my wooing is done.

Oh, the woods and the meadows,
    Woods where we hid from the wet,
Stiles where we stay'd to be kind,
    Meadows in which we met!

Light, so low in the vale,
    You flash and lighten afar,
For this is the golden morning of love,
    And you are his morning star.

Flash, I am coming, I come,
    By meadow and stile and wood;
Oh, lighten into my eyes and my heart,
    Into my heart and my blood!

Heart, are you great enough,
   For a love that never tires ?
O heart, are you great enough for love ?
   I have heard of thorns and briars.

Over the thorns and briars,
   Over the meadows and stiles,
Over the world to the end of it
   Flash for a million miles.

ALFRED TENNYSON.

LXXIX.

ONE so fair—none so fair.
　　In her eyes so true
　　Love's most inner heaven bare
　　To the balmiest blue !

One so fair—none so fair.
　　In the skies no Star
Like my Star of Earth so near—
　　They but shine afar.

One so fair—none so fair.
　　All too sweet it seems ;
Wake me not, O world of care,
　　If I walk in dreams.

One so fair—none so fair.
　　O my bosom-guest,
Love ne'er smiled a happier pair
　　To the bridal-nest.

One so fair—none so fair.
  Lean to me, sweet Wife ;
Light will be the load we bear ;
  Two hearts in one life.

GERALD MASSEY.

LXXX.

JOHN ANDERSON'S ANSWER.

I CANNOT kiss thee as I used to kiss;
　Time, who is lord of love, must answer this.
　Shall I believe thine eyes have grown less sweet?
　Nay, but my life-blood fails on heavier feet.
Time goes, old girl, time goes.

I cannot hold as once I held thy hand;
Youth is a tree whose leaves fall light as sand.
Hast thou known many trees that shed them so?
Ay me, sweetheart, I know, ay me, I know.
Time goes, my bird, time goes.

I cannot love thee as I used to love.
Age comes, and little Love takes flight above.
If our eyes fail, have his the deeper glow?
I do not know, sweetheart, I do not know.
Time goes, old girl, time goes.

Why, the gold cloud grows leaden, as the eve
Deepens, and one by one its glories leave.
And, if you press me, dear, why this is so,
That this is worth a tear is all I know.
Time flows and rows and goes.

In that old day the subtle child-god came;
Meek were his eyelids, but his eyeballs flame,
With sandals of desire his light feet shod,
With eyes and breath of fire a perfect god
. He rose, my girl, he rose.

He went, my girl, and raised your hand and sighed,
" Would that my spirit always could abide."
And whispered " Go your ways and play your day,
Would I were god of time, but my brief sway
Is briefer than a rose."

Old wife, old love; there is a something yet
That makes amends, though all the glory set;
The after-love that holds thee trebly mine,
Though thy lips fade, my dove, and we decline,
And time, dear heart, still goes.

HON. JOHN LEICESTER WARREN.

LXXXI.

RENUNCIATION.

H no! you shall not catch me in the snare—
    I will not love, I say!
Life might become a terror, a despair,
    If you were ta'en away.

Nothing is given here, 'tis only lent,—
    I will not, dare not, trust:
For joy might strike at once his heaven-built tent,
    And leave me but its dust.

What horror, after all my life was given,
    Adventured on one barque,
If that should go, even to the joy of heaven,
    And I left in the dark!

Left on a wreck of sorrow, with no power
    My losses to repair;
With death denied, and every torturing hour
    By memory made a snare.

Left with the dregs of life, its wine poured out;
    Left to the past a prey;
From its sad ghosts that haunt my heart about,
    Helpless to flee away.

No! I renounce life's bliss—love's perfect flower,
    Sweet though it be!—I choose
The lower, lasting lot, and keep the power,
    Without a pang, to lose.

                        W. W. STORY.

LXXXII.

WINDLE-STRAWS.

I.

ERE life to last for ever, love,
    We might go hand in hand,
      And pause and pull the flowers that blow
      In all the idle land ;
And we might lie in sunny fields
    And while the hours away
With fallings-out and fallings-in
    For half a summer day.

But since we two must sever, love,
    Since some dim hour we part,
I have no time to give thee much
    But quickly take my heart,
" For ever thine," and " thine my love,"—
    O Death may come apace.
What more of love could life bestow,
    Dearest, than this embrace ?

II.

SHE kissed me on the forehead,
  She spake not any word,
The silence flowed between us,
  And I nor spoke nor stirred.

So hopeless for my sake it was,
  So full of ruth, so sweet,
My whole heart rose and blessed her,
  —Then died before her feet.

EDWARD DOWDEN.

LXXXIII.

BAGATELLES.

THE wanton bee that suck'd the rose
    Has lured a leaf away ;
The love that in my bosom glows
    Must stay, and stay, and stay.

And when the rose began to die,
    The bee ran up away ;
But Kitty in my love shall lie
    Beyond the dying day.

————

I'd like to be the lavender
    That makes her linen sweet,
And swoon and sweeten in her breast,
    And faint around her feet.

She'd hardly think of me at all,
    And shake out lawn and sheet ;
And yet I'd be the lavender
    And make her linen sweet.

THEOPHILE MARZIALS.

I

TRAGEDIES.

SHE reach'd a rosebud from the tree,
 And bit the tip and threw it by ;
My little rose, for you and me,
 The worst is over when we die !

———

For love is like the China-rose
 That leafs so quickly from the tree ;—
And life, though all the honey goes,
 Lasts ever, like the pot pourri.

———

She was only a woman, famish'd for loving,
 Mad with devotion, and such slight things
And he was a very great musician,
 And used to finger his fiddle-strings.

Her heart's sweet gamut is cracking and breaking
 For a look, for a touch,—for such slight things ;
But he's such a very great musician,
 Grimacing and fing'ring his fiddle-strings.

———

In the middle of my garden-bed,
   There stands a tall rose-tree ;
I took the stem, and shook and shook it,
   Thick the flowers kept covering me.

And oh ! I said, you sweet large roses,
   Red as rose can be,
Just drop into my bosom here,
   And die along with me !

THEOPHILE MARZIALS.

LXXXV.

MAJOLICA AND ROCOCO.

WHEN I was by Chloe kiss'd,
　　Ceased or 'gan I to exist?
　　If 'twas life before without her,
　　What is this to be about her?

———

If angels love above in heaven,
　　Then death must be too oversweet,
For this dear love thy lips have given,
　　Has made this life, my love, replete.

———

The rose of her cheek may wane and die,
　　Her hair's gold fibre dull and decay;
But love has a colour not fused to fly,
　　In the fabric that never shall wear away.

THEOPHILE MARZIALS.

LXXXVI.

BABY.

WHERE did you come from, baby dear?
Out of the everywhere into here.

Where did you get those eyes so blue?
Out of the sky as I came through.

What makes the light in them sparkle and spin?
Some of the starry spikes left in.

Where did you get that little tear?
I found it waiting when I got here.

What makes your forehead so smooth and high?
A soft hand stroked it as I went by.

What makes your cheek like a warm white rose?
I saw something better than any one knows.

Whence that three-cornered smile of bliss?
Three angels gave me at once a kiss.

Where did you get this pearly ear?
God spoke and it came out to hear.

Where did you get those arms and hands?
Love made itself into bonds and bands.

Feet, whence did you come, you darling things?
From the same box as the cherubs' wings.

How did they all just come to be you?
God thought about me, and so I grew.

But how did you come to us, you dear?
God thought about you, and so I am here.

GEORGE MACDONALD.

LXXXVII.

TO A CHILD.

IF by any device or knowledge
    The rosebud its beauty could know,
  It would stay a rosebud for ever,
    Nor into its fulness grow.

And if thou could'st know thy own sweetness,
  O little one, perfect and sweet,
Thou would'st be a child for ever,
    Completer whilst incomplete.

FRANCIS TURNER PALGRAVE.

LXXXVIII.

PARIS A MACON.

I SAW, I saw the lovely child,
    I watched her by the way,
    I learnt her gestures sweet and wild,
    Her loving eyes and gay.

Her name?—I heard not, nay, nor care,—
    Enough it was for me
To find her innocently fair
    And delicately free.

Oh cease and go ere dreams be done,
    Nor trace the angel's birth,
Nor find the paradisal one
    A blossom of the earth!

Thus it is with our subtlest joys,—
    How quick the soul's alarm!
How lightly deed or word destroys
    That evanescent charm!

It comes unbidden, comes unbought,
    Unfettered flees away,—
His swiftest and his sweetest thought
    Can never poet say.

FREDERICK MYERS.

LXXXIX.

UNREFLECTING CHILDHOOD.

IT is, indeed, a little while
    Since you were born, my happy pet ;
  Your future beckons with a smile,
    Your bygones don't exist as yet.
Is all the world with beauty rife?
  Are you a little bird that sings
Her simple gratitude for life,
    And lovely things?

The ocean, and the waning moons,
  And starry skies, and starry dells,
And winter sport, and golden Junes,
  Art, and divinest Beauty-spells :-
Festa and song, and frolic wit,
  And banter, and domestic mirth,—
They all are ours !—dear child, is it
    A pleasant earth?

And poet friends, and poesy,
   And precious books, for any mood :
And then that best of company,
   Those graver thoughts in solitude
That hold us fast and never pall :
   Then there is You, my own, my fair—
And I . . . soon I must leave it all,
     —And much you care.

FREDERICK LOCKER.

XC.

NATURÆ REPARATRICI.

GRAY cloud, gray veil 'twixt me and youth
    And youth's unclouded weather,
Well mayst thou blot the golden days
    And skies effaced for ever.

In vain the veil to silver melts,
    And flakes of sun and shadow
Once more invite these alien steps
    To chase them o'er the meadow.

Yet nature holds a gracious hand,
    Her ancient way pursuing;
And spreads the charms we loved of old,
    To aid the heart's renewing.

Here her long crests of fringèd crag
    Allure the sky-ward swallows;
Here the still dove's low love-note floats
    Above her leafy hollows.

Here its calm strength her hillside rears
    From heaving slopes of clover ;
Here still the pewit pipes and flits
    Within his furzy cover.

Here hums the wild-bee in the thyme,
    Here glows the royal heather ;
And youth comes back upon the breeze,
    And youth's unclouded weather.

              FRANCIS TURNER PALGRAVE.

XCI.

FLOWERS WITHOUT FRUIT.

PRUNE thou thy words, the thoughts control
    That o'er thee swell and throng;
They will condense within thy soul,
    And change to purpose strong.

But he who lets his feelings run
    In soft luxurious flow,
Shrinks when hard service must be done,
    And faints at every ·woe.

Faith's meanest deed more favour bears,
    Where hearts and wills are weigh'd,
Than brightest transports, choicest prayers,
    Which bloom their hour and fade.

JOHN HENRY NEWMAN.

XCII.

PLEASURE AND PAIN.

HO can determine the frontier of Pleasure?
    Who can distinguish the limits of Pain?
    Where is the moment the feeling to
        measure?
    Where is experience repeated again?

Ye who have felt the delirium of passion—
    Say, can ye sever its joys and its pangs?
Is there a power in calm contemplation
    To indicate each upon each as it hangs?

I would believe not ;—for spirit will lanquish
    While sense is most blest and creation most bright ;
And life will be dearer and clearer in anguish
    Than ever was felt in the throbs of delight.

See the Fakeer as he swings on his iron,
    See the thin Hermit that starves in the wild ;
Think ye no pleasures the penance environ,
    And hope the sole bliss by which pain is beguiled?

No! in the kingdom those spirits are reaching,
  Vain are our words the emotions to tell;
Vain the distinctions our senses are teaching,
  For Pain has its Heaven and Pleasure its Hell!

RICHARD, LORD HOUGHTON.

THE HIDDEN SELF.

I KNOW not if a keener smart
   Can come to finer souls than his
  Who hears men praise him, mind or heart,
   For something higher than he is ;—

Who fain would say : " Behold me, friends,
  That which I am, not what you deem
A thing of low and narrow ends,
  Sordid, not golden as I seem ;

" See here the hidden blot of shame,
  The weak thought that you take for strong,
The brain too dull to merit fame,
  The faint and imitative song ;"

But dares not, lest discovery foul
  Not his name only, but degrade
Heights closed but to the soaring soul,
  Names which scorn trembles to invade ;

K

And doth his inner self conceal
From all men in his own despite,
Hiding what he would fain reveal,
And a most innocent hypocrite.

LEWIS MORRIS.

XCIV.

A GENIAL moment oft has given
   What years of toil and pain,
Of long industrious toil, have striven
   To win, and all in vain.

Yet count not, when thine end is won,
   That labour merely lost;
Nor say it had been wiser done
   To spare the painful cost.

When heaped upon the altar lie
   All things to feed the fire—
One spark alighting from on high—
   The flames at once aspire;

But those sweet gums and fragrant woods,
   Its rich materials rare,
By tedious quest o'er lands and floods
   Had first been gathered there.

RICHARD CHENEVIX TRENCH.

THE TOYS.

MY little Son, who look'd from thoughtful eyes,
  And moved and spoke in quiet grown-up
    wise,
      Having my law the seventh time disobey'd,
I struck him, and dismiss'd
With hard words and unkiss'd,
His Mother, who was patient, being dead.
Then, fearing lest his grief should hinder sleep,
I visited his bed,
But found him slumbering deep,
With darken'd eyelids, and their lashes yet
From his late sobbing wet.
And I, with moan,
Kissing away his tears, left others of my own ;
For, on a table drawn beside his head,
He had put, within his reach,
A box of counters and a red-vein'd stone,
A piece of glass abraded by the beach,

And six or seven shells,
A bottle with bluebells
And two French copper coins, ranged there with
    careful art,
To comfort his sad heart.
So when that night I pray'd
To God, I wept, and said :
Ah, when at last we die with trancèd breath,
Not vexing Thee in death,
And Thou rememberest of what toys
We made our joys,
How weakly understood,
Thy great commanded good,
Then, fatherly not less
Than I whom Thou hast moulded from the clay,
Thou'lt leave Thy wrath, and say,
" I will be sorry for their childishness."

COVENTRY PATMORE.

XCVI.

LOSS AND GAIN.

MYRIAD Roses, unregretted, perish in their
    vernal bloom,
        That the essence of their sweetness *once*
    your beauty may perfume.

Myriad Veins of richest life-blood empty for their
    priceless worth,
To exalt *one* Will imperial over spacious realms of
    earth.

Myriad Hearts are pained and broken that *one* Poet
    may be taught
To discern the shapes of passion and describe them
    as he ought.

Myriad Minds of heavenly temper pass as passes
    moon or star,
That *one* philosophic Spirit may ascend the solar car.

Sacrifice and Self-Devotion hallow earth and fill the
    skies,
And the meanest life is sacred whence the highest
    may arise.

RICHARD, LORD HOUGHTON.

XCVII.

FEBRUARY.

OON—and the north-west sweeps the empty
   road,
  The rain-washed fields from hedge to hedge
   are bare ;
Beneath the leafless elms some hind's abode
Looks small and void, and no smoke meets the air
From its poor hearth : one lonely rook doth dare
The gale, and beats above the unseen corn,
Then turns, and whirling down the wind is borne.

Shall it not hap that on some dawn of May
Thou shalt awake, and, thinking of days dead,
See nothing clear but this same dreary day,
Of all the days that have passed o'er thine head ?
Shalt thou not wonder, looking from thy bed,
Through green leaves on the windless east afire,
That this day too thine heart doth still desire ?

Shalt thou not wonder that it liveth yet,
The useless hope, the useless craving pain,
That made thy face, that lonely noontide, wet
With more than beating of the chilly rain?
Shalt thou not hope for joy new born again,
Since no grief ever born can ever die
Through changeless change of seasons passing by?

WILLIAM MORRIS.

MARCH.

LAYER of the winter, art thou here again ?
    O welcome, thou that bring'st the summer nigh!
    The bitter wind makes not thy victory vain,
    Nor will we mock thee for thy faint blue sky.
Welcome, O March ! whose kindly days and dry
Make April ready for the throstle's song,
Thou first redresser of the winter's wrong !

Yea, welcome March ! and though I die ere June,
Yet for the hope of life I give thee praise,
Striving to swell the burden of the tune
That even now I hear thy brown birds raise,
Unmindful of the past or coming days ;
Who sing : "O joy ! a new year is begun :
What happiness to look upon the sun ! "

Ah, what begetteth all this storm of bliss
But Death himself, who crying solemnly,
E'en from the heart of sweet Forgetfulness,
Bids us "Rejoice, lest treasureless ye die.
Within a little time must ye go by.
Stretch forth your open hands, and while ye live
Take all the gifts that Death and Life may give."

WILLIAM MORRIS.

APRIL.

FAIR midspring, besung so oft and oft,
    How can I praise thy loveliness enow?
    Thy sun that burns not, and thy breezes soft
    That o'er the blossoms of the orchard blow,
The thousand things that 'neath the young leaves grow,
The hopes and chances of the growing year,
Winter forgotten long, and summer near.

When Summer brings the lily and the rose,
She brings us fear; her very death she brings
Hid in her anxious heart, the forge of woes;
And, dull with fear, no more the mavis sings.
But thou! thou diest not, but thy fresh life clings ·
About the fainting autumn's sweet decay,
When in the earth the hopeful seed they lay.

Ah ! life of all the year, why yet do I
Amid thy snowy blossoms' fragrant drift,
Still long for that which never draweth nigh,
Striving my pleasure from my pain to sift,
Some weight from off my fluttering mirth to lift?
—Now, when far bells are ringing, " Come again,
Come back, past years ! why will ye pass in vain?"

WILLIAM MORRIS.

C.

SPRING IS COMING.

BY the bursting of the leaves,
   By the lengthening of the eves,
      Spring is coming ;
   By the flowers that scent the air,
By the skies more blue and fair,
By the singing everywhere ;
     Spring is coming.

All the woods and fields rejoice :
     Spring is coming.
Only here and there a voice—
Here of buds the worm has worn,
Here of birds whose nest is torn,
There of those whose life is pent
Far from pleasant sight and scent—
Wails, as if their life's distress
Won a new wild bitterness ;
     Spring is coming.

F. W. BOURDILLON.

CI.

A SPRING EVENING.

ACROSS the glory of the evening skies
    A veil is drawn of shadowed mists, that rise
    From lavishness of God's late gift, the rain.

So after farewell said, fond memories
Of words and looks the sweetest come again
Across the glowing heart, a veil of pain.

F. W. BOURDILLON.

IN SPRING.

SWEET primrose-time ! when thou art here
    I go by grassy ledges
Of long lane-side, and pasture-mead,
    And moss-entangled hedges :

And all about her army gay
    The primrose weather musters,
In single knots, and scatter'd files,
    And constellated clusters.

And golden-headed children go
    Among the golden blossoms,
And harvest a whole meadow's wealth,
    Heap'd on their dainty bosoms.

Ah ! play your play, sweet little ones,
    Whose life is gladness only :
Nor ask an equal mirth from hearts
    Which, e'en with you, are lonely.

God to His flowers His flowers gives,
　Pure happiness uncloying :
Whilst they, whose primrose time is past,
　Enjoy in your enjoying.

FRANCIS TURNER PALGRAVE.

CIII.

THE year's at the spring,
    And day's at the morn;
    Morning's at seven;
    The hill-side's dew-pearled;
The lark's on the wing;
The snail's on the thorn;
God's in His heaven—
All's right with the world.

ROBERT BROWNING.

CIV.

IT was in the prime
   Of the sweet Spring-time.
      In the linnet's throat
      Trembled the love-note;
And the love-stirred air
Thrilled the blossoms there.
      Little shadows danced
      Each a tiny elf,
      Happy in large light
      And the thinnest self.

It was but a minute
      In a far-off Spring,
      But each gentle thing,
Sweetly-wooing linnet,
   Soft-thrilled hawthorn tree,
      Happy shadowy elf
      With the thinnest self,
   Live still on in me.
Oh the sweet, sweet prime
Of the past Spring-time.

GEORGE ELIOT.

A GLEE FOR WINTER.

I.

HENCE, rude Winter ! crabbed old fellow,
    Never merry, never mellow !
    Well-a-day ! in rain and snow
    What will keep one's heart aglow ?
Groups of kinsmen, old and young,
Oldest they old friends among !
Groups of friends, so old and true,
That they seem our kinsmen too !
These all merry all together,
Charm away chill Winter weather !

II.

What will kill this dull old fellow ?
Ale that's bright, and wine that's mellow !
Dear old songs for ever new ;
Sometimes love, and laughter too ;
Pleasant wit, and harmless fun,
And a dance when day is done !

Music-friends so true and tried—
Whispered love by warm fireside—
Mirth at all times all together—
Make sweet May of Winter weather !

ALFRED DOMETT.

CVI.

MY STAR.

ALL that I know
    Of a certain star
    Is, it can throw
      (Like the angled spar)
Now a dart of red,
  Now a dart of blue ;
Till my friends have said
  They would fain see, too,
My star that dartles the red and the blue!
Then it stops like a bird ; like a flower, hangs furled:
  They must solace themselves with the Saturn
    above it.
What matter to me if their star is a world ?
  Mine has opened its soul to me ; therefore I love it.

ROBERT BROWNING.

CVII.

I WOULD thou might'st not vex me with thine
        eyes,
    Thou fair Ideal Beauty, nor would'st shame
  All lower thoughts and visions as they rise,
    As in mid-noon a flame.

For now thy presence leaves no prospect fair,
  Nor joy in act, nor charm in any maid,
Nor end to be desired, for which men dare,
  Thou making me afraid.

Because life seems through thee a thing too great
  To spend on these, which else might grow to thee;
So that fast bound, I idly hesitate :
  I prithee set me free ;

Or, hold me, if thou wilt, but come not near,
  Let me pursue thee still in ghostly grace ;
Far off let me pursue thee, for I fear
  To faint before thy face.

LEWIS MORRIS.

CVIII.

THE UNREALIZED IDEAL.

MY only love is always near,—
    In country or in town
    I see her twinkling feet, I hear
    The whisper of her gown.

She foots it ever fair and young,
    Her locks are tied in haste,
And one is o'er her shoulder flung,
    And hangs below her waist.

She ran before me in the meads ;
    And down this world-worn track
She leads me on ; but while she leads
    She never gazes back.

And yet her voice is in my dreams,
    To witch me more and more ;
That wooing voice ! Ah me, it seems
    Less near me than of yore.

Lightly I sped when hope was high,
  And youth beguiled the chase,—
I follow, follow still ; but I
  Shall never see her face.

FREDERICK LOCKER.

CIX.

WARM whispering through the slender olive
      leaves
          Came to me a gentle sound,
          Whispering of a secret found
In the clear sunshine 'mid the golden sheaves:

Said it was sleeping for me in the morn,
          Called it gladness, called it joy,
          Drew me on —" Come hither, boy "—
To where the blue wings rested on the corn.

I thought the gentle sound had whispered true—
          Thought the little heaven mine,
          Leaned to clutch the thing divine,
And saw the blue wings melt within the blue.

GEORGE ELIOT.

AFTER-THOUGHT.

MAN dwells apart, though not alone,
    He walks among his peers unread ;
The best of thoughts which he hath known,
    For lack of listeners are not said.

Yet dreaming on earth's clustered isles,
    He saith, "They dwell not lone like men,"
Forgetful that their sun-flecked smiles
    Flash far beyond each other's ken.

He looks on God's eternal suns,
    That sprinkle the celestial blue,
And saith, " Ah ! happy shining ones,
    I would that men were grouped like you ! "

Yet this is sure : the loveliest star
    That clustered with its peers we see,
Only because from us so far
    Doth near its fellows seem to be.

JEAN INGELOW.

ISOLATION.

YES ! in the sea of life enisled,
 With echoing straits between us thrown,
 Dotting the shoreless watery wild,
 We mortal millions live *alone.*
The islands feel the enclasping flow,
And then their endless bounds they know.

But when the moon their billows lights,
And they are swept by balms of spring,
And in their glens, on starry nights,
 The nightingales divinely sing ;
And lovely notes, from shore to shore,
Across the sounds and channels pour—

Oh ! then a longing like despair
Is to their farthest caverns sent ;
For surely once, they feel, we were
 Parts of a single continent !
Now round us spreads the watery plain—
Oh might our marges meet again !

Who order'd that their longing's fire
Should be, as soon as kindled, cool'd?
Who renders vain their deep desire?
A God, a God their severance ruled!
And bade betwixt their shores to be
The unplumb'd, salt, estranging sea.

MATTHEW ARNOLD.

CXII.

THE SOLITUDE OF LIFE.

WHEN Fancy's exhalations rise
    From youth's delicious morn,
    Our eyes seem made for others' eyes,
    Spirit for spirit born :
But time the truthful faith controls,—
We learn too soon, alas!
How wide the gulf between two souls,
How difficult to pass !

In twilight and in fearfulness
We feel our path along
From heart to heart, yet none the less
Our way is often wrong.
And then new dangers must be faced,
New doubts must be dispelled,—
For not one step can be retraced
That once the Past has held.

To some 'tis given to walk awhile
In Love's unshaded noon,
But clouds are gathering while they smile,
And night is coming soon !
Most happy he whose journey lies
Beneath the starlight sheen
Of unregretful memories
Of glory that has been.

We live together years and years,
And leave unsounded still
Each other's springs of hopes and fears,
Each other's depths of will :
We live together day by day,
And some chance look or tone
Lights up with instantaneous ray
An inner world unknown.

Then wonder not that they who love
The longest and the best,
Are parted by some sudden move
Of passion or unrest :
Nor marvel that the wise and good
Should oft apart remain,
Nor dare, when once misunderstood,
To sympathise again.

Come, Death! and match thy quiet gloom
With being's darkling strife,
Come, set beside the lonely Tomb,
The Solitude of Life ;
And henceforth none who see can fear
Thy hour, which some will crave,
Who feel their hearts, while beating here,
Already in the grave.

RICHARD, LORD HOUGHTON.

NOT TO BE.

SHE rose said, " Let but this long rain be past,
    And I shall feel my sweetness in the sun,
  And pour its fulness into life at last ; "
    But when the rain was done,
But when dawn sparkled through unclouded air,
    She was not there.

The lark said, " Let but winter be away,
  And blossoms come, and light, and I will soar,
And lose the earth, and be the voice of day ; "
    But when the snows were o'er,
But when spring broke in blueness overhead,
    The lark was dead.

And myriad roses made the garden glow,
  And skylarks carolled all the summer long—
What lack of birds to sing and flowers to blow ?
    Yet, ah, lost scent, lost song !
Poor empty rose, poor lark that never trilled !
    Dead unfulfilled !

AUGUSTA WEBSTER.
M

CXIV.

OO soon so fair, fair lilies ;
    To bloom is then to wane ;
      The folded bud has still
        To-morrows at its will,
Blown flowers can never blow again.

    Too soon so bright, bright noontide ;
The sun that now is high
    Will henceforth only sink
    Towards the western brink ;
Day that's at prime begins to die.

    Too soon so rich, ripe summer,
For autumn tracks thee fast ;
    Lo, death-marks on the leaf !
    Sweet summer, and my grief ;
For summer come is summer past.

Too soon, too soon, lost summer ;
Some hours and thou art o'er.
Ah ! death is part of birth :
Summer leaves not the earth
But last year's summer lives no more.

AUGUSTA WEBSTER.

CXV.

NOTHING LOST.

WHERE are last year's snows,
Where the summer's rose,—
Who is there who knows?

Or the glorious note
Of some singer's throat
Heard in years remote?

Or the love they bore
Who, in days of yore,
Loved, but are no more?

Or the faiths men knew
When, before mind grew,
All strange things seemed true?

.   .   .   .

The snows are sweet spring rain,
The dead rose blooms again,
Young voices keep the strain.

The old affection mild
Still springs up undefiled
For love, and friend, and child.

The old faiths grown more wide,
Purer and glorified,
Are still our life-long guide.

Nothing that once has been,
Tho' ages roll between
And it be no more seen,

Can perish, for the Will
Which doth our being fulfil
Sustains and keeps it still.

LEWIS MORRIS.

CXVI.

LIFE knows no dead so beautiful
        As is the white cold-coffin'd past;
    This I may love nor be betray'd:
    The dead are faithful to the last.
I am not spouseless—I have wed
A memory—a life that's dead.

JOAQUIN MILLER.

CXVII.

CHANGED.

FROM the outskirts of the town,
    Where of old the milestone stood,
Now a stranger, looking down,
I behold the shadowy crown
    Of the dark and haunted wood.

Is it changed, or am I changed?
    Ah, the oaks are fresh and green,
But the friends with whom I ranged
Through their thickets are estranged
    By the years that intervene.

Bright as ever flows the sea,
    Bright as ever shines the sun,
But, alas! they seem to me
Not the sun that used to be,
    Not the tides that used to run.

HENRY WADSWORTH LONGFELLOW.

CXVIII.

LIKE to the moan of buried rivers,
    Heard faintly as they roam,
    While the wild rock around them shivers
    Through sheets of sunless foam ;
Beneath the life that weighs and presses,
  With muffled undertone,
Throbs in the spirit's worn recesses,
  The voice of years long flown.

If, in the tumult of existence,
  It whisper soft and low,
Yea seem, scarce heard through depths of distance,
  To melt away and go :
Yet oft, when stars more whitely glitter,
  When moons are waning chill,
That tide unseen grows loud and bitter,
  The caverned heart to fill.

And, as the other night, unbroken
   And starless, hangs around,
Old words, half thought, old thoughts, half spoken,
   Pour in to swell the sound.
Though Death's dumb frost all else is hushing,
   From that undying past,
The voice not lost, the stream still rushing,
   Shall murmur to the last.

                  SIR FRANCIS HASTINGS DOYLE.

CXIX.

LEAFLESS HOURS.

THE pale sun, through the spectral wood,
　　Gleams sparely, where I pass ;
My footstep, silent as my mood,
　　Falls in the silent grass.

Only my shadow points before me,
　　Where I am moving now ;
Only sad memories murmur o'er me
　　From every leafless bough :
And out of the nest of last year's Redbreast
　　Is stolen the very snow.

ROBERT, LORD LYTTON.

CXX.

H roses for the flush of youth,
    And laurel for the perfect prime ;
But pluck an ivy branch for me
    Grown old before my time.

Oh violets for the grave of youth,
    And bay for those dead ere their prime ;
Give me the withered leaves I chose
    Before in the old time.

CHRISTINA ROSSETTI.

CXXI.

I.

FOR me no roseate garlands twine,
  But wear them, Dearest, in my stead ;
Time has a whiter hand than thine,
  And lays it on my head.

II.

Enough to know thy place on earth
  Is there where roses latest die ;
To know the steps of youth and mirth
  Are thine, that pass me by.

AUBREY DE VERE.
SIR HENRY TAYLOR.

CXXII.

I BRING a garland for your head,
    Of blossoms fresh and fair,
    My own hands wound their white and red
        To ring about your hair·;
Here is a lily, here a rose,
A warm narcissus that scarce blows,
And fairer blossoms no man knows.

So crowned and chapleted with flowers,
    I pray you be not proud ;
For after brief and summer hours
    Comes autumn with a shroud ;—
Though fragrant as a flower you lie,
You and your garland, by and by,
Will fade and wither up and die !

EDMUND W. GOSSE.

THE FALLING ROSE.

PASS, falling rose !
 Not now the glory of the spring is round thee;
  Not now the air of summer round thee
   blows ;
Pallid and chill the autumn's mists have found thee ;
 Pass, falling rose !

 Pass, falling rose !
Where are the songs that wooed thy glad unfolding ?
 Only the south the wood-dove's soft wail knows ;
Far southern eaves the swallow's nest are holding ;
 Pass, falling rose !

 Pass, falling rose !
Linger the blooms to birth thy glory wooing ?
 Linger the hues that lured thee to unclose ?
Long, long, their leaves the dark earth have been
 strewing ;
  Pass, falling rose !

WILLIAM COX BENNETT.

CXXIV.

THE ROSE IN OCTOBER.

LATE and sweet, too sweet, too late!
What nightingale will sing to thee?
The empty nest, the shivering tree,
The dead leaves by the garden gate,
And cawing crows for thee will wait,
O sweet and late!

Where wert thou when the soft June nights
Were faint with perfume, glad with song?
Where wert thou when the days were long
And steeped in summer's young delights?
What hopest thou now but checks and slights,
Brief days, lone nights?

Stay, there's a gleam of winter wheat
Far on the hill; down in the woods
A very heaven of stillness broods;
And through the mellow sun's noon heat,
Lo, tender pulses round thee beat,
O late and sweet!

MARY TOWNLEY.

CXXV.

DOVER BEACH.

THE sea is calm to-night,
    The tide is full, the moon lies fair
    Upon the straits ;—on the French coast, the
       light
Gleams, and is gone ; the cliffs of England stand
Glimmering and vast, out in the tranquil bay.
Come to the window, sweet is the night air !
Only, from the long line of spray
Where the ebb meets the moon-blanch'd sand,
Listen ! you hear the grating roar
Of pebbles which the waves draw back, and fling,
At their return, up the high strand,
Begin, and cease, and then again begin,
With tremulous cadence slow, and bring
The eternal note of sadness in.

Sophocles long ago
Heard it on the Ægæan, and it brought

Into his mind the turbid ebb and flow
Of human misery ; we
Find also in the sound a thought,
Hearing it by this distant northern sea.

    The Sea of Faith
Was once, too, at the full, and round earth's shore
Lay like the folds of a bright girdle furl'd ;
But now I only hear
Its melancholy, long, withdrawing roar,
Retreating to the breath
Of the night-wind down the vast edges drear
And naked shingles of the world.

Ah, love, let us be true
To one another ! for the world, which seems
To lie before us like a land of dreams,
So various, so beautiful, so new,
Hath really neither joy, nor love, nor light,
Nor certitude, nor peace, nor help for pain ;
And we are here as on a darkling plain
Swept with confused alarm of struggle and fight,
Where ignorant armies clash by night !

                    MATTHEW ARNOLD.

CXXVI.

BURDENS.

ARE sorrows hard to bear,—the ruin
 Of flowers, the rotting of red fruit,
A love's decease, a life's undoing,
 And summer slain, and song-birds mute,
And skies of snow and bitter air?
These things, you deem, are hard to bear.

But ah the burden, the delight
 Of dreadful joys!   Noon opening wide,
Golden and great; the gulfs of night,
 Fair deaths, and rent veils cast aside,
Strong soul to strong soul rendered up,
And silence filling like a cup.

EDWARD DOWDEN.

CXXVII.

ON THE SHORE.

THE angry sunset fades from out the west,
    A glimmering greyness creeps along the
        sea ;
    Wild waves be hushed and moan into your
        rest,
Soon will all earth be sleeping, why not ye ?

Far off the heavens deaden o'er with sleep,
    The purple twilight darkens on the hill ;
Why will ye only ever wake and weep ?
    I weary of your sighing, oh ! be still.

But ever, ever, moan ye by the shore,
    While all your trouble surges in my breast ;
Oh, waves of trouble surge in me no more,
    Or be but still awhile and let me rest.

AUGUSTA WEBSTER.

CXXVIII.

THE waters are rising and flowing
　　Over the weedy stone—
Over it, over it going;
　　It is never gone.

Over it joys go sweeping,
　　'Tis there—the ancient pain :
Yea, drowned in waves and waves of weeping,
　　It will rise again.

GEORGE MACDONALD.

CXXIX.

 LIFE, O death, O world, O time,
O grave, where all things flow,
'Tis yours to make our lot sublime
With your great weight of woe.

Though sharpest anguish hearts may wring,
Though bosoms torn may be,
Yet suffering is a holy thing;
Without it what were we?

RICHARD CHENEVIX TRENCH.

CXXX.

OASIS.

LET them go by — the heats, the doubts, the
   strife;
   I can sit here and care not for them now,
   Dreaming beside the glimmering wave of life
Once more,—I know not how.

There is a murmur in my heart, I hear
Faint, O so faint, some air I used to sing;
It stirs my sense; and odours dim and dear
The meadow-breezes bring.

Just this way did the quiet twilights fade
Over the fields and happy homes of men,
While one bird sang as now, piercing the shade,
Long since,—I know not when.

EDWARD DOWDEN.

CXXXI.

THE EPICUREAN.

OW gently, beautiful, and calm,
  The quiet river murmurs by ;
How soft the light, how full of balm,
  The breeze that soothes the dark'ning sky!

In every clime, in every state,
  We may be happy if we will ;
Man wrestles against iron fate,
  And then complains of pain and ill.

The flowers, the beasts, the very heaven,
  Calmly their destined paths pursue ;
All take the pleasures that are given,
  We only find them short and few.

Oh that mankind, alive to truth,
  Would cease a hopeless war to wage ;
Would reap in youth the joys of youth,—
  In age the peacefulness of age !

Upon an everlasting tide
  Into the silent seas we go ; ·
But verdure laughs along the side,
  And roses on the margin blow.

Nor life, nor death, nor aught they hold,
  Rate thou above their natural height ;
Yet learn that all our eyes behold,
  Has value, if we mete it right.

Pluck then the·flowers that line the stream,
  Instead of fighting with its power ;
But pluck as flowers, not gems, nor deem
  That they will bloom beyond their hour.

Whate'er betides, from day to day,
  An even pulse and spirit keep ;
And, like a child, worn out with play,
  When wearied with existence, sleep.

SIR FRANCIS HASTINGS DOYLE.

DEPARTURE.

IT was not like your great and gracious ways !
    Do you, that have naught other to lament,
    Never, my Love, repent
    Of how, that July afternoon,
You went,
With sudden, unintelligible phrase,
And frighten'd eye,
Upon your journey of so many days,
Without a single kiss or a good-bye ?
I knew, indeed, that you were parting soon ;
And so we sate, within the low sun's rays,
You whispering to me, for your voice was weak,
Your harrowing praise.
Well, it was well, my Wife,
To hear you such things speak,
And see your love
Make of your eyes a growing gloom of life,
As a warm South wind sombres a March grove.
And it was like your great and gracious ways
To turn your talk on daily things, my Dear,

Lifting the luminous, pathetic lash
To let the laughter flash,
Whilst I drew near,
Because you spoke so low that I could scarcely hear.
But all at once to leave me at the last,
More at the wonder than the loss aghast,
With huddled, unintelligible phrase,
And frighten'd eye,
And go your journey of all days
With not one kiss or a good-bye,
And the only loveless look the look with which you
    pass'd,
'Twas all unlike your great and gracious ways.

COVENTRY PATMORE.

CXXXIII.

BEFORE SEDAN.

HERE, in this leafy place,
  Quiet he lies,
 Cold, with his sightless face
  Turned to the skies ;
'Tis but another dead ;
All you can say is said.

Carry his body hence,—
  Kings must have slaves ;
Kings climb to eminence
  Over men's graves :
So this man's eye is dim ;—
Throw the earth over him.

What was the white you touched,
  There, at his side ?
Paper his hand had clutched
  Tight e'er he died ;—
Message or wish, may be ;—
Smooth the folds out and see.

Hardly the worst of us
    Here could have smiled !—
Only the tremulous
    Words of a child ;—
Prattle, that has for stops
Just a few ruddy drops.

Look. She is sad to miss,
    Morning and night,
His—her dead father's—kiss ;
    Tries to be bright,
Good to mamma, and sweet.
That is all. " Marguerite."

Ah, if beside the dead
    Slumbered the pain !
Ah, if the hearts that bled
    Slept with the slain !
If the grief died ;—But no ;—
Death will not have it so.

AUSTIN DOBSON.

CXXXIV.

" BAI RN, when I am dead,
How shall ye keep frae harm ?
What hand shall gie ye bread ?
What fire will keep ye warm ?
How shall ye dwell on earth awa' frae me ? "—
" O Mither, dinna dee ! "

" O bairn, by night or day
I hear nae sounds ava',
But voices of winds that blaw,
And the voices of ghaists that say,
'Come awa ! come awa ! '
The Lord that made the wind, and made the sea,
Is sore on my son and me,
And I melt in His breath like snaw."—
" O Mither, dinna dee ! "

"O bairn, it is but closing up the een,
    And lying down never to rise again.
Many a strong man's sleeping hae I seen,—
    There is nae pain!
I'm weary, weary, and I scarce ken why;
    My summer has gone by,
And sweet were sleep, but for the sake o' thee."—
    "O Mither, dinna dee!"

                    ROBERT BUCHANAN.

CXXXV.

(From "'Tis Pity She's a Queen,"—a.d. 1610),
ACT IV. SCENE 2.

The Lady Margaret, *with* Susan *and* Lucy ; Lady
M. *at her embroidery frame, singing.*

GIRLS, when I am gone away,
 On this bosom strew
 Only flowers meek and pale,
  And the yew.

Lay these hands down by my side,
 Let my face be bare ;
Bind a kerchief round the face,
 Smooth my hair.

Let my bier be borne at dawn,
 Summer grows so sweet,
Deep into the forest green
 Where boughs meet.

Then pass away, and let me lie
　　One long, warm, sweet day
There alone with face upturn'd,
　　One sweet day.

When the morning light grows broad,
　　While noon sleepeth sound,
While the evening falls and faints,
　　While the world goes round.

EDWARD DOWDEN.

CXXXVI.

PASSING away, saith the World, passing away :
Chances, beauty and youth sapped day by
day :
Thy life never continueth in one stay.
Is the eye waxen dim, is the dark hair changing to
grey
That hath won neither laurel nor bay ?
I shall clothe myself in Spring and bud in May ;
Thou, root-stricken, shalt not rebuild thy decay
On my bosom for aye.
Then I answered : Yea.

Passing away, saith my Soul, passing away :
With its burden of fear and hope, of labour and play ;
Hearken what the past doth witness and say :
Rust in thy gold, a moth is in thine array,
A canker is in thy bud, thy leaf must decay.
At midnight, at cockcrow, at morning, one certain
day
Lo, the Bridegroom shall come and shall not delay :
Watch thou and pray.
Then I answered : Yea.

Passing away, saith my God, passing away :
Winter passeth after the long delay :
New grapes on the vine, new figs on the tender spray,
Turtle calleth- turtle in Heaven's May.
Though I tarry, wait for Me, trust Me, watch and pray,
Arise, come away, night is past and lo it is day.
My Love, My Sister, My Spouse, thou shalt hear me
     say.
Then I answered : Yea.

CHRISTINA ROSSETTI.

CXXXVII.

PUSH off the boat,
  Quit, quit the shore,
    The stars will guide us back : —
O gathering cloud,
  O wide, wide sea,
    O waves that keep no track !

On through the pines !
  The pillared woods,
    Where silence breathes sweet breath :—
O labyrinth,
  O sunless gloom,
    The other side of death !

GEORGE ELIOT.

"*THE UNDISCOVERED COUNTRY.*"

COULD we but know
      The land that ends our dark, uncer-
            tain travel,
Where lie those happier hills and meadows low,—
Ah, if beyond the spirit's inmost cavil,
   Aught of that country could we surely know,
         Who would not go ?

      Might we but hear
The hovering angels' high imagined chorus,
   Or catch, betimes, with wakeful eyes and clear,
One radiant vista of the realm before us,—
   With one rapt moment given to see and hear,
         Ah, who would fear ?

      Were we quite sure
To find the peerless friend who left us lonely,
   Or there, by some celestial stream as pure,
To gaze in eyes that here were lovelit only,—
   This weary mortal coil, were we quite sure,
         Who would endure ?

EDMUND CLARENCE STEDMAN.

CXXXIX.

NOT YET.

NOT yet, not yet, the light;
Underground, out of sight,
· Like moles, we blindly toil.
On, though we know not where;
Some day the upper air,
The sun, and all things fair,
We reach through the dark soil.

BEATRIX TOLLEMACHE.

CXI.

BY-AND-BY.

WAITING, waiting. 'Tis so far
    To the day that is to come :
One by one the days that are
    All to tell their countless sum ;
Each to dawn and each to die—
What so far as by-and-by ?

Waiting, waiting. 'Tis not ours
    This to-day that flies so fast :
Let them go, the shadowy hours
    Floating, floated, into Past.
Our day wears to-morrow's sky,—
What so near as by-and-by ?

                    AUGUSTA WEBSTER.

CXLI.

AFTER.

LITTLE time for laughter,
  A little time to sing,
  A little time to kiss and cling,
And no more kissing after.

A little while for scheming
  Love's unperfected schemes ;
  A little time for golden dreams, ·
Then no more any dreaming.

A little while 'twas given
  To me to have thy love ;
  Now, like a ghost, alone I move
About a ruined heaven.

A little time for speaking,
  Things sweet to say and hear ;
  A time to seek, and find thee near,
Then no more any seeking.

A little time for saying
  Words the heart breaks to say,
  A short, sharp time wherein to pray,
Then no more need for praying;

But long, long years to weep in,
  And comprehend the whole
  Great grief that desolates the soul,
And eternity to sleep in.

PHILIP BOURKE MARSTON.

THE SICK MAN AND THE BIRDS.

THE SICK MAN.

SPRING,—art thou come, O Spring !
   I am too sick for words ;
How hast thou heart to sing,
   O Spring, with all thy birds ?

THE BLACKBIRD.

I sing for joy to see again
The merry leaves along the lane,
   The little bud grown ripe ;
And look, my love upon the bough !
Hark, how she calleth to me now,—
          " Pipe ! Pipe ! "

THE SICK MAN.

Ah ! weary is the sun ;
   Love is an idle thing :
But, Bird, thou restless one,
   What ails thee, wandering ?

THE SWALLOW.

By shore and sea I come and go,
To seek I know not what—and lo !
On no man's eaves I sit
But voices bid me rise once more,
To flit again by sea and shore,—
"Flit ! Flit !"

THE SICK MAN.

This is Earth's bitter cup :—
Only to seek, not know.
But Thou, that strivest up,
Why dost thou carol so ?

THE LARK.

A secret Spirit gifteth me
With song, and wing that lifteth me,
A Spirit for whose sake,
Striving amain to reach the sky,
Still to the old dark earth I cry—
"Wake ! Wake !"

THE SICK MAN.

My hope hath lost its wing.
Thou, that to Night dost call,
How hast thou heart to sing,
Thy tears made musical ?

THE NIGHTINGALE.

Alas for me ! a dry desire
Is all my song,—a waste of fire
  That will not fade or fail ;
To me, dim shapes of ancient crime
Moan through the windy ways of Time,
    " Wail ! wail ! "

THE SICK MAN.

Thine is the sick man's song,—
  Mournful, in sooth, and fit ;
Unrest that cries " How long ? "
  And the Night answers it.

AUSTIN DOBSON.

CXLIII.

REST.

HEN the tumult of day is done,
    And the winds are at rest,
When the glory is all but gone
    In the wonderful west.

Why, heart, is thy trouble so deep?
  . Why, spirit, thy care?
Full soon thou shalt quieter sleep
    Than the quietest there.

                    JAMES RHOADES.

CXLIV.

A VOICE FROM AFAR.

WEEP not for me :—
    Be blithe as wont, nor tinge
        with gloom
The stream of love that circles home,
    Light hearts and free !
Joy in the gifts Heaven's bounty lends ;
    Nor miss my face, dear friends !

    I still am near ;—
Watching the smiles I prized on earth,
Your converse mild, your blameless mirth ;
    Now too I hear
Of whisper'd sounds the tale complete,
    Low prayers, and musings sweet.

A sea before
The throne is spread ;—its pure still glass
Pictures all earth-scenes as they pass.
We on its shore,
Share, in the bosom of our rest,
God's knowledge, and are blest.

JOHN HENRY NEWMAN.

CXLV.

THE world is great : the birds all fly from me,
The stars are golden fruit upon a tree
All out of reach : my little sister went,
And I am lonely.

The world is great : I tried to mount the hill
Above the pines, where the light lies so still,
But it rose higher : little Lisa went,
And I am lonely.

The world is great : the wind comes rushing by,
I wonder where it comes from ; sea-birds cry
And hurt my heart : my little sister went,
And I am lonely.

The world is great : the people laugh and talk,
And make loud holiday : how fast they walk !
I'm lame, they push me : little Lisa went,
And I am lonely.

GEORGE ELIOT.

CXLVI.

IF but thy heart were stone—
   Strong stone or steel— ·
It never had made this moan,
   It never had learnt to feel.

The storm should never have swept
   Over the place of its rest ;
It never had listened and leapt
   At the cry of a life opprest.

It had never been shaken and torn
   At the sight of a loved one's pain ;
It had never stood still, forlorn,
   At the thought " Is there meeting again ? "

It had stood by itself secure,
   Bound round and beneath and above,
Fenced from the plaint of the poor,
   And free from the fires of love.

Thou hadst smiled in god-like mirth,
   Thou hadst lived serene, alone,
Thou hadst lived a lord of earth,
   If but thy heart were stone.

                    ERNEST MYERS.

THE SEA-LIMITS.

CONSIDER the sea's listless chime;
    Tune's self it is, inaudible,—
    The murmur of the earth's own shell.
Secret continuance sublime
    Is the sea's end : our sight may pass
    No furlong further.   Since time was,
This sound hath told the lapse of time.

No quiet, which is death's,—it hath
    The mournfulness of ancient life,
    Enduring always at dull strife.
As the world's heart of rest and wrath,
    Its painful pulse is in the sands.
    Last utterly, the whole sky stands,
Grey and not known, along its path.

Listen alone beside the sea,
    Listen alone among the woods;
    Those voices of twin's solitudes
Shall have one sound alike to thee:

Hark ! where the murmurs of thronged men
    Surge and smile back, and surge again,—
Still the one voice of wave and tree.

Gather a shell from the strown beach
    And listen at its lips : they sigh
    The same desire and mystery,
The echo of the whole sea's speech.
    And all mankind is thus at heart
    Not anything but what thou art :
And Earth, Sea, Man, are all in each.

DANTE GABRIEL ROSSETTI.

VIOLETS.

VIOLETS, shy violets !
　　How many hearts with thee compare !
　　　Who hide themselves in thickest green,
　　　　　And thence unseen,
　　　Ravish the enraptured air
　　With sweetness, dewy fresh and rare !

Violets, shy violets !
　　Human hearts to me shall be
　　　Viewless violets in the grass,
　　　　　And as I pass,
　　Odours and sweet imagery
　　Will wait on mine and gladden me !

GEORGE MEREDITH.

CXLIX.

THE APOLOGY.

THINK me not unkind and rude
  That I walk alone in grove and glen;
I go to the god of the wood
  To fetch his word to men.

Tax not my sloth that I
  Fold my arms beside the brook;
Each cloud that floated in the sky
  Writes a letter in my book.

Chide me not, laborious band,
  For the idle flowers I brought;
Every aster in my hand
  Goes home loaded with a thought.

There was never mystery
  But 'tis figured in the flowers;
Was never secret history
  But birds tell it in the bowers.

One harvest in thy field
   Homeward brought the oxen strong;
A second crop thine acres yield,
   Which I gather in a song.

RALPH WALDO EMERSON.

CL.

L'ENVOI.

I HOLD within my hand a lute,
　　A lute that hath not many strings.
　　A little bird above it sings,
　　And singing soars and claps its wings;
　Sing, little bird; when thou art mute,
　The music dies within my lute.

　Sing on, thou little bird, until
　I hear a voice expected long,
　That bids an after-silence fill
　The space that once was filled with song.
　Then fold thy wings upon my breast,
　Upon my heart, and give it rest.

DORA GREENWELL.

BOOK II.

Sonnets.

CLI.

THE SINGER'S PLEA.

HY do I sing?   I know not why, my friend ;
     The ancient rivers, rivers of renown,
     A royal largess to the sea roll down,
     And on those liberal highways nations send
Their tributes to the world,—stored corn and wine,
Gold-dust, the wealth of pearls, and orient spar,
And myrrh, and ivory, and cinnabar,
And dyes to make a presence-chamber shine.
But in the woodlands, where the wild flowers are,
The rivulets, they must have their innocent will·
Who all the summer hours are singing still ;
The birds care for them, and sometimes a star,
And should a tired child rest beside the stream,
Sweet memories would slide into his dream.

EDWARD DOWDEN.

CLII.

SHAKSPEARE.

OTHERS abide our question—Thou art free !
We ask and ask—Thou smilest and art still,
Out-topping knowledge ! So some sovran hill
Who to the stars uncrowns his majesty,

Planting his steadfast footsteps in the sea,
Making the heaven of heavens his dwelling-place,
Spares but the border, often, of his base
To the foil'd searching of mortality ;

And thou, whose head did stars and sunbeams know,
Self-school'd, self-scann'd, self-honour'd, self-secure,
Didst walk on earth unguess'd at.—Better so !

All pains the immortal spirit must endure,
All weakness which impairs, all griefs which bow,
Find their sole voice in that victorious brow.

MATTHEW ARNOLD.

CLIII.

LETTY'S GLOBE.

WHEN Letty had scarce pass'd her third glad
    year,
  And her young artless words began to flow,
  One day we gave the child a colour'd
    sphere
Of the wide earth, that she might mark and know
By tint and outline all its sea and land.
She patted all the world; old empires peep'd
Between her baby-fingers ; her soft hand
Was welcome at all frontiers ; how she leap'd,
And laugh'd, and prattled in her pride of bliss !
But when we turn'd her sweet unlearnèd eye
On our own isle, she rais'd a joyous cry,
" Oh yes ! I see it, Letty's home is there ! "
And while she hid all England with a kiss,
Bright over Europe fell her golden hair.

CHARLES TENNYSON TURNER.

CLIV.

LOVE THE MUSICIAN.

LOVE is the Minstrel; for in God's own sight,
    The master of all melody, he stands,
    And holds a golden rebeck in his hands,
And leads the chorus of the saints in light;
But ever and anon those chambers bright
    Detain him not, for down to these low lands
    He flies, and spreads his musical commands,
And teaches men some fresh divine delight.
For with his bow he strikes a single chord
    Across a soul, and wakes in it desire
    To grow more pure and lovely, and aspire
To that ethereal country where, outpoured
From myriad stars that stand before the Lord,
    Love's harmonies are like a flame of fire.

EDMUND W. GOSSE.

CLV.

LOVE PASSING.

H wherefore ever onward, Love ! Oh why
Not rest with me awhile, and bid me take
Thine own sweet flowers that everywhere grow
    high
In meadows glorious made by that deep lake,
Reflecting clear the heaven of thy sweet grace :
Teach me, O Love, to pluck these flowers of thine,
Give me to see and know thy blessed face,
That everlasting wisdom may be mine :—
I feel the charm of sweetest misery,
I know the mountain-land of quick extremes,
Thick flowers and deepest snows I also see,
I feel great sorrow mix with brightest dreams :—
Sweet Love ! Oh rush not thus so quickly by,
But live with me that joy may never die.

J. W. INCHBOLD.

CLVI.

LOVE'S QUEST.

LOVE walks with weary feet the upward way,
  Love without joy and led by suffering ;
  Love's unkissed lips have now no song to
   sing,
Love's eyes are blind and cannot see the day.
Love walks in utter darkness, and I say :
  "Oh, Love, 'tis summer ;" or, "Behold the spring ;"
  Or, " Love, 'tis autumn, and leaves withering ;"
And " Now it is the winter bleak and gray ; "
And still Love heedeth not. " Oh, Love," I cry,
  " Wilt thou not rest ? the path is over steep : "
Love answers not, but passeth all things by ;
  Nor will he stay, for those who laugh or weep.
I follow Love who follows Grief ; but lo,
Where the way ends, not Love himself can know.

PHILIP BOURKE MARSTON.

CLVII.

LOVE'S ANSWER.

I SAID to Love, " Lo one thing troubles me !
    How shall I show the way in which I love?
    Is any word, or look, or kiss enough
    To show to her my love's extremity ?
What is there I can say, or do, that she
    May know the strength and utter depth thereof ?
For words are weak, such love as mine to prove,
    Though I should pour them forth unceasingly."
Then fell Love's smile upon me as he said,
    " Thou art a child in love, not knowing this ;
    That could she know thy love by word or kiss,
Or gauge it by its show, 'twere all but dead :
    For not by bounds, but shoreless distances,
Full knowledge of the sea is compassèd."

PHILIP BOURKE MARSTON.

Q

CLVIII.

WINGED HOURS.

EACH hour until we meet is as a bird
    That wings from far his gradual way along
    The rustling covert of my soul,—his song
Still loudlier trilled through leaves more deeply
      stirr'd.

But at the hour of meeting, a clear word
    Is every note he sings, in Love's own tongue;
    Yet, Love, thou know'st the sweet strain suffers
      wrong,
Through our contending kisses oft unheard.

What of that hour at last, when for her sake
    No wing may fly to me nor song may flow;
    When, wandering round my life unleaved, I know
The blooded feathers scattered in the brake,
    And think how she, far from me, with like eyes
    Sees through the tuneful bough the wingless
      skies?

DANTE GABRIEL ROSSETTI.

CLIX.

BROKEN MUSIC.

HE mother will not turn, who thinks she hears
    Her nursling's speech first grow articulate ;
    But breathless with averted eyes elate
    She sits, with open lips and open ears,
That it may call her twice. 'Mid doubts and fears
    Thus oft my soul has hearkened ; till the song,
    A central moan for days, at length found tongue.
And the sweet music welled and the sweet tears.

But now, whatever while the soul is fain
    To list that wonted murmur, as it were
The speech-bound sea-shell's low importunate strain,—
    No breath of song, thy voice alone is there,
Oh bitterly beloved ! and all her gain
    Is but the pang of unpermitted prayer.

                    DANTE GABRIEL ROSSETTI.

CLX.

NIGHTINGALES.

HAT spirit moves the quiring nightingales
    To utter forth their notes so soft and clear?
    What purport hath their music, which pre-
        vails
At midnight, thrilling all the darkened air?
'Tis said, some weeks before the hen-birds land
Upon our shores, their tuneful mates appear;
And, in that space, by hope and sorrow spann'd,
Their sweetest melodies 'tis ours to hear;
And is it so? for solace till they meet,
Does this most perfect chorus charm the grove?
Do these wild voices, round me and above,
Of amorous forethought and condolence treat?
Well may such lays be sweetest of the sweet,
That aim to fill the intervals of Love!

CHARLES TENNYSON TURNER.

CLXI.

LILITH.

(FOR A PICTURE.)

F Adam's first wife, Lilith, it is told
 (The witch he loved before the gift of Eve),
  That, ere the snake's, her sweet tongue
   could deceive,
And her enchanted hair was the first gold.
And still she sits, young, while the earth is old,
 And, subtly of herself contemplative,
  Draws men to watch the bright web she can
   weave,
Till heart and body and life are in its hold.

The rose and poppy are her flowers; for where
 Is he not found, O Lilith, whom shed scent
And soft-shed kisses and soft sleep shall snare?
  Lo! as that youth's eyes burned at thine, so went
  Thy spell through him, and left his straight neck
   bent,
And round his heart one strangling golden hair.

DANTE GABRIEL ROSSETTI.

LOVE-SWEETNESS.

SWEET dimness of her loosened hair's downfall
    About thy face; her sweet hands round thy
      head
    In gracious fostering union garlanded;
Her tremulous smiles; her glances' sweet recall
Of love; her murmuring sighs memorial;
    Her mouth's culled sweetness by thy kisses shed
    On cheeks and neck and eyelids, and so led
Back to her mouth which answers there for all;—

What sweeter than these things, except the thing
    In lacking which all these would lose their
      sweet:—
    The confident heart's still fervour; the swift beat
And soft subsidence of the spirit's wing,
Then when it feels, in cloud-girt wayfaring,
    The breath of kindred plumes against its feet?

DANTE GABRIEL ROSSETTI.

CLXIII.

THE BRIDESMAID.

 BRIDESMAID, ere the happy knot was tied,
    Thine eyes so wept that they could scarcely
        see;
    Thy sister smiled and said, "No tears for
        me!
A happy bridesmaid makes a happy bride."
And then, the couple standing side by side,
    Love lighted down between them full of glee,
    And over his left shoulder laugh'd at thee,
"O happy bridesmaid, make a happy bride."
And all at once a pleasant truth I learn'd,
    For while the tender service made thee weep,
I loved thee for the tear thou couldst not hide,
And prest thy hand, and knew the press return'd,
    And thought, "My life is sick of single sleep;
O happy bridesmaid, make a happy bride!"

ALFRED TENNYSON.

SPRING LOVE.

FROM morn to evening, this day, yesterday,
  We've walked within the garden'd paths
   of love,
  Till the moon rose the darkening woods
   above:
We've seen the blossoming apple's crimson spray,
And watched the hiving bees work lustily,
  As if their time was short as it was sweet:
  Along love's meadow-lands too, with glad feet,
We've welcomed all the wild flowers come with May.

Bend thy sweet head; I've strung this long woodbine
  With primroses and cowslips—golden fringe
   For golden hair, the flowers that best express
The opening of the year, the mild sunshine,
  And the frank clearness of those thoughtless eyes,
   Through which there gleams scarce-trusted
   blessedness.

WILLIAM BELL SCOTT.

CLXV.

W H Y.

"WHY do I love thee?" Thus, in earnest wise,
　　I answer: Sweet! I love thee for thy
　　　face
　　Of rarest beauty; and for every grace
That in thy voice and air and motion lies;
I love thee for the love-look in thine eyes,—
　　The melting glance which only one may see
　　Of all who mark how beautiful they be;
I love thee for thy mind (which yet denies,
For modesty, how wonderful it is!)
　　I love thee for thy heart so true and warm,
　　I love thee for thy bosom's hidden charm;
I love thee for thy mouth so sweet to kiss;
　　Because of these I love thee; yet above
　　All else, because I cannot choose but love!

JOHN GODFREY SAXE.

CLXVI.

REMEMBRANCE.

O think of thee ! it was thy fond request
        When yesterweek we parted.   Ah ! how well
        I heed thy bidding only Love may tell
Beneath his roses.   As, for welcome rest,
The bird, wing-weary, seeks her downy nest,
        So oft, dear heart ! from toil and care I flee,
        And, nestling in my happy thought of thee,
With sweet repose my weary soul is blest.
To think of thee—who evermore art near
        My conscious spirit, like the halo spread
        In altar-pictures round some stately head,
As 'twere of Heaven the golden atmosphere—
        What can I else, until in death I sink,
        And, thinking of my darling, cease to think?

JOHN GODFREY SAXE.

CLXVII.

LET not our lips pronounce the word Farewell
　　To those we cherish ;—if one needs must part,
　　On hope's illusion let the fancy dwell,
　　　Nor deem that distance can make cold the
　　　　heart !
Though I should look through sorrow's dim eclipse,
And print warm partings on the loved one's lips—
To speak the last sad word my tongue were dumb ;
Or, if it syllabled my soul's emotion,
'Twould be to tell how pilgrim steps have come
To worship at the shrine of love's devotion !
So be the language of despair unspoken
By those whose hearts, nor time, nor space can sever—
A fountain seal'd till hope be lost for ever,
And only gushing when the heart is broken.

JAMES HEDDERWICK.

CLXVIII.

I WOULD not have this perfect love of ours
  Grow from a single root, a single stem,
   Bearing no goodly fruit, but only flowers
   That idly hide life's iron diadem :
It should grow alway like that eastern tree
Whose limbs take root and spread forth constantly;
That love for one, from which there doth not spring
Wide love for all, is but a worthless thing.
Not in another world, as poets prate,
Dwell we apart above the tide of things,
High floating o'er earth's clouds our faëry wings :
But our pure love doth ever elevate
Into a holy bond of brotherhood
All earthly things, making them pure and good.

JAMES RUSSELL LOWELL.

CLXIX.

UR love is not a fading, earthly flower :
　　Its wingèd seed dropped down from Paradise,
　　And, nursed by day and night, by sun and
　　　shower,
Doth momently to fresher beauty rise :
To us the leafless autumn is not bare,
Nor winter's rattling boughs lack lusty green.
Our summer hearts make summer's fulness, where
No leaf, or bud, or blossom may be seen :
For nature's life in love's deep life doth lie,
Love,—whose forgetfulness is beauty's death,
Whose mystic key these cells of Thou and I
Into the infinite freedom openeth,
And makes the body's dark and narrow grate
The wide-flung leaves of Heaven's palace-gate.

JAMES RUSSELL LOWELL.

CLXX.

AFTER DEATH.

THE curtains were half drawn, the floor was swept
        And strewn with rushes, rosémary and may
        Lay thick upon the bed on which I lay,
Where through the lattice ivy-shadows crept.
He leaned above me, thinking that I slept
        And could not hear him ; but I heard him say :
        " Poor child, poor child ! " and as he turned away
Came a deep silence, and I knew he wept.
He did not touch the shroud, or raise the fold
        That hid my face, or take my hand in his,
                Or ruffle the smooth pillows for my head :
                He did not love me living ; but once dead
        He pitied me ; and very sweet it is
To know he still is warm, though I am cold.

CHRISTINA ROSSETTI.

CLXXI.

LOVE, TIME, AND DEATH.

AH me, dread friends of mine,—Love, Time,
 and Death :
 Sweet Love, who came to me on sheeny wing,
And gave her to my arms—her lips, her breath,
 And all her golden ringlets clustering :
And Time, who gathers in the flying years,
 He gave me all, but where is all he gave?
He took my love and left me barren tears,
 Weary and lone I follow to the grave.
There Death will end this vision half divine,
 Wan Death, who waits in shadow evermore,
And silent, ere he gave the sudden sign ;
 Oh, gently lead me thro' thy narrow door,
Thou gentle Death, thou trustiest friend of mine—
 Ah me, for Love—will Death my love restore?

FREDERICK LOCKER.

CLXXII.

HOARDED JOY.

I SAID: "Nay, pluck not,—let the first fruit be;
　　Even as thou sayest, it is sweet and red,
　　But let it ripen still.　The tree's bent head
Sees in the stream its own fecundity
And bides the day of fulness.　Shall not we
　　At the sun's hour that day possess the shade,
　　And claim our fruit before its ripeness fade,
And eat it from the branch and praise the tree?"

I say: "Alas! our fruit hath wooed the sun
　　Too long,—'tis fallen and floats adown the stream.
Lo, the last clusters!　Pluck them every one,
　　And let us sup with summer; ere the gleam
Of autumn set the year's pent sorrow free,
And the woods wail like echoes from the sea."

DANTE GABRIEL ROSSETTI.

CLXXIII.

RURAL NATURE.

WHERE art thou loveliest, O Nature, tell!
    Oh where may be thy Paradise? Where
      grow
Thy happiest groves? And down what woody dell
    Do thy most fancy-winning waters flow?
    Tell where thy softest breezes longest blow?
And where thy ever blissful mountains swell
    Upon whose sides the cloudless sun may throw
Eternal summer, while the air may quell

His fury. Is it 'neath his morning car,
    Where jewell'd palaces, and golden thrones,
Have aw'd the eastern nations through all time?

Or o'er the western seas, or where afar
    Our winter sun warms up the southern zones
With summer? Where can be the happy climes?

WILLIAM BARNES.
R

CLXXIV.

WHEN man alone, or leagued in governments,
  The works of Christian duty would fulfil,
  His faltering steps defeat his anxious will,
  As heights attain'd reveal but fresh ascents :
How poor his efforts to his high intents !
Fain would he uproot every human ill ;
But fields neglected open to him still,
And woe on woe its piteous tale presents.
Nature alone succeeds in all she tries :
She drops her dews, and not a flower is miss'd ;
She bids the universal grass arise,
Till stony ways and wilds antagonist
Are into emerald beauty softly kiss'd,
To show the power in gentleness that lies.

                                JAMES HEDDERWICK.

CLXXV.

HERE never yet was flower fair in vain,
　　Let classic poets rhyme it as they will :
　　The seasons toil that it may blow again,
　　And summer's heart doth feel its every ill ;
Nor is a true soul ever born for naught ;
Wherever any such hath lived and died,
There hath been something for true freedom wrought,
Some bulwark levelled on the evil side :
Toil on, then, Greatness ! thou art in the right,
However narrow souls may call thee wrong ;
Be as thou wouldst be in thine own clear sight
And so thou wilt in all the world's ere long ;
For worldlings cannot, struggle as they may,
From man's great soul one great thought hide away.

JAMES RUSSELL LOWELL.

CLXXVI.

IT may be that our homeward longings made
 That other lands were judged with partial eyes ;
 But fairer in my sight the mottled skies,
 With pleasant interchange of sun and shade,
And more desired the meadow and deep glade
Of sylvan England, green with frequent showers,
Than all the beauty which the vaunted bowers
Of the parched South have in mine eyes displayed ;
Fairer and more desired !— this well might be,
For let the South have beauty's utmost dower
And yet my heart might well have turned to thee,
My home, my country, when a delicate flower
Within thy pleasant borders was for me
Tended, and growing up thro' sun and shower.

RICHARD CHENEVIX TRENCH.

CLXXVII.

I SAW in dream where met proud rivers twain
    From the East and West—one without storm
       or stain,
    Clear-eyed and paved with crystal, as to glass
The merest speck that in the air might pass
Above it ; the other, from remoter springs,
Soil'd with long travel and passionate outgoings,
Full-vein'd and swoll'n with ore from the iron rock,
Impetuous sped to meet it : at the shock
Earth reeled, and heaven grew dark with sudden gloam
Above the unpenetrable spray.   What wonder,
If men's eyes, baffled by the blinding foam,
Saw not beyond, where, 'scaped the smoke and thunder,
Through prosperous fields, bright blazon'd fold on fold,
One clear strong stream their glorious course they hold.

JAMES RHOADES.

CLXXVIII.

BELOW THE OLD HOUSE.

BENEATH those buttressed walls with lichen
grey,
    Beneath the slopes of trees whose flickering
shade
Darkens the pools by dun green velveted,
The stream leaps like a living thing at play,—
In haste it seems; it cannot, cannot stay!
    The great boughs changing there from year to
year,
    And the high jackdaw-haunted eaves, still hear
The burden of the rivulet,—Passing away!

And sometime certainly that oak no more
    Will keep the winds in check; his breadth of
beam

Will go to rib some ship for some far shore ;
    Those coigns and eaves will crumble, while that
        stream
Will still run whispering, whispering night and day,
That over-song of Father Time,—Passing away !

                    WILLIAM BELL SCOTT.

PROJECTED SHADOWS.

AH, memory! ah, ruthless memory!
    Shall I not have one hour unfill'd for thee?
    Why wilt thou thus usurp the days to be,
Unsatisfied with all thy realms that lie
Behind the Present? why o'ercloud the sky,
    Glad with gold star-scripts of Futurity?
    Hast thou not made the fleeting hours for me
Sunless enough, that thou must flicker by
    The shrouding years, and hovering on the verge
Of my horizon's blue, blot out the forms
    Of all my pleasant creatures of delight,
    Won with much wrestling from the haggard
        night,—
And in their stead paint up a sky of storms
    And the stern Fury sworded with the scourge?

JOHN PAYNE.

CLXXX.

COUNT each affliction, whether light or grave,
    God's messenger sent down to thee; do thou
    With courtesy receive him; rise and bow;
    And, ere his shadow pass thy threshold, crave
Permission first his heavenly feet to lave;
Then lay before him all thou hast; allow
No cloud of passion to usurp thy brow,
Or mar thy hospitality; no wave
Of mortal tumult to obliterate
The soul's marmoreal calmness: Grief should be
Like joy, majestic, equable, sedate;
Confirming, cleansing, raising, making free;
Strong to consume small troubles; to commend
Great thoughts, grave thoughts, thoughts lasting to the
    end.

AUBREY DE VERE.

CLXXXI.

BLESSED is he who hath not trod the ways
    Of secular delights, nor learned the lore
    Which loftier minds are studious to abhor :
    Blessed is he who hath not sought the praise
That perishes, the rapture that betrays;
Who hath not spent in Time's vainglorious war
His youth; and found, a schoolboy at fourscore,
How fatal are those victories which raise
Their iron trophies to a temple's height
On trampled Justice; who desires not bliss,
But peace; and yet when summoned to the fight,
Combats as one who combats in the sight
Of God and of His Angels, seeking this
Alone, how best to glorify the right.

AUBREY DE VERE.

CLXXXII.

NOW OR WHEN.

N the tall buttress of a Minster gray,
    The glorious work of long-forgotten men,
    I read this Dial-legend,—" Now or When."
Well had these builders used their little day
Of service—witness this sublime display
    Of blossom'd stone, dazzling the gazer's ken.
    These towers attest they knew 'twas there and then,
Not some vague morrow, they must work and pray.
Oh ! let us seize this transitory Now
    From which to build a life-work that shall last :
In humble prayer and worship let us bow
    Ere fleeting opportunity is past.
When once Life's sun forsakes the Dial-plate,
For work and for repentance 'tis too late !

RICHARD WILTON.

THE HAWTHORN AND THE WILD ROSE.

I LEARNT a lesson from the flowers to-day :—
    As o'er the fading hawthorn-blooms I sighed,
    Whose petals fair lay scattered far and wide,
  Lo, suddenly upon a dancing spray
I saw the first wild roses clustered gay.
    What though the smile I loved, so soon had died
    From one sweet flower—there, shining at its side,
The blushing Rose surpassed the snowy May.
So, if as Life glides on, we miss some flowers
    Which once shed light and fragrance on our way,
Yet still the kindly-compensating hours
    Weave us fresh wreaths in beautiful array ;
    And long as in the paths of peace we stay,
Successive benedictions shall be ours !

RICHARD WILTON.

CLXXXIV.

THE SOUND OF THE SEA.

THE sea awoke at midnight from its sleep,
  And round the pebbly beaches far and wide
  I heard the first wave of the rising tide
  Rush onward with uninterrupted sweep ;
A voice out of the silence of the deep,
  A sound mysteriously multiplied
  As of a cataract from the mountain's side,
  Or roar of winds upon a wooded steep.
So comes to us at times, from the unknown
  And inaccessible solitudes of being,
  The rushing of the sea-tides of the soul ;
And inspirations, that we deem our own,
  Are one divine foreshadowing and foreseeing
  Of things beyond our reason and control.

HENRY WADSWORTH LONGFELLOW.

CLXXXV.

ASK not for those thoughts, that sudden leap
From being's sea, like the isle-seeming Kraken,
With whose great rise the ocean all is shaken
And a heart-tremble quivers through the deep;
Give me that growth which some perchance deem sleep,
Wherewith the steadfast coral-stems uprise,
Which, by the toil of gathering energies,
Their upward way into clear sunshine keep,
Until, by Heaven's sweetest influences,
Slowly and slowly spreads a speck of green
Into a pleasant island in the seas,
Where, 'mid tall palms, the cane-roofed home is seen,
And wearied men shall sit at sunset's hour,
Hearing the leaves and loving God's dear power.

JAMES RUSSELL LOWELL.

CLXXXVI.

GRIEVE not that ripe Knowledge takes away
The charm that Nature to my childhood wore,
For, with that insight, cometh, day by day,
A greater bliss than wonder was before ;
The real doth not clip the poet's wing,—
To win the secret of a weed's plain heart
Reveals some clew to spiritual things,
And stumbling guess becomes firm-footed art :
Flowers are not flowers unto the poet's eyes,
Their beauty thrills him by an inward sense ;
He knows that outward seemings are but lies,
Or, at the most, but earthly shadows, whence
The soul that looks within for truth may guess
The presence of some wondrous heavenliness.

JAMES RUSSELL LOWELL.

CLXXXVII.

TO HELEN.

A MOMENTARY wish passed through my
    brain,
    To be the monarch of some magic place,
    Thick-sown with burning gems, or to con-
        strain
The uncouth help of some half-demon race,
Vexing the pearl-paved billows of the main
    For thee, and starry caverns in far space.
It was a wish unwisely formed, and vain ;
    Even in the humblest trifles, love can trace
That which no mine can give, no Geni's wing
From depths beneath or heights above can bring ;
The memories of each kind look and tone,
    Gestures, and glancing smiles, into the gift
    Pass like a living spirit, and uplift
Its value, to the level of their own.

SIR FRANCIS HASTINGS DOYLE.

CLXXXVIII.

AUTUMN.

NOW Autumn's fire burns slowly along the woods,
   And day by day the dead leaves fall and melt,
      And night by night the monitory blast
      Wails in the key-hole, telling how it pass'd
O'er empty fields, or upland solitudes,
   Or grim wide wave ; and now the power is felt
Of melancholy, tenderer in its moods
   Than any joy indulgent summer dealt.
Dear friends, together in the glimmering eve,
   Pensive and glad, with tones that recognise
   The soft invisible dew in each one's eyes,
It may be, somewhat thus we shall have leave
   To walk with memory, when distant lies
Poor Earth, where we were wont to live and grieve.

WILLIAM ALLINGHAM.

S

CLXXXIX.

OCTOBER.

AY, thou art welcome, heaven's delicious breath!
 When woods begin to wear the crimson leaf,
 And suns grow meek, and the meek suns
  grow brief,
And the year smiles as it draws near its death.
Wind of the sunny south! oh, still delay
 In the gay woods and in the golden air,
 Like to a good old age released from care,
Journeying, in long serenity, away.
In such a bright, late quiet, would that I
 Might wear out life like thee, 'mid bowers and
  brooks,
 And, dearer yet, the sunshine of soft looks,
And music of kind voices ever nigh;
And when my last sand twinkled in the glass,
Pass silently from men, as thou dost pass.

WILLIAM CULLEN BRYANT.

CXC.

WORLDLY PLACE.

E VEN in a palace, life may be led well!
So spoke the imperial sage, purest of men,
Marcus Aurelius.—But the stifling den
Of common life, where, crowded up pell-mell,

Our freedom for a little bread we sell,
And drudge under some foolish master's ken,
Who rates us, if we peer outside our pen—
Match'd with a palace, is not this a hell?

Even in a palace! On his truth sincere,
Who spoke these words, no shadow ever came;
And when my ill-school'd spirit is aflame

Some nobler, ampler stage of life to win,
I'll stop, and say : " There were no succour here !
The aids to noble life are all within."

MATTHEW ARNOLD.

THE GOOD SHEPHERD WITH THE KID.

*H*E saves the sheep, the goats he doth not save!
    So rang Tertullian's sentence, on the side
    Of that unpitying Phrygian sect which cried:
      " Him can no fount of fresh forgiveness lave,

Who sins, once wash'd by the baptismal wave!"
    So spake the fierce Tertullian.   But she sigh'd,
    The infant Church! of love she felt the tide
    Stream on her from her Lord's yet recent grave.

And then she smil'd; and in the Catacombs,
    With eye suffused but heart inspired true,
    On those walls subterranean, where she hid

Her head in ignominy, death, and tombs,
    She her Good Shepherd's hasty image drew—
    And on his shoulders, not a lamb, a kid.

                    MATTHEW ARNOLD.

CXCII.

EAST LONDON.

'TWAS August, and the fierce sun overhead
    Smote on the squalid streets of Bethnal
        Green,
    And the pale weaver, through his window
        seen
In Spitalfields, look'd thrice dispirited ;

I met a preacher there I knew, and said :
" Ill and o'erwork'd, how fare you in this scene ? "
" Bravely ! " said he ; " for I of late have been
Much cheer'd with thoughts of Christ, *the living
    bread.*"

O human soul ! as long as thou canst so
Set up a mark of everlasting light,
Above the howling senses' ebb and flow,

To cheer thee, and to right thee if thou roam,
Not with lost toil thou labourest through the night !
Thou mak'st the heaven thou hop'st indeed thy home.

MATTHEW ARNOLD.

CXCIII.

THE BETTER PART.

LONG fed on boundless hopes, O race of man,
    How angrily thou spurn'st all simpler fare !
    "Christ," some one says, "was human as we
        are.
    No judge eyes us from Heaven, our sin to
        scan.

We live no more, when we have done our span."—
"Well, then, for Christ," thou answerest, "who can
    care ?
From sin, which Heaven records not, why forbear ?
Live we like brutes our life without a plan !"

So answerest thou ; but why not rather say :
" Hath man no second life ?—*Pitch this one high !*
Sits there no judge in Heaven, our sin to see ?—

More strictly, then, the inward judge obey !
Was Christ a man like us ?—*Ah ! let us try*
If we then, too, can be such men as He !"

MATTHEW ARNOLD.

CXCIV.

IMMORTALITY.

FOIL'D by our fellow-men, depress'd, outworn,
  We leave the brutal world to take its way,
  And, *Patience ! in another life,* we say,
  The world shall be thrust down, and we
    up-borne !

And will not, then, the immortal armies scorn
The world's poor, routed leavings? or will they,
Who fail'd under the heat of this life's day,
Support the fervours of the heavenly morn?

No, no ! the energy of life may be
Kept on after the grave, but not begun !
And he who flagg'd not in the earthly strife,

From strength to strength advancing—only he,
His soul well-knit, and all his battles won,
Mounts, and that hardly, to eternal life.

MATTHEW ARNOLD.

DEVELOPMENT IN NATURE.

ALLED up in sense we know no general plan:
    Æons long past creative power went on,
    Evolving lights and forces round the
        throne,
And in the ordered nucleus of the plan
Blossomed and brightened the umbrageous span
    Of this our world, beneath the Fates' fell care,
    The Tree of Life outspreading everywhere,
And seedling fruits from short-lived blooms began.

Have these old mysteries ceased? from fiery steeps,
    From deepening swamps the mute snake writhed
        along;
Anon the bird screamed—then the furred beast creeps
    Growling; then Adam speaks erect and strong.
Shall there not rise again from Nature's deeps
    One more, whose voice shall be the perfect song?

WILLIAM BELL SCOTT.

CXCVI.

SCIENCE ·ABORTIVE.

WITH what vain speculations do we slake
  The mental thirst ! What matter, cycles hence,
  If Higher Creatures at mankind's expense
Start into life with senses broad awake
To truths we only dream of; hands to shake
  The pillars of the temple we but grope
  Feebly about, who will gain entrance, cope
With the dæmon, and all prison-fetters break ?

The churchyard dust a thousand times blown wide
  Would see them, hear them not ; the question men
  Ten hundred various creeds and gods have raised
To answer, by Death's door we must abide ;
  Blinded by life itself, by fears half-crazed,
  We raise another god and ask again !

WILLIAM BELL SCOTT.

CXCVII.

SELF-DECEPTION.

THERE'S a Seer's peak on Ararat, they say,
    From which we can descry the better
       world;
    Not that supernal kingdom whence were
       hurled
The rebel-angels ere Creation's day,
But Eden-garden, Adam's first array,
    Round which the Flood-waves stood back like a
      wall,
    And whither still are sent the souls of all
The good dead, where the cherubim sing and play.

Dear lovely land we wait for and desire,
    Whence fondly-loved lost faces look back still,
      Waiting for us, so distant and apart;
But from the depths between what mists aspire—
    What wrinkled sea rolls severing hill from hill—
      Vision! 'tis but the reflex of the heart!

WILLIAM BELL SCOTT.

PAST AND FUTURE.

FAIR garden, where the man and woman dwelt,
    And lov'd, and work'd, and where, in work's
      reprieve,
    The sabbath of each day, the restful eve,
They sat in silence, with lock'd hands, and felt
The voice which compass'd them, a-near, a-far,
    Which murmur'd in the fountains and the breeze,
    Which breathed in spices from the laden trees,
And sent a silvery shout from each lone star.
Sweet dream of Paradise! and if a dream,
    One that has help'd us when our faith was weak ;
We wake, and still it holds us, but would seem
    Before us, not behind,—the good we seek,—
The good from lowest root which waxes ever,
The golden age of science and endeavour.

EMILY PFEIFFER.

CXCIX.

FAITH.

"FOLLOW Me," Jesus said ; and they uprose,
 Peter and Andrew rose and followed Him,
 Followed Him even to heaven through
  death most grim,
And through a long hard life without repose,
Save in the grand ideal of its close.
 "Take up your cross and come with Me," He
  said ;
 And the world listens yet through all her dead,
And still would answer had we faith like those.

But who can light again such beacon-fire !
 With gladsome haste and with rejoicing souls—
  How would men gird themselves for the emprise ?
Leaving their black boats by the dead lake's mire,
 Leaving their slimy nets by the cold shoals,
  . Leaving their old oars, nor once turn their eyes.

WILLIAM BELL SCOTT.

CC.

THE FOOTPRINTS.

COME to green under-glooms,—and in your hair
    Weave night-shade, foxglove red, and rank
       wolf's-bane ;
    And slumber and forget Him ; if in vain
Ye try to slumber off your sorrow there,
Arise once more and openly repair
    To busy haunts where men and women sigh,
And if all things but echo back your care,
    Cry out aloud, "There is no God !" and die.
But if upon a day when all is dark,
Thou, stooping in the public ways, shalt mark
    Strange luminous footprints as of feet that shine,
Follow them ! follow them! O soul bereaven !
God had a Son,—He hath passed that way to heaven ;
    Follow and look upon that Face divine !

ROBERT BUCHANAN.

BOOK III.

English Examples

OF

French Forms of Verse.

CCI.

[TRIOLET.]

WHEN first we met we did not guess
    That Love would prove so hard a master;
Of more than common friendliness
When first we met we did not guess.
Who could foretell this sore distress,
    This irretrievable disaster,
When first we met?—We did not guess
    That Love would prove so hard a master.

ROBERT BRIDGES.

T

CCII.

A KISS.

[TRIOLET.]

ROSE kissed me to-day.
　　Will she kiss me to-morrow?
　Let it be as it may,
　Rose kissed me to-day.
But the pleasure gives way
　To a savour of sorrow;
Rose kissed me to-day,—
　Will she kiss me to-morrow?

AUSTIN DOBSON.

CCIII.

[RONDEL.]

KISS me, sweetheart; the Spring is here,
 And Love is Lord of you and me!
 The blue-bells beckon each passing bee;
 The wild wood laughs to the flowered year:
There is no bird in brake or brere,
 But to his little mate sings he,
"Kiss me, sweetheart; the Spring is here,
 And Love is Lord of you and me!"

The blue sky laughs out sweet and clear;
 The missel-thrush upon the tree
 Pipes for sheer gladness, loud and free;
And I go singing to my dear,
"Kiss me, sweetheart; the Spring is here,
 And Love is Lord of you and me!"

JOHN PAYNE.

CCIV.

[RONDEAU.]

HIS poisoned shafts, that fresh he dips
In juice of plants that no bee sips,
He takes, and with his bow renown'd,
Goes out upon his hunting ground,
Hanging his quiver at his hips.

He draws them one by one, and clips
Their heads between his finger tips,
And looses with a twanging sound
His poisoned shafts.

But if a maiden with her lips
Suck from the wound the blood that drips,
And drink the poison from the wound,
The simple remedy is found
That of their deadly terror strips
His poisoned shafts.

ROBERT BRIDGES.

CCV.

[RONDEAU.]

ITH pipe and flute the rustic Pan
    Of old made music sweet for man ;
        And wonder hushed the warbling bird,
        And closer drew the calm-eyed herd,—
The rolling river slowlier ran.

Ah ! would,—ah ! would, a little span,
Some air of Arcady could fan
        This age of ours, too seldom stirred
                With pipe and flute !

But now for gold we plot and plan ;
And from Beersheba unto Dan,
        Apollo's self might pass unheard,
        Or find the night-jar's note preferred. . .
Not so it fared, when time began,
                With pipe and flute !

AUSTIN DOBSON.

CCVI.

[RONDEAU.]

IF Love should faint, and hálf decline
    Below the fit meridian sign,
       And, shorn of all his golden dress,
       His regal state and loveliness,
Be no more worth a heart like thine,

Let not thy nobler passion pine,
But, with a charity divine,
       Let Memory ply her soft address
          If Love should faint.

And oh! this laggard soul of mine,
Like some halt pilgrim stirred with wine,
       Shall ache in pity's dear distress
       Until the balms of thy caress
To work the finished cure combine,
          If Love should faint.

EDMUND W. GOSSE.

CCVII.

[RONDEAU.]

IFE lapses by for you and me;
    Our sweet days pass us by and flee;
      And evermore death draws us nigh;
      The blue fades fast out of our sky;
The ripple ceases from our sea.

What would we not give, you and I,
The early sweet of life to buy!
    Alas! sweetheart, that cannot we:
      Life lapses by.

But though our young years buried lie,
Shall Love with Spring and Summer die?
    What if the roses faded be?
    We in each other's eyes will see
New Springs, nor question how or why
      Life lapses by.

JOHN PAYNE.

THE COQUETTE.

[RONDEAU.]

THIS pirate bold upon Love's sea
　　Will let no passing heart go free ;
　　　　No barque by those bright eyes espied
　　　　May sail away o'er life's blue tide
Till all its treasure yielded be.

Her craft, the *Conquest*, waits for thee
Where her swift rapine none may see ;—
　　　　From shadowy coves on thee will glide
　　　　　　This pirate bold.

Yet thou, if thou her power wouldst flee,
Go, feign thyself love's refugee,
　　　　And crave sweet shelter ; she'll deride
　　　　Thy piteous suit with scornful pride ;
And thou, thou shalt escape in glee
　　　　　　This pirate bold !

SAMUEL WADDINGTON.

CCIX.

CARPE DIEM.

[RONDEAU.]

TO-DAY, what is there in the air
    That makes December seem sweet May?
    There are no swallows anywhere,
    Nor crocuses to crown your hair,
And hail you down my garden way.

Last night the full moon's frozen stare
    Struck me, perhaps; or did you say
Really, you'd come, sweet friend and fair,
                                    To-day?

To-day is here;—come, crown to-day
    With Spring's delight or Spring's despair!
Love cannot bide old Time's delay—
Down my glad gardens light winds play,
  And my whole life shall bloom and bear
                                    To-day.

THEOPHILE MARZIALS.

CCX.

[RONDEAU REDOUBLÉ.]

MY day and night are in my lady's hand;
I have no other sunrise than her sight;
 For me her favour glorifies the land;
Her anger darkens all the cheerful light.

Her face is fairer than the hawthorn white,
When all a-flower in May the hedgerows stand;
 Whilst she is kind, I know of no affright;
My day and night are in my lady's hand.

 All heaven in her glorious eyes is spanned;
Her smile is softer than the Summer night,
 Gladder than daybreak on the Faery strand;
I have no other sunrise than her sight.

 Her silver speech is like the singing flight
Of runnels rippling o'er the jewelled sand;
 Her kiss, a dream of delicate delight;
For me, her favour glorifies the land.

What if the Winter chase the Summer bland !
The gold sun in her hair burns ever bright.
    If she be sad, straightway all joy is banned ;
Her anger darkens all the cheerful light.

    Come weal or woe, I am my lady's knight,
And in her service every ill withstand ;
    Love is my Lord in all the world's despite,
And holdeth in the hollow of his hand
             My day and night.

JOHN PAYNE.

CCXI.

[RONDEAU REDOUBLÉ.]

MY soul is sick of nightingale and rose,
    The perfume and the darkness of the
      grove ;
    I weary of the fevers and the throes,
And all the enervating dreams of love.

    At morn I love to hear the lark, and rove
The meadows, where the simple daisy shows
    Her guiltless bosom to the skies above—
My soul is sick of nightingale and rose.

    The afternoon is sweet, and sweet repose,
But let me lie where breeze-blown branches move.
    I hate the stillness where the sunbeams doze,
The perfume and the darkness of the grove.

    I love to hear at eve the gentle dove
Contented coo the day's delightful close.
    She sings of joy and all the calm thereof,—
I weary of the fevers and the throes.

I love the night who like a mother throws
Her arms round hearts that throbbed and limbs
    that strove,
  As kind as Death, that puts an end to woes
And all the enervating dreams of Love.

  Because my soul is sick of fancies wove
Of fervid ecstacies and crimson glows,
  Because the taste of cinnamon and clove
Palls on my palate—let no man suppose
    My soul is sick.

W. COSMO MONKHOUSE.

CCXII.

[KYRIELLE.]

LARK in the mesh of the tangled vine,
A bee that drowns in the flower-cup's wine,
A fly in the sunshine,—such is man.
All things must end, as all began.

A little pain, a little pleasure,
A little heaping up of treasure,
Then no more gazing upon the sun.
All things must end that have begun

Where is the time for hope or doubt
A puff of the wind, and life is out.
A turn of the wheel, and rest is won.
All things must end that have begun.

Golden morning and purple night,
Life that fails with the failing light!
Death is the only deathless one.
All things must end that have begun.

Ending waits on the brief beginning;
Is the prize worth the stress of winning?
E'en in the dawning the day is done.
All things must end that have begun.

Weary waiting and weary striving,
Glad outsetting and sad arriving;
What is it worth when the goal is won?
All things must end that have begun.

Speedily fades the morning glitter;
Love grows irksome and wine grows bitter.
Two are parted from what was one.
All things must end that have begun.

Toil and pain and the evening rest;
Joy is weary and sleep is best;
Fair and softly the day is done.
All things must end that have begun.

JOHN PAYNE.

SPRING SADNESS..

[VIRELAI.]

S I sat sorrowing
  Love came and bade me sing
   A joyous song and meet ;
  For see (said he) each thing
Is merry for the Spring,
  And every bird doth greet
The break of blossoming,
That all the woodlands ring
  Unto the young hours' feet.

Wherefore put off defeat,
And rouse thee to repeat
  The chime of merles that go,
With flutings shrill and sweet,
In every green retreat,
  The tune of streams that flow
And mark the fair hours' beat,
With running ripples fleet
  And breezes soft and low.

For who should have, I trow,
Such joyance in the glow
  And pleasance of the May,—
In all sweet bells that blow,
In death of Winter's woe
  And birth of Springtide gay,
When in woodwalk and row
Hand-linked the lovers go,—
  As he to whom alway

God giveth day by day
To set to roundelay
  Life's sad and sunny hours,—
To weave into a lay
Life's golden years and gray,
  Its sweet and bitter flowers,—
To sweep, with hands that stray
In many a devious way,
  Its harp of sun and showers?

Nor in this life of ours,
Whereon the sky oft lowers,
  Is any lovelier thing
Than in the wild wood bowers
The cloud of green that towers,
  The blithe birds welcoming
The vivid vernal hours
Among the painted flowers
  And all the pomp of Spring.

U

True, Life is on the wing,
And all the birds that sing,
　　And all the flowers that be
Amid the glow and ring,
The pomp and glittering
　　　Of Spring's sweet pageantry,
Have here small sojourning,—
And all our sweet hours bring
　　　Death nearer, as they flee.

Yet this thing learn of me :
The sweet hours fair and free
　　　That we have had of yore,
The fair things we did see,
The linkèd melody
　　　Of waves upon the shore
That rippled in their glee,—
Are not lost utterly,
　　　Though they return no more.

But in the true heart's core
Thought treasures evermore
　　　The tune of birds and breeze ;
And there the slow years store
The flowers our dead Springs wore
　　　And scent of blossomed leas :
There murmur o'er and o'er
The sound of woodlands hoar
　　　With newly burgeoned trees.

So for the sad soul's ease
Remembrance treasures these
    Against Time's harvesting,
That so, when mild Death frees
The soul from Life's disease
    Of strife and sorrowing,
In glass of memories
The new hope looks and sees
    Through Death a brighter Spring.

JOHN PAYNE

CCXIV.

[VILLANELLE.]'

WHEN I saw you last, Rose,
          You were only so high ;—
How fast the time goes !

Like a bud ere it blows,
          You just peeped at the sky
When I saw you last, Rose !

Now your petals unclose,
          Now your May-time is nigh ;—
How fast the time goes !

You would prattle your woes,
          All the wherefore and why,
When I saw you last, Rose !

Now you leave me to prose,
          And you seldom reply ;—
How fast the time goes !

And a life,—how it grows !
    You were scarcely so shy
When I saw you last, Rose !

In your bosom it shows
    There's a guest on the sly ;
(How fast the time goes !)

Is it Cupid ?   Who knows !
    Yet you used not to sigh
When I saw you last, Rose !
How fast the time goes !

                    AUSTIN DOBSON.

CCXV.

[VILLANELLE.]

 SUMMER-TIME, so passing sweet,
 But heavy with the breath of flowers,
But languid with the fervent heat,

They chide amiss who call thee fleet,—
 Thee, with thy weight of daylight hours,
O Summer-time, so passing sweet!

Young Summer, thou art too replete,
 Toō rich in choice of joys and powers,
But languid with the fervent heat.

Adieu! my face is set to meet
 Bleak Winter, with his pallid showers—
O Summer-time, so passing sweet!

Old Winter steps with swifter feet,
 He lingers not in wayside bowers,
He is not languid with the heat;

His rounded day, a pearl complete,
   Gleams on the unknown night that lowers ;
O Summer-time, so passing sweet,
But languid with the fervent heat !

EMILY PFEIFFER.

CCXVI.

[VILLANELLE.]

OULDST thou not be content to die
  When low-hung fruit is hardly
      clinging,
And golden Autumn passes by?

If we could vanish, thou and I,
  While the last woodland bird is singing,
Wouldst thou not be content to die?

Deep drifts of leaves in the forest lie,
  Red vintage that the frost is flinging,
And golden Autumn passes by.

Beneath this delicate rose-gray sky,
  While sunset bells are faintly ringing,
Wouldst thou not be content to die?

For wintry webs of mist on high
  Out of the muffled earth are springing,
And golden Autumn passes by.

O now when pleasures fade and fly,
  And Hope her southward flight is winging,
Wouldst thou not be content to die?

Lest Winter come, with wailing cry,
  His cruel icy bondage bringing,
When golden Autumn hath passed by,

And thou with many a tear and sigh,
  While Life her wasted hands is wringing,
Shalt pray in vain for leave to die
When golden Autumn hath passed by.

EDMUND W. GOSSE.

CCXVII.

[VILLANELLE.]

THE air is white with snow-flakes clinging;
    Between the gusts that come and go,
    Methinks I hear the woodlark singing;

Methinks I see the primrose springing
    On many a bank and hedge, although
The air is white with snowflakes clinging.

Surely, the hands of Spring are flinging
    Woodscents to all the winds that blow;
Methinks I hear the woodlark singing;

Methinks I see the swallow winging
    Across the woodlands sad with snow;
The air is white with snowflakes clinging.

Was that the cuckoo's woodchime swinging?
    Was that the linnet fluting low?
Methinks I hear the woodlark singing.

Or can it be the breeze is bringing
    The breath of violets?—Ah no !
The air is white with snow-flakes clinging.

It is my lady's voice that's stringing
    Its beads of gold to song—and so
Methinks I hear the woodlark singing.

The violets I see upspringing
    Are in my lady's eyes, I trow :
The air is white with snow-flakes clinging.

Dear, while thy tender tones are ringing,—
    Even though amidst the winter's woe
The air is white with snow-flakes clinging,
Methinks I hear the woodlark singing.

JOHN PAYNE.

THE PRODIGALS.

[BALLADE.]

"PRINCES!—and you, most valorous,
  Nobles and barons of all degrees!
  Hearken awhile to the prayer of us,—
  Prodigals driven of destinies!
  Nothing we ask or of gold or fees;
Harry us not with the hounds we pray;
  Lo,—for the surcote's hem we seize,—
Give us—ah! give us—but Yesterday."

"Dames most delicate, amorous!
  Damosels blithe as the belted bees!
Beggars are we that pray thee thus,—
  Beggars outworn of miseries!
  Nothing we ask of the things that please;
Weary are we, and old, and gray;
  Lo,—for we clutch and we clasp your knees,—
Give us—ah! give us—but Yesterday!"

"Damosels—Dames, be piteous!"
    (But the dames rode fast by the roadway trees.)
"Hear us, O Knights, magnanimous!"
    (But the knights pricked on in their panoplies.)
    Nothing they gat of hope or ease,
But only to beat on the breast and say :—
    " Life we drank to the dregs and lees ;
Give us—ah ! give us—but Yesterday!"

ENVOY.

    Youth, take heed to the prayer of these !
Many there be by the dusty way,—
    Many that cry to the rocks and seas
"Give us—ah ! give us—but Yesterday !"

AUSTIN DOBSON.

CCXIX.

[BALLADE.]

1.

HAT do we here who with reverted eyes
    Turn back our longing from the modern
      air
To the dim gold of long-evanished skies,
When other songs in other mouths were fair ?
Why do we stay the load of life to bear,
To measure still the weary worldly ways,
    Waiting upon the still-recurring sun,
That ushers in another waste of days,
Of roseless Junes and unenchanted Mays,
    Why but because our task is yet undone ?

11.

Were it not thus, could but our high emprise
    Be once fulfilled, which of us would forbear
To seek that haven where contentment lies ?
    Who would not doff at once life's load of care
    To be at peace among the silence there ?

Ah, who alas ?—Across the heat and haze
 Death beckons to us in the shadow dun—
Favouring and fair—" My rest is sweet," he says :
But we, reluctantly, avert our gaze,
 Why but because our task is yet undone ?

III.

Songs have we sung, and many melodies
 Have from our lips had issue rich and rare :
But never yet the conquering chant did rise,
 That should ascend the very heaven's stair,
 To rescue life from anguish and despair.
Often and again, drunk with delight of lays,
 " Lo ! " have we cried, " this is the golden one
That shall deliver us ! "—Alas ! Hope's rays
Die in the distance, and Life's sadness stays,
 Why but because our task is yet undone ?

ENVOY.

Great God of Love, thou whom all poets praise,
 Grant that the aim of rest for us be won ;
Let the light shine upon our life that strays
Disconsolate within the desert maze ;
 Why but because our task is yet undone ?

JOHN PAYNE.

THE BALLAD OF PROSE AND RHYME.

[BALLADE À DOUBLE REFRAIN.]

WHEN the roads are heavy with mire and rut,
　　In November fogs, in December snows,
　　When the North Wind howls, and the
　　　doors are shut,
　There is place and enough for the pains of prose ;—
　But whenever a scent from the whitethorn blows,
And the jasmine-stars to the lattice climb,
　And a Rosalind-face at the casement shows,
Then hey !—for the ripple of laughing rhyme !

When the brain gets dry as an empty nut,
　When the reason stands on its squarest toes,
When the mind (like a beard) has a " formal cut,"
　There is place and enough for the pains of prose ;—
　But whenever the May-blood stirs and glows,
And the young year draws to the "golden prime,"—
　And Sir Romeo sticks in his ear a rose,
Then hey !—for the ripple of laughing rhyme !

In a theme where the thoughts have a pedant-strut,
   In a changing quarrel of " Ayes " and " Noes,"
In a starched procession of " If " and " But,"
   There is place and enough for the pains of prose ;—
   But whenever a soft glance softer grows;
And the light hours dance to the trysting time,
   And the secret is told " that no one knows,"
Then hey !—for the ripple of laughing rhyme !

ENVOY.

In the work-a-day world,—for its needs and woes,
There is place and enough for the pains of prose ;
But whenever the May-bells clash and chime,
Then hey !—for the ripple of laughing rhyme !

AUSTIN DOBSON.

CCXXI.

THE GOD OF WINE.

[CHANT ROYAL.]

1.

BEHOLD, above the mountains there is light,
 A streak of gold, a line of gathering fire,
 And the dim East hath suddenly grown
  bright
With pale aëreal flame, that drives up higher
The lurid airs that all the long night were
Breasting the dark ravines and coverts bare ;
 Behold, behold! the granite gates unclose,
 And down the vales a lyric people flows,
Who dance to music, and in dancing fling
 Their frantic robes to every wind that blows,
And deathless praises to the Vine-god sing.

II.

Nearer they press, and nearer still in sight,
  Still dancing blithely in a seemly choir ;
Tossing on high the symbol of their rite,
  The cone-tipped thyrsus of a god's desire ;
Nearer they come, tall damsels flushed and fair,
With ivy circling their abundant hair,
  Onward, with even pace, in stately rows
  With eye that flashes, and with cheek that glows,
And all the while their tribute-songs they bring,
  And newer glories of the past disclose,
And deathless praises to the Vine-god sing.

III.

The pure luxuriance of their limbs is white,
  And flashes clearer as they draw the nigher,
Bathed in an air of infinite delight,
  Smooth without wound of thorn, or fleck of mire,
Borne up by song as by a trumpet's blare,
Leading the van to conquest, on they fare,
  Fearless and bold, whoever comes and goes,
  These shining cohorts of Bacchantes close,
Shouting and shouting till the mountains ring,
  And forests grim forget their ancient woes,
And deathless praises to the Vine-god sing.

IV.

And youths are there for whom full many a night
   Brought dreams of bliss, vague dreams that haunt
      and tire,
Who rose in their own ecstasy bedight,
   And wandered forth through many a scourging brier,
And waited shivering in the icy air,
And wrapped the leopard-skin about them there,
   Knowing, for all the bitter air that froze,
   The time must come, that every poet knows,
When he shall rise and feel himself a king,
   And follow, follow where the ivy grows,
And deathless praises to the Vine-god sing.

V.

But oh ! within the heart of this great flight,
   Whose ivory arms hold up the golden lyre,
What form is this of more than mortal height ?
   What matchless beauty, what inspired ire !
The brindled panthers know the prize they bear,
And harmonise their steps with stately care ;
   Bent to the morning, like a living rose,
   The immortal splendour of his face he shows.
And, where he glances, leaf, and flower, and wing
   Tremble with rapture, stirred in their repose,
And deathless praises to the Vine-god sing.

ENVOY.

Prince of the flute and ivy, all thy foes
Record the bounty that thy grace bestows,
    But we, thy servants, to thy glory cling,
And with no frigid lips our songs compose,
    And deathless praises to the Vine-god sing.

EDMUND W. GOSSE.

CCXXII.

THE GOD OF LOVE.

[CHANT ROYAL.]

I.

 MOST fair God, O Love both new and old,
     That wert before the flowers of morn-
        ing blew,
Before the glad sun in his mail of gold
     Leapt into light across the first day's dew!
That art the first and last of our delight,
That in the blue day and the purple night
     Holdest the hearts of servant and of king :
     Lord of liesse, sovran of sorrowing,
That in thy hand hast heaven's golden key,
     And Hell beneath the shadow of thy wing,
Thou art my Lord to whom I bend the knee !

II.

What thing rejects thy mastery? who so bold
    But at thine altars in the dusk they sue?
Even the strait pale goddess, silver-stoled,
    That kissed Endymion when the Spring was new,
To thee did homage in her own despite,
When in the shadow of her wings of white
    She slid down trembling from her moonèd ring
    To where the Latmian boy lay slumbering,
And in that kiss put off cold chastity.
    Who but acclaim with voice and pipe and string,
" Thou art my Lord to whom I bend the knee ? "

III.

Master of men and gods, in every fold
    Of thy wide vans the sorceries that renew
The labouring earth tranced with the winter's cold
    Lie hid,—the quintessential charms that woo
The souls of flowers, slain with the sullen might
Of the dead year, and draw them to the light.
    Balsam and blessing to thy garments cling :
    Skyward and seaward, when thy white hands
        fling
Their spells of healing over land and sea,
    One shout of homage makes the welkin ring,
" Thou art my Lord to whom I bend the knee ! "

IV.

I see thee throned aloft : thy fair hands hold
    Myrtles for joy, and euphrasy and rue :
Laurels and roses round thy white brows rolled,
    And in thine eyes the royal heaven's hue :
But in thy lips' clear colour, ruddy bright,
The heart's-blood shines of many a hapless wight.
    Thou art not only fair and sweet as Spring ;
    Terror and beauty, fear and wondering
Meet on thy brow, amazing all that see :
    All men do praise thee, ay ! and everything ;
Thou art my Lord to whom I bend the knee !

V.

I fear thee, though I love.   Who can behold
    The sheer sun burning in the orbèd blue,
What while the noontide over hill and wold
    Flames like a fire, except his mazèd view
Wither and tremble ?   So thy splendid sight
Fills me with mingled gladness and affright.
    Thy visage haunts me in the wavering
    Of dreams, and in the dawn awakening,
I feel thy radiance streaming full on me.
    Both joy and fear unto thy feet I bring ;
Thou art my Lord to whom I bend the knee !

ENVOY.

God above gods, High and Eternal King,
To whom the spheral symphonies do sing,
  I find no whither from thy power to flee,
Save in thy pinions' vast o'ershadowing.
  Thou art my Lord to whom I bend the knee!

JOHN PAYNE.

A NOTE ON SOME FOREIGN FORMS
OF VERSE.

" They are a school to win
The fair French daughter to learn English in ;
And, graced with her song,
To make the language sweet upon her tongue."
—BEN JONSON, *Underwoods.*

SOME FOREIGN FORMS OF VERSE.

BY way of Appendix to the foregoing selection of later English lyrics, I have been asked by the Editor to supply some brief notes as to the rules for writing the old French forms, of which the book contains sundry English examples. The request is in a measure embarrassing, because the pieces of this kind in our language are not very numerous, and being few in number, can scarcely be held to be fairly representative. They come, not "in battalions," but rather as "single spies,"—with something on them of the strangeness born of another air and sun. They have, besides, a little of that hesitation which betokens those who are not quite sure of the welcome they will receive. To quit metaphor, it has been urged, and by some whose opinions are entitled to the utmost consideration, that the austere and lofty spirit of our island Muse is averse to the poetry of art pure and simple;—that genuine inspiration and emotion do not express or exhibit themselves in stereotyped shapes and set refrains;—and it must be candidly admitted that it is by no means easy to combat such objections. Then

again, there are opponents of less weight, to whom
(it may be), in the words of the "great Author" in
Fielding's "Amelia,"—"Rhymes are difficult things,
—they are stubborn things, Sir!"—and to such,
committed (perchance) to the comfortable but
falsely-seductive immunities of blank verse, the introduction of outlandish complications is a gratuitous
injury.   To them it appears conclusive to say—
"These forms are certainly not new: if they are
so excellent, why were they not introduced before?"
There is, at all events, one answer, which once held
equally good of not a few foreign products which
have since become domestic necessaries—"Because
no one has introduced them."   When the English
sonnet was in leading-strings, there were doubtless
contemporary critics who regarded it as a merely
new-fangled Italian conceit, suitable enough for the
fantastic gallantries of Provençal "Courts of Love,"
but affording little or no room for earnest or serious
effort.   They could not foresee "Avenge, O Lord,
thy slaughter'd saints,"—in the primitive essays of
Surrey and Wyatt.   And who shall say that some
Shakespeare of the future (or the present) shall not
"unlock his heart" with a *Rondeau?*   Not that it is
for a moment proposed to put the *Rondeau* on a level
with the Sonnet.   Still, it must not be forgotten that
the Sonnet, however deservedly popular with English
writers, is nevertheless a "foreign product" and an
"arbitrary form."

But without entering further into these considera-
tions, it may be conceded that the majority of the
forms now in question are not at present suited for,

nor are they intended to rival the more approved national rhythms in, the treatment of grave or elevated themes. What is modestly advanced for some of them (by the present writer at least) is that they may add a new charm of buoyancy,—a lyric freshness,—to amatory and familiar verse, already too much condemned to faded measures and out-worn cadences. Further, upon the assumption that merely graceful or tuneful trifles may be sometimes written (and even read), that they are admirable vehicles for the expression of trifles or *jeux d'esprit.* * They have also a humbler and obscurer use. If, to quote the once-hackneyed, but now too-much-forgotten maxim of Pope—

"Those move easiest that have learned to dance,"

what better discipline, among others, could possibly be devised for "those about to versify" than a course of *Rondeaux, Triolets,* and *Ballades?* After all, it is chiefly as an aid in this direction that the following rules for writing the six principal forms, as given by French authorities, are here reproduced. Into their history and origin it is not proposed to enter minutely; but those curious in these respects are referred

---

* Do we not just a little forget, now-a-days, that our "*nugæ*" should be "*canoræ*"?—that one requisite, at least, of a song is that it shall be musical?—

"Parnassus' peaks still catch the sun;
But why—O lyric brother!—
Why build a Pulpit on the one,
A Platform on the other?"

We can never want for lectures or sermons, in their proper places.

to an article in the *Cornhill Magazine* for July 1877,* as also to the *Odes Funambulesques*, the *Petit Traité de Poésie Française*, and other works of M. Théodore de Banville.   To M. de Banville in particular, and to the second French Romantic School in general, the happy modernisation in France of the old measures of Marot, Villon, and Charles of Orleans is mainly to be ascribed.

TRIOLET, RONDEL, RONDEAU.—These three are classed together, because originally the names appear to have been used indifferently.   For example, in his " History of English Rhythms," Dr. Guest quotes,— from an old French authority, the "*Jardin de Plaisance,*"—a poem of *eight* lines corresponding to the modern *Triolet*, but commencing thus :—

> " *Ainsi se font communs* rondeaulx
> *Ne plus ne moins que cestuy ci.*"

And Charles of Orleans seems to have called what we now style his *Rondels, Rondeaux* or *Chansons*. What is less intelligible is, that M. Gustave Masson in " *La Lyre Française*" (Macmillan) unaccountably prints a pair of these as " *Triolets.*"   The fact would appear to be, that the *Rondel* and the *Triolet* are the earlier forms, and the *Rondeau* is an evolved product of both.   The natural tendency, in the first instance, would be to somewhat overwork the refrain, then afterwards to make it less prominent, and finally to enlarge the field of operation.   This is exactly what appears to have taken place.

* By Mr. E. W. Gosse.

The modern Triolet consists of *eight* lines with *two* rhymes. The first pair of lines are repeated as the seventh and eighth, while the first is repeated as the fourth. The order of rhymes is thus as follows :—*a,b,a,a,a,b,a,b.* The following example by, of all persons in the world, a grave French magistrate, Jacques Ranchin, has been christened by Ménage the " King of *Triolets ;* "—

> " *Le premier jour du mois de mai*
>   *Fut le plus heureux de ma vie.*
> *Le beau dessein que je formai,*
> *Le premier jour du mois de mai.*
> *Je vous vis et je vous aimai :*
>   *Si ce dessein vous plut, Silvie,*
> *Le premier jour du mois de mai*
>   *Fut le plus heureux de ma vie.*"

Here is another, and a less sentimental one, by M. Alexis Piron—"*qui ne fut rien, Pas même acade-micien.*" It is, in fact, addressed to the Academy, against whom—"*semper ardentes acuens sagittas* "— he discharged quite a quiver of arrowy little epi-grams :—

> " *Grâce à monsieur l'abbé Ségui,*
>   *Messieurs, vous revoilà quarante.*
> *On dit que vous faites aussi*
> *Grâce à monsieur l'abbé Ségui.*
> *Par la mort de je ne sais qui,*
>   *Vous n'étiez plus que neuf et trente :*
> *Grâce à monsieur l'abbé Ségui,*
>   *Messieurs, vous revoilà quarante.*"

As far as can be ascertained, the *Triolet* has not

been written at all in English until quite recently. Mr. Swinburne's admirable " Match " (" Poems and Ballads," 1st series, 1866), is apparently reminiscent of this form; but the pair of *Triolets* * by Mr. Robert Bridges (" Poems," Pickering, 1873) seem the first of their kind. The *Triolet* is perhaps best adapted for Epigram. The weight of its *raison d'être* rests upon the fifth and sixth line, while the perfection of its execution lies in the skill with which the third line is connected with the fourth, and the final couplet with the one preceding it. If, as in Piron's, the writer is able to give a new sense to the fourth line, the general effect is increased.

The modern RONDEL is a poem of *fourteen* lines with *two* rhymes. As in the *Triolet*, the initial couplet is repeated at the close. It is also repeated after the sixth line, forming the seventh and eighth lines. Thus the whole falls naturally into three groups or stanzas, two of four lines and one of six. The usual arrangement of the rhymes is—*a,b,b,a ; a,b,a,b ;— a,b,b,a,a,b,* as in the following from Charles of Orleans :—

> " *Alez vous en, alez, alez,*
>   *Soussy, Soing, et Merencolie,*
>   *Me cuidez sous* (pensez-vous) *toute ma vie*
>   *Gouverner, comme fait avez ?*

> " *Je vous prometz que non ferez,*
>   *Raison aura sur vous maistrie.*
> *Alez vous en, alez, alez,*
>   *Soussy, Soing, et Merencolie.*

---

* *Vide* No. cci.—[ED.]

" *Se jamais plus vous retournez*
Avecques vostre compaignie,
Je pri à Dieu qu'il vous maudie,
Et ce par qui vous revendrez.
Alez vous en, alez, alez,
Soussy, Soing, et Merencolie."

Mr. John Payne's "Kiss me, Sweetheart," which appeared in the "Athenæum" for August 18, 1877, is a correct English example.* Some writers content themselves with repeating one line only, the first, at the close, thus making the *Rondel* of *thirteen* lines. But as M. de Banville gives the rule in one way, and writes the poem in another, it may be assumed that this is a matter in which his English followers are also at liberty to use their discretion.

The beauty of the *Rondel* lies in the skilful management of the refrain. In the most successful specimens it will be found to recur without effort, and with a certain indefinable air of novelty at each recurrence. Most of the masterpieces in this form are contained in the works of Charles of Orleans, although M. de Banville has written some graceful examples. Beyond the English *Rondels* attributed to the former writer, one of which is printed in Cary's "Early French Poets," there would appear to be but few antique *Rondels* in our language. Guest, it is true, speaks of a "Roundle" by Lidgate ; and a very clumsy one by Hoccleve is quoted by Professor Morley in his "Shorter English Poems." It is possible, as Chaucer, in the "Legende of Good Women," expressly speaks to his own authorship of—

* *Vide* No. cciii.—[ED.]

> " Many a himpne for your holy daies
> That highten balades, *roundels*, virelaies,"—

that further search would reveal others.   Meanwhile, it is matter for speculation whether Sidney's " My true love hath my heart and I have his," quoted in Puttenham's " Arte of English Poesie," is not in form a memory of the *Rondel.*

As has been already said, the modern RONDEAU is a modification of the *Rondel.*   It is made up of *thirteen* lines with *two* rhymes and two *unrhyming* refrains, generally the first half of the first line, sometimes only the first word.*   As in the *Rondel,* the lines fall into three groups, a first of five lines, a second of three (and refrain), and a third of five (and refrain).   The usual sequence of the rhymes is *a,a,b,b,a ;—a,a,b* (and refrain) ;—*a,a,b,b,a* (and refrain), as shown in the following early example by Victor Brodeau.   It is in ten-syllable lines ; most modern *Rondeaux* are in eight :—

> " *Au bon vieux temps, que l'amour par bouquets*
> *Se démenoit, et par joyeux caquets,*
>   *La femme étoit trop sotte, ou trop peu fine :*
>   *Le temps depuis, qui tout fine et affine,*
>   *Lui a montré à faire ses acquets.*

> " *Lors les seigneurs étoient petits naquets* (garçons) ;
> *D'aulx et oignons se faisoient les banquets ;*
>   *Et n'étoit bruit de ruer en cuisine,*
>   *Au bon vieux temps.*

> " *Dames aux huis n'avoient clefs ni loquets ;*
> *Leur garderobe étoit petits paquets*

---

* *Vide* Nos. cciv. to ccix.—[ED.]

> *De canevas, ou de grosse etamine :*
> *Or, diamants, on laissoit en leur mine,*
> *Et les couleurs porter aux perroquets,*
> *Au bon vieux temps."*

But Marot and Villon, and even Voiture, occasionally wrote a shorter *Rondeau* of ten lines, thus— *a,b,b,a ;—a,b* (and refrain) ;—*a,b,b,a* (and refrain). A very beautiful English example of this latter form is Mr. D. G. Rossetti's translation of the *"Lay, ou plustost Rondeau,"* in Villon's *Grand Testament—*

> " Death, of thee do I make my moan,
>   Who had'st my lady away from me,
>   Nor wilt assuage thine enmity
>   Till with her life thou hast mine own ;
>   For since that hour my strength has flown.
>   Lo ! what wrong was her life to thee,
>   Death ?

> " Two we were, and the heart was one ;
>   Which now being dead, dead I must be,
>   Or seem alive as lifelessly
>   As in the choir the painted stone,
>   Death ! "

The *Rondel*, it will be seen, is well suited for the expression of brief emotions, and sportive or amatory incident ; in short, for any light lyrical theme of defined extent, which is rather enhanced than impaired by the iteration of its keynote. The *Rondeau* offers the ,same advantages, with this in addition — that it may be more successfully employed in playful irony or satire. Probably it is the latter characteristic which makes it more popular in France than the elder form. An ingenious anti-climax is frequently obtained by the introduction of a play of words into the refrain. Thus Prépétit de Grammont, addressing Benserade upon that egregious performance of his,— the translation of the whole of Ovid's Metamorphoses into *Rondeaux* (the very "Table of Errata" is a *Rondeau*),—takes for refrain "*À la fontaine*," which he skilfully converts at the close into a reference to the famous fabulist. In the efforts of Vincent de Voiture, the master of what Voltaire called "*baladinages*," the inner secrets of the modern *Rondeau* are to be studied at their best. Nothing can be more successful than his management of the refrain, whether for play of words or otherwise, while he thoroughly understands the difficult art of giving that difficult stepping-stone, the second stanza, its precise import and value. Furthermore, he is careful to make the refrain, as it should be, the natural overflow of the eighth and thirteenth lines, and not, as it is too often, a merely detachable and meaningless phrase. As to the arrangement of rhymes, however, it should be added, that some writers, and particularly that "spoiled child of the Muses," Alfred de Musset, do not exactly follow Marot and Voiture ; and in one of the most happy of our English specimens, the "Carpe Diem" * of Mr. Theo. Marzials, its author has apparently followed M. de Musset. On the other hand, M. Maurice Bouchor, a young French poet of whom much is expected, appears to favour the second form, of which Mr. Rossetti's translation furnished our example.

There were a few *Rondeaux* written in English

* *Vide* No. ccix.—[ED.]

during the seventeenth and eighteenth century, in the " Rolliad" and elsewhere. The well-known " Jenny kiss'd me " of Leigh Hunt is of course irregular ; but, like the splendid and also irregular sonnet of Keats—" Bright Star, would I were steadfast as thou art,"—it will survive that disadvantage.

Before quitting the *Rondeau*, it should be noted that there is a variety of it called the "*Rondeau Redoublé*."* It consists of *six* quatrains (*a,b,a,b*), with *two* rhymes only. The first four lines form in succession the last lines of the second, third, fourth, and fifth quatrains. At the end of the final quatrain, the first words of the poem are added as an unrhyming and independent refrain. Sometimes the final quatrain is styled the *Envoi*.

VIRELAI, VILLANELLE.—The *Virelai* (*lai*, a lay, and *virer*, to turn), need not long detain us. In its modern form it appears as a poem of *two* rhymes, and of uncertain length, in which the lines forming the initial couplet are alternately repeated at the close of a paragraph, or at the pleasure of the writer.† Of the VILLANELLE, a regularised *Virelai*, we shall give the typical example, that of Jean Passerat (1534-1602)—

> " *J'ai perdu ma tourterelle.*
> *N'est-ce-point elle que j'oi* (j'entends),
> *Je veux aller après elle.*

> " *Tu regrettes ta femelle :*
> *Hélas ! aussi fais-je, moi :*
> *J'ai perdu ma tourterelle.*

---

* See Nos. ccx., ccxi.—[Ed.]
† See No. ccxiii. for the early form.—[ED.]

" *Si ton amour est fidèle*
Aussi est ferme ma foi :
Je veux aller après elle.

" *Ta plainte se renouvelle :*
Toujours plaindre je me doi :
J'ai perdu ma tourterelle.

" *En ne voyant plus ma belle*
Plus rien de beau je ne voi ;
Je veux aller après elle.

" *Mort, que tant de fois j'appelle,*
Prends ce qui se donne à toi.
J'ai perdu ma tourterelle.
Je veux aller après elle."

" *Ipsa mollities !*" as Sir Henry Wotton said of
" Comus." One might almost fancy it, with its
tender cooing burden, to be taken from the purer
pages of that charming pastoral, the " Daphnis and
Chloe " of Longus, more charming still in the quaint
old French of Amyot. The primitive *Villanelle* was,
in truth, a " shepherd's song ;" and, according to rule,
" the thoughts should be full of sweetness and simpli-
city." The arrangement of rhymes requires no further explanation. The first and third line must form
the final couplet, but there is no restriction as to the
number of stanzas.* A good modern example is that
entitled " *La Marquise Aurore*" in the " *Deux Sai-
sons*" of the late Philoxène Boyer ; but we have not
met with many French poems in this form.

BALLADE, CHANT ROYAL.—The BALLADE † is a

* See Nos. ccxiv. to ccxvii.—[ED.]
† See Nos. ccxviii. to ccxx.—[ED.]

poem of three stanzas and a half stanza styled the
Envoi, the last line being identical in each, and forming a refrain.   The rhymes of the first stanza must
be repeated throughout.   The formula is generally as
follows :—*a,b,a,b,b,c,b,c,* for the first, second, and third
stanzas, and *b,c,b,c,* for the *Envoi.*   Or the stanzas
may be dixains, thus *a,b,a,b,b,c,c,d,c,d,* and *c,c,d,c,d,* for
Envoi.   They may even consist of a larger or smaller
number of lines, so long as the rhymes are continued
throughout.   Strictly, the *Envoi* should commence
" Prince," " Princess," &c., as the older *Ballades* were
generally dedicated, or " *envoyées,*" to some one or
other dignitary, actual or symbolical.   Another rule
of the early *Ballade* writers was that the number of
lines in the stanzas should be regulated by the
number of syllables in the refrain.   This is no
longer rigorously observed; but as it assumes the
conception of the refrain to precede everything else,
   affords a hint (if hint be needed) of the paramount
importance of the refrain in this form.   To give the
reader a French specimen, here is De Banville's
"*Ballade des Pendus,*" * which more than any other
shows him to be, in his own words,—" *vieux Gaulois et
fils du bon Villon :*"—

> " *Sur ses larges bras étendus,*
>   *La forêt où s'éveille Flore,*

---

* From the comedy of " *Gringoire.*"   Perhaps Mr. A. Lang,
whose charming " Ballads and Lyrics of Old France " (Long-
mans, 1872) virtually led the van in the matter of these forms,
will one day give us a version of this sombre poem.

A des chapelets de pendus
   Que le matin caresse et dore.
   Ce bois sombre, où le chêne arbore
Des grappes de fruits inouïs
   Même chez le Turc et le More,
C'est le verger du roi Louis.

" *Tous ces pauvres gens morfondus,*
   Roulant des pensers qu'on ignore,
Dans les tourbillons éperdus
   Voltigent, palpitants encore.
   Le soleil levant les devore.
Regardez-les, cieux éblouis,
   Danser dans les feux de l'aurore.
C'est le verger du roi Louis.

" *Ces pendus, du diable entendus,*
   Appellent dès pendus encore.
Tandis qu'aux cieux, d'azur tendus,
   Où semble luire un météore,
   La rosée en l'air s'évapore,
Un essaim d'oiseaux réjouis
   Par dessus leur tête picore.
C'est le verger du roi Louis.

Envoi.
" *Prince, il est un bois que décore*
   Un tas de pendus enfouis
Dans le doux feuillage sonore,
   C'est le verger du roi Louis."

There is, if we mistake not, a certain plate in Callot's " Miseries of War" which might serve as a fitting headpiece to the above. This wood, with its "*fruits inouïs*" bathed in the morning sun and swinging in the morning breeze; the grim suggestion of—

   " *Ces pendus, du diable entendus,*
      Appellent des pendus encore ;"—

the black birds blown about above, and the rumbling of "*rs*" in the refrain, as of distant thunder through the leaves ;—all combine to make a most striking and effective picture. Other specimens as fine will be found in De Banville's "*Trente-six Ballades Joyevses*" (Alphonse Lemerre, 1873) ; or the curious may consult the beautiful "*Livre des Ballades*," issued by the same publisher in 1876, which contains a choice selection from Froissart downwards. In England *Ballades* have been written by Mr. Swinburne and others. A large number, mostly on political themes, have also been printed in the " London " newspaper, and prove conclusively that this form presents no insurmountable difficulties to skilful writers. Many sprightly examples of most of the other forms, it should be added, are to be found in the same periodical.

There is a variety of the *Ballade* called the *Double Ballade*. This is simply a ballad of six huitains or dixains in lieu of three, generally without "*Envoi.*" De Banville has written several. The unique English specimen is the "*Ballade of Dead Lions*," which recently appeared in the " London " for January 12, 1878. Another variety is the *Ballade à double refrain,** which the "*Art Poëtique*" of Thomas Sibilet, 1555, declares to be "*autant rare que plaisante.*" Indeed there seems to be but one well-known French example,—the "*Frère Lubin*" of Clement Marot.

The CHANT ROYAL may be defined as a *ballade* of five stanzas of eleven lines with an "*Envoi*" of five.

---

* See No. ccxx.—[Ed.]

According to the strict rules it should be an Allegory, the solution of which is contained in the *Envoi.* Such is Marot's "*Chant Royal de la Concepcion.*" The examples in English are at present (we believe) confined to three or four. One is the splendid *Chant Royal* of the God of Wine, published by Mr. E. W. Gosse in his article in the "Cornhill Magazine," already referred to,* which has the additional distinction of being the first of its class.

The rhymes play so important a part in the foregoing rules, that a few words on this head may not unfitly close these notes, especially as those who write the forms do not appear to be wholly agreed in the matter. On the one hand, it is advanced that the forms are sufficiently difficult in French, and that to transfer them to our tongue without at the same time adopting the French system of rhyming is to hamper them with superfluous difficulties. By the French system of rhyming, is meant the license used by French writers to rhyme words of exactly similar sound and spelling so long as they have different meanings. This is not held to be admissible in English, although cases might be cited. ·Milton,ʹfor example, has " Ruth " and " ruth " in one of his sonnets. On the other hand, it is contended that if we import these forms, we must, to make them really English, adopt them with all their native difficulties, and add our own as well. It will be clear, however, to both sides that so long as these forms remain in the category of *tours-de-force*, which they must do if the latter view be taken,

* See No. ccxxi. —[Ed.]

they will be of little or no service as popular additions to our stock of forms.   As a middle course the
present writer would suggest that it should be allowable to rhyme such words as "hail" and "hale;"
but not allowable to rhyme such words as "prove,"
"approve," "reprove," in which the philological rela-
tionship is of the closest.   Even in the former case,
however, the skilful writer will be careful not to bring
the rhymes into close proximity ; and, in the shorter
forms, will probably find it best to avoid them altogether.   The purist would never employ them under
any circumstances.

A. D.

Notes to the Poems.

NOTES TO THE POEMS.

No. 1.—*Page 3.*

From the *Romance of the Scarlet Leaf and other Poems* (1865). The author describes it as having been "suggested by a Sketch of E. Jones's." It has been set to music by M. Blumenthal. Mr. Aïdé himself is well known as one of the most versatile of our living writers, having been successful alike as poet, novelist, and dramatist. He is also a musical composer.

No. 2.—*Page 5.*

From *Now and Then* (1876); a collection of miscellaneous verse by Mr. Ashe, whose poetry has generally an old-fashioned quaintness about it which is very delightful. See also Nos. 33, 44, and 58.

No. 3.—*Page 6.*

From *Harold* (1876), act i., scene 2, where it is sung by Edith. It is a worthy addition to the long and splendid roll of Mr. Tennyson's songs, which, like those of Shakespeare and Shelley, may be said to be "set" to their own music.

No. 4.—*Page* 7.

From *Searching the Net* (1873). This poem, in some passages, reminds one of the fine old lyric, beginning

" Over the mountains
And over the waves,"

in which the following lines occur :—

" Some think to lose him
By having him confined,
And some do suppose him,
Poor thing, to be blind ;
But if ne'er so close ye wall him,
Do the best that you may,
Blind Love, if so ye call him,
Will find out his way."

Mr. Warren's poetry may be said to belong, in style and tone, to the Swinburnian school, but has nevertheless a distinct note of its own. There are some very happy passages in " Love gives all Away."

No. 5.—*Page* 10.

This originally appeared in the *Cornhill Magazine*, and may be compared with Miss Rossetti's lines, *An End :*—

" Love, strong as Death, is dead ;
Come, let us make his bed
Among the dying flowers :
A green turf at his head ;
And a stone at his feet,
Whereon we may sit
In the quiet evening hours."

Mr. Austin has a decidedly original lyrical faculty, which he has exercised admirably in this and No. 46. His longer poems are noticeable for their lofty aim and well-sustained power.

No. 6—*Page* 11.

From *Poems and Romances* (1869). Mr. Simcox may be described as another disciple of Mr. Swinburne, also with a distinct "note" of his own, to save him from the charge of imitation.

No. 7.—*Page* 12.

From one of Mr. Edwin Arnold's earlier volumes. Compare the idea running through it with the well-known lines of Longfellow :—

> " No one is so accursed by fate,
>   No one so utterly desolate,
>   But some heart, though unknown,
>   Responds unto his own."

The idea itself, of course, is as old as Plato.

No. 8.—*Page* 13.

From *Flower and Thorn* (1877). This, as well as No. 42, by the same writer, has an airy grace not very frequent in the works of Transatlantic writers. Mr. Aldrich deserves to be better known in this country than he is.

No. 9.—*Page* 14.

This poem, which first appeared in *Scribner's*

Monthly Magazine, is quite in the style of our own Sedley and Rochester.   Mr. Stedman is another of those American writers who ought to have more readers in Great Britain than they have, for his verse is very agreeable, if not powerful.   Perhaps the best of his lighter poetic efforts is his " Pan in Wall Street."

No. 10.—*Page* 16.

From *The Wanderer* (1859) ; a series of poems written in the cynical period of the writer's literary career.   Lord Lytton's later work is of a much sounder quality ; *vide* his *Fables in Song* (1874).   *The Wanderer,* nevertheless, contains perhaps the truest poetry, *quâ* poetry, that he has written or will ever write.   There can be no question of the superiority of his poetic powers over those of·his more famous father, though the latter's verse is perhaps too sternly slighted in these superfine days.

No. 11.—*Page* 18.

From *Queen Mary* (1875), act v., scene 2, where it is sung by the heroine of the play ; the play itself being, in spite of the swifter movement of *Harold,* the better of the two dramas Mr. Tennyson has yet given to the world.

No. 12.—*Page* 19.

From *Poems and Ballads,* first series (1866).   In point of melody this lyric is far surpassed by its (companion ?) poem, *At Parting,* of which the first verse runs :—

" For a night and a day Love sang to us, played with us,
   Folded us round from the dark and the light,
And our hearts were full-filled of the music he made with us,
Made with our lips and our hearts while he stayed with us,
   Stayed in mid-passage his pinions from flight,
      For a day and a night."

No. 14.—*Page 22.*

From *The Unknown Eros and other Odes* (1877);
a volume of striking poetry from the pen of one
whose previous works had hardly prepared the
public for a book of such peculiar power. The contrast between these *Odes* and *The Angel in the House*
is, indeed, so great, that those who have formed their
estimate of Mr. Patmore's poetical capacity, after a
perusal of the latter volume, will now find it necessary
to revise it. The writer handles the metre of the *Odes*
with great success. See Nos. 95 and 132.

No. 15.—*Page 24.*

From *The Red Flag and other Poems* (1872). Mr.
Roden Noel has recently produced a drama, called
The House of Ravensburg, which does more justice
to his unmistakeable powers than any one of his previous publications. It contains at least one charming
lyric.

No. 16.—*Page 26.*

Mr. Lowell's serious poetry has not yet filtered
through the hands of the select few in Britain, into
those of the "ordinary reader"—either on account of
its generally didactic character, or because Mr.

Lowell's reputation as a "sentimental" poet has been obscured by the popularity of his "Biglow Papers." As in the case of the elder Hood, the American writer suffers from his success in humorous work; the public does not seem able to conceive of the same man as at once a great humorist and an imaginative poet of decided genius.

No. 17.—*Page* 28.

From the *Poems* (1870), and one of the most happy of the poet's efforts. It is both clear and musical. Mr. Rossetti's work is generally musical, but not always clear. He is seen perhaps at his strongest in his sonnets, for a selection from which see Book III., *passim.* The most obvious characteristic of Mr. Rossetti's poetry generally is the impression of power it conveys.

No. 18.—*Page* 29.

From *Music and Moonlight, and other Poems* (1874). Mr. O'Shaughnessy is another of the Swinburnian school. This is one of his most admirable pieces.

No. 19.—*Page* 31.

From *Song of Two Worlds*, third series (1875), and the production of a writer who, on the publication of the first series of the *Songs*, at once took a high position as one of the most vigorous of our younger poets. He is perhaps more original in his lyric forms than in the ideas embodied in them, though the latter have frequently a suggestiveness of their own. His *Epic of Hades*, if in style too reminiscent of the Tennysonian manner, is a very interesting poem, full of fine thoughts and felicitous expressions.

No. 20.—*Page* 32.

One of the most characteristic of Mr. Browning's shorter lyrics.

No. 21.—*Page* 33.

From *On Viol and Flute* (1873) ; a volume of short poems by a writer, who, showing in this early book a keen sense of style, afterwards essayed a higher and not less successful flight in his drama of *King Erik* (1876), a work of great imaginative power. The few lyrics in it are quite Elizabethan in their tone. Mr. Gosse is further notable as one of the few living writers who have handled old French measures with skill. He is undoubtedly one of the most able of the new generation of poets.

No. 22.—*Page* 35.

From *The Spectator;* to which Mr. Bourdillon has contributed a series of short lyrics, worthy of remark for their completeness of idea and form.

No. 23.—*Page* 36.

From *Pelleas and Ettarre*, in *The Idylls of the King.*

No. 25.—*Page* 38.

From the *Poems* (1877) of a writer who ranks, with his brother, Mr. Frederick Myers, among the most thoughtful of the younger singers.

No. 26.—*Page* 39.

From *The Infant Bridal and other Poems* (1864) of Mr. Aubrey de Vere, who is one of the most attractive of our meditative poets. His verse is more nearly Wordsworthian than that of any of his contemporaries, except Mr. Matthew Arnold in some moods.

No. 27.—*Page* 40.

From *Festus* (1839); a work of which the interpolated lyrics are not, of course, the strongest feature. Still, they are interesting as the productions of a poet who has written one of the most striking works of modern times, and is yet one of the least known and understood of living writers.

No. 28.—*Page* 41.

A pleasing specimen of the verse of a lady whose greatest literary successes have been achieved in the path of prose fiction.

No. 30.—*Page* 45.

By the most dramatic of living lady poets, as well as one of the most tender of feminine lyrists. It is from *A Woman Sold, and other Poems* (1867). Mrs.

Webster has a large number of admirers, but her merits have yet to be made known to "the many." Her chief notes are sounded on the chord of the evanescent character of human joys.

No. 31.—*Page* 46.

From *Flotsam and Jetsam* (1877) ; a collection of poems old and new, by the poet to whom his friend Robert Browning has given fame as " Waring." Mr. Domett's poetry deserves to be read, however, for its own sake. See, especially, No. 105.

No. 32.—*Page* 47.

From *Spindrift* (1867). Sir Noel Paton is like Mr. D. G. Rossetti, a painter-poet, and is almost as successful on paper as he is on canvass in perpetuating the delicacy of his fancy.

No. 34.—*Page* 49.

One of the most musical things Mr. Buchanan has written : it appeared originally in a magazine.

No. 36.—*Page* 54.

Miss Rossetti is unquestionably the most popular female poet of the day, and well deserves her laurels. Her work is, on the whole, the best poetic soil on which the sentiment of her own sex could be nurtured, for, although it is melancholy in its general cast, it has many moments of spiritual elevation. See, notably, No. 136.

No. 38.—*Page* 58.

This appeared first in *The Argosy.*

No. 41.—*Page* 63.

One of the happiest passages in Lord Houghton's volumes. Here, as elsewhere in this poet's writings, there is a distinct tone as of the best verse of the seventeenth century.

No. 43.—*Page* 65.

From *Queen Mary*, act iii., scene 5 ; where it is supposed to be sung behind the scenes by a milkmaid.

No. 45.—*Page* 67.

From the collected *Poems* (1877) of Mr. Allingham, who is one of the freshest and most idyllic of our poets. The last two lines in this lyric are charming.

No. 46.—*Page* 69.

From the *Human Tragedy*, act iv.

No. 47.—*Page* 71.

From *London Lyrics* (1877) ; a volume of delightful verse, which has already gone into eight or nine editions, and seems destined to go into a dozen more. It will always be a valued possession of every true lover of the alternately vivacious and pathetic, limpid and pointed in modern poetry. Mr. Locker is too often regarded as only a society-poet—that is, as exclusively a laureate of Mayfair, its doings and its sayings. He is this, but he is more, for he has written some of the most successful " serious " poetry of the day.

No. 50.—Page 76.

From *Songs before Sunrise* (1871). Mr. Swinburne is seen at his best, perhaps, in brief lyric flights like this.

No. 51.—Page 77.

The production of a poet the amount of whose lyric work has been but small, whilst its excellence is sufficient to make us wish for more. From the fact that a new edition of Sir Henry Taylor's poems has recently been issued, it is safe to argue that they are now more appreciated by the "general" than they were. There is a solid and sonorous beauty about them which the present generation seems to find it difficult to appreciate. The plays are emphatically for the closet, but they are none the worse for that in an age when theatrical representations are beset by so many drawbacks for poetic work.

No. 52.—Page 78.

From *Pegasus Resaddled* (1877); a mélange of verse, full of fluency and verve.

No. 53.—Page 80.

From *Greenwood's Farewell, and other Poems* (1876); a volume which worthily maintained the reputation won by *Jonas Fisher* (1875) and since confirmed by *The Meda Maiden and other Poems* (1877).

No. 54.—*Page 82.*

The work of one whose reputation is greater in the field of criticism than in the field of song, but whose verse has nevertheless much spontaneity of fancy as well as depth of thought. The refrain of this particular poem recalls, in its peculiar lilt, that of one of Sir Walter Scott's most happy lyrics :—

> " Adieu for evermore,
> My Love !
> And adieu for evermore."

No. 55.—*Page 84.*

From *St. Paul and other Poems* (1870). *St. Paul* itself is a soliloquy, supposed to be uttered by the Apostle, and marked by fervid and melodious rhetoric. It represents the highest level to which, up to the present time, the writer's powers have attained.

No. 56.—*Page 85.*

From *A Tale of Eternity and other Poems* (1869). This lyric reminds one a little both of Charles Lamb's *Hester* and Frederick Locker's *My Neighbour Rose.* Its best praise is, that it is not unworthy to rank near those masterpieces. It has a pathetic quaintness which is very pleasing.

No. 57.—*Page 87.*

From *Lays of Middle Age and other Poems* (1859),

by a Scotch journalist, who has for too many years "given up" to the Press the talents which were "meant for" Literature in its more permanent forms.

No. 59.—*Page* 90.

By a writer who has of recent years preferred to cultivate the field of fiction, rather than that of poetry, in which he was once so noticeable a labourer. This, and No. 148, are taken from Mr. Meredith's earliest volume (1851). His strongest verse, perhaps, is to be found in *Modern Love* (1862).

No. 61.—*Page* 92.

There is a touch of Carew about this lyric.

No. 64.—*Page* 99.

From *Proverbs in Porcelain* (1877). Mr. Austin Dobson is, like Mr. Locker, too often looked upon as merely a producer of society-verse. He has certainly written some of the best specimens in English of that difficult *genre;* he has, in fact, displayed in *vers de société* an originality of style and tone which proclaims him one of its most accomplished masters. Like Mr. Locker, however—though in quite a different way, for Mr. Dobson is thoroughly individual in his work—he has done admirable things in the poetry both of "sentiment" and "reflection." (See, for example, Nos. 133 and 142.) His efforts in the direction of French forms in English speak for themselves. Altogether, Mr. Dobson has a high and secure position among the singers of the day.

No. 65.—*Page* 101.

From *My Beautiful Lady* (1863); a series of well-wrought cameos by a poet-sculptor.

No. 66.—*Page* 103.

From *Boudoir Ballads* (1876); the work of a facile and agreeable writer.

No. 68.—*Page* 105.

From *A Year of Song* (1872). This, and the "Rose Song," are perhaps Mr. Sawyer's happiest performances in verse. "Angelica" has been set to music.

No. 69.—*Page* 107.

This used to be called *Geraldine and I*, and originally appeared in *Macmillan's Magazine* for 1868. In revising it for his edition of 1876, Mr. Locker gave it its present title, which, by the way, is also the title of one of Mr. Austin Dobson's *Vignettes in Rhyme* (1873).

No. 77.—*Page* 118.

This and the following poem are from *The Window, or the Songs of the Wrens* (1870); a little lyrical drama, so to speak, which has hardly attained to the popularity that might have been anticipated for it. Yet it contains some of the Laureate's most delicate work.

No. 81.—*Page* 125.

From *Graffiti d'Italia* (1869), by another poet-sculptor. Mr. Story is, however, rather a poet of rhetoric than of magic, having vigour but not charm.

No. 82.—*Page* 127.

From the *Poems* (1876) of a writer who, like Mr. Palgrave, is best known and appreciated as a critic, in which character he has added at least one permanent work to our literature, in the shape of his essay upon *Shakspere's Mind and Art.* His verse is that of a man of culture, who thinks for himself, and has considerable powers of rhythmical expression.

No. 83.—*Page* 129.

From *The Gallery of Pigeons, and other Poems* (1873). Mr. Marzials' poetry deals perhaps too much in fantasy to be very popular; yet it contains some charming things, among which these "Bagatelles," and Nos. 84 and 85, may be fairly ranked. If Mr. Marzials' belongs to any school at all, it is to that over which Mr. Browning presides, and in which Mr. Meredith is a highly-placed scholar.

No. 86—*Page* 133.

The work of a poet, novelist, and essayist, whose most enduring verse is probably that which is to be read in *Phantastes* and *The Disciple.*

No. 89.—*Page* 138.

The success with which Mr. Locker treats the subject of childhood in his poetry has been often noted.

No. 91.—*Page* 142.

From *Verses on Various Occasions* (1868); a volume of strong-pithed if not melodious writing. Dr. Newman's ablest poetic performance is, of course, . *The Dream of Gerontius.*

No. 92.—*Page* 143.

Another instance, and an excellent one, of the poetry of rhetoric, of which Lord Houghton has given us so many valuable examples.

No. 94.—*Page* 147.

The note immediately above may be applied to this poem also, which is a fair specimen of the Archbishop's thoughtful and cultivated muse.

No. 97.—*Page* 152.

This, with the two following lyrics, is from *The Earthly Paradise* (1868), and is sufficiently indicative of Mr. Morris's reflective tone. The poet has all Jaques' power of sucking melancholy out of song, or rather, of permeating song with melancholy. His Muse is certainly not an inspiring one, but it is musical and tender, and has attractiveness if not charm. Mr. Morris is more successful perhaps in narrative than in reflection.

No. 104.—*Page* 163.

From *The Spanish Gypsy* (1868); a dramatic poem from which, also, Nos. 109 and 137 are taken. These lyrics have a light and graceful flow about them, which ought to make them popular. The blank verse in which they are enshrined has the qualities of sonority and strength; and indeed the poem altogether is worthy of far more attention than the critics generally have accorded to it.

No. 105.—*Page* 164.

This is usually looked upon as Mr. Domett's most excellent piece of work. It was originally published many years ago.

No. 110.—*Page* 171.

Compare this poem with the one that follows, and compare both with Mr. Arnold's "Self-Dependence."

No. 111.—*Page* 172.

From the series entitled "Switzerland," which includes some of the writer's most delightful pieces.

No. 112.—*Page* 174.

The fourth verse of this poem recalls a passage in Mr. Arnold's "Buried Life," whilst the fifth verse seems to re-echo more than one passage in others of the latter writer's poems.

No. 113.—*Page* 177.

Originally printed in *The Cornhill Magazine.*

2 A

No. 114.—*Page* 178.

This and No. 140 are extracted from *Yu-pe-ya's Lute* (1874), a Chinese story of pathetic interest.

No. 116.—*Page* 182.

From *Songs of the Sierras* (1871). Mr. Miller's poetry is, as a rule, as wild and lawless in character as the life he sings about.

No. 117.—*Page* 183.

One of the poet's later lyrics, and quite in his old familiar style.

No. 118.—*Page* 184.

This, like No. 112, recalls some lines by Mr. Arnold. Note the last four of the first verse : how irresistibly they suggest to us the following :—

> " Through the deep recesses of our breast
> The unregarded river of our life
> Pursues with indiscernible flow its way."

No. 121.—*Page* 188.

A very happy specimen of collaboration. It is difficult to say which verse is the prettier in idea.

No. 122.—*Page* 189.

From *King Erik.* See the Note to No. 21.

No. 123.—*Page* 190.

Mr. Bennett is most at home in song-writing, to

which he has almost wholly given himself up, and in which his successes have been many.

No. 124.—*Page* 191.

From *The Atlantic Monthly* (1877).

No. 125:—*Page* 192.

In every way a characteristic poem ; notable for its thoroughly Arnoldian sentiment, and the happy way in which the irregular metre is managed.

No. 129.—*Page* 197.

The idea of this little lyric may be found in Long-fellow's familiar lines :—

> " Learn how sublime a thing it is
> To suffer and be strong."

But how much nearer adequacy is the Archbishop's treatment of it !

No. 131.—*Page* 199.

Here is another instance in which Mr. Arnold's "notes" find an echo in a contemporary's song. Compare the second verse with a very similar passage in *Empedocles on Etna.*

No. 133.—*Page* 203.

This originally appeared in *Macmillan's Magazine.* It has been slightly retouched.

No. 134.—*Page* 205.

From "Meg Blane," a poem first published in
North Coast and other Poems (1867).　　The inter-
locutors are Meg and her half-witted son.

No. 135.—*Page* 207.

An excellent imitation of the Elizabethan manner;
directly reminding us, indeed, of Beaumont and
Fletcher's "Lay a garland on my hearse."

No. 136.—*Page* 209.

This has been highly praised by Mr. Swinburne.

No. 139.—*Page* 213.

From *The Spectator*.

No. 141.—*Page* 215.

From *All in All* (1874).　　See, also, Nos. 156 and
157, which are derived from the same volume.

No. 143.—*Page* 220.

From Mr. Rhoades' single volume of *Poems*, from
which, also, No. 177 is taken.　　Mr. Rhoades used to
be a frequent contributor to *The Spectator*; he now
rarely publishes.

No. 145.—*Page* 223.

From the volume of miscellaneous verse entitled
Tubal (1874).　　This volume contains what is perhaps

George Eliot's highest flight in poetry—the lines about " the choir invisible."

No. 149.—*Page 229.*

Mr. Emerson's verse is thoroughly individual, and well worthy of study ; but it lacks genuine inspiration, and has none of the glamour of true poetry.

No. 150.—*Page 231.*

From *Camera Obscura* (1876) ; a little volume of verse and prose, by a writer who is always tender and graceful.

No. 152.—*Page 236.*

The finest tribute to Shakespeare since Milton's.

No. 153.—*Page 237.*

Originally published in *Macmillan's Magazine.*

No. 155.—*Page 239.*

From *Annus Amoris* (1876) ; a book of sonnets, which are not, however, in strict sonnet form, as regards the position of the rhymes. This specimen follows the Shakespearean arrangement.

No. 158.—*Page 242.*

Mr. Rossetti, strange to say, is not always true to the Italian model, in which the last six lines have but two rhymes between them. His sonnets are, however, full of masterly expression.

No. 159.—*Page* 243.

Note, here, the fine sweep of the eleventh line.

No. 160.—*Page* 244.

Not so thoroughly satisfying as No. 153, but elegant nevertheless.

No. 163.—*Page* 247.

Mr. Tennyson's sonnets are not quite so highly esteemed as they deserve to be. This is one of his best.

No. 165.—*Page* 249.

Reminiscent, surely, of one of Mrs. Browning's sonnets. No. 166 is more original.

No. 173.—*Page* 257.

By a writer who is best known as a poet in dialect, and that dialect the Dorsetshire. His literary English is, however, very interesting, as this poem testifies.

No. 177.—*Page* 261.

A sonnet only in the sense that it consists of fourteen lines. The idea is excellent.

No. 179.—*Page* 264.

From *Intaglios* (1871); a volume of vigorously-written sonnets.

No. 182.—*Page 267.*

This and No. 183 are two hitherto unpublished pieces by the author of *Wood-Notes and Church Bells.* Mr. Wilton handles the sonnet form with great ease and effect.

No. 184.—*Page 269.*

From one of Mr. Longfellow's later volumes. The ninth, tenth, and eleventh lines may be paralleled by these of Mr. Matthew Arnold's :—

> " From the soul's subterranean depth upborne
> As from an infinitely distant land,
> Come airs and floating echoes, and convey
> A melancholy into all our day."

No. 189.—*Page 274.*

Mr. Bryant is perhaps the most truly national of all American poets. He is certainly more so than Mr. Longfellow, who has, however, outstripped him in popularity in Britain.

No. 190.—*Page 275.*

This and the following specimens of Mr. Arnold's sonnet-writing show how skilfully he adapts himself to a kind of verse which can no longer be called "foreign ;" which could not, indeed, be called so after Shakespeare and Milton had adopted it.

No. 195.—*Page 280.*

Apart altogether from the intrinsic value of his poetry, which (in regard especially to the sonnets and the ballads) is obviously great, Mr. Scott may be regarded as the Nestor of the school of writers in which Messrs. Swinburne and Rossetti are the leading masters. He is happier, perhaps, in his ballads than in his sonnets, though the latter are original in subject and bold in treatment. His proper place among contemporaries is a high one.

No. 198.—*Page* 283.

A fair example of Mrs. Pfeiffer's work. This lady has imagination, if not fancy; and the matter of her verse is always valuable.

No. 201.—*Page* 289.

From *Poems* (1873). This triolet is so neatly turned that it is to be regretted Mr. Bridges has not written more in this form than he has. As it is, he is entitled to the credit of having been the first to use it in English poetry.

No. 202.—*Page* 290.

This is one of several examples of the same form, printed in *Proverbs in Porcelain* (1877). Here is another specimen :—

> " Oh, Love's but a dance,
> Where Time plays the fiddle !
> See the couples advance,—
> Oh, Love's but a dance !
> A whisper, a glance,—
> 'Shall we twirl down the middle?'
> Oh, Love's but a dance,
> Where Time plays the fiddle ! "

No. 203.—*Page* 291.

From *The Athenæum.* The reader will remark how largely and successfully Mr. Payne figures in this volume as an imitator of the old French forms. His facility in rhyme and rhythm is not more remarkable than the intrinsic poetry of his work. This rondel especially has a happy charm. So has the rondeau which forms No. 207. Nos. 210, 213, 217, 219, and 222 are here printed, by Mr. Payne's permission, for the first time. It may be mentioned that Mr. Payne has achieved, and is about to publish, a translation into English, in the original metres, of the whole poetical works of François Villon.

No. 204.—*Page* 292.

From *Poems* (1873), where it is accompanied by two other rondeaux.

No. 206.—*Page* 294.

Kindly written for this volume by Mr. Gosse, who is one of the leaders in the new movement for the Anglicisation of French metres.

No. 208.—*Page* 296.

Hitherto unprinted. Mr. Waddington is known as a graceful contributor to the magazines.

No. 209.—*Page* 297.

From *The Athenæum.* See Mr. Dobson's *Note* (page 342). Mr. Dobson has himself written a rondeau in this form ; *i.e.*, the following lines, originally printed in *The Spectator*, but not repub-lished in his recent volume :—

> Rose, in the hedge-row grown,
>   Where the scent of the fresh sweet hay
> Comes up from the fields new-mown,
> You know it—you know it—alone,
>   So I gather you here to-day.
>
> For here—was it not here, say ?—
> That she came by the woodland way,
>   And my heart with a hope unknown
>   Rose ?
>
> Ah, yes !—with her bright hair blown,
>   And her eyes like the skies of May,
> And her steps like the rose-leaves strewn
>   When the winds in the rose-trees play—
> It was here—O my love—my own
>   Rose !

No. 211.—*Page* 300.

Hitherto unpublished, also. Mr. Monkhouse has written more than one " old form " in English, and always skilfully. They will no doubt appear among his forthcoming *Poems*.

No. 212.—*Page* 302.

This originally appeared in *St. Paul's Magazine*. The form in which it is written is one of the most ancient of French measures.

No. 215.—*Page* 310.

First printed in *The Spectator* (1877), and since republished in *Gerard's Monument* (second edition,

1878). It is Mrs. Pfeiffer's most successful effort in this way.

No. 216.—Page 312.

Originally given in an article contributed by Mr. Gosse to *The Cornhill* (1877).

No. 218.—Page 316.

From *Proverbs in Porcelain* (1877), and the first original piece of its kind in English. It has been slightly retouched for this volume.

No. 220.—Page 320.

First published in *Belgravia* (1878), and, up to the present time, the only one of its kind in English.

No. 221.—Page 322.

Reproduced from *The Cornhill* article, by Mr. Gosse, above mentioned. Also the first of its kind published in English.

INDEX OF WRITERS.

Aïdé, Hamilton, i.
Aldrich, Thomas Bailey, viii. xlii.
Allingham, William, xlv. clxxxviii.
Arnold, Edwin, vii. lxxiv.
Arnold, Matthew, cxi. cxxv. clii. cxc. cxci. cxcii. cxciii. cxciv.
Ashby-Sterry, J., lxvi.
Ashe, Thomas, ii. xxxiii. xliv. lviii.
Austin, Alfred, v. xlvi.

Bailey, Philip James, xxvii. lx.
Barnes, Rev. William, clxxiii.
Bennett, William Cox, cxxiii.
Bourdillon, F. W., xxii. c. ci.
Bridges, Robert, cci. cciv.
Browning, Robert, xiii. xx. xxiv. xlix. lxxiii. ciii. cvi.
Bryant, William Cullen, clxxxix.
Buchanan, Robert, xxxiv. cxxxiv. cc.

Craik, Dinah Maria, xxviii.

Dobson, Austin, lxiv. cxxxiii. cxlii. ccii. ccv. ccxiv. ccxviii. ccxx.
Domett, Alfred, xxxi. lxxv. cv.
Dowden, Edward, lxxxii. cxxvi. cxxx. cxxxv. cli.
Doyle, Sir Francis Hastings, cxviii. cxxxi. clxxxvii.

Eliot, George, civ. cix. cxxxvii. cxlv.
Emerson, Ralph Waldo, cxlix.

Gosse, Edmund W., xxi. cxxii. cliv. ccvi. ccxvi. ccxxi.
Greenwell, Dora, cl.

Hedderwick, James, lvii. clxvii. clxxiv.
Houghton, Lord, xli. lxi. xcii. xcvi. cxii.

Inchbold, J. W., clv.
Ingelow, Jean, cx.

Locker, Frederick, xlvii. lxvii. lxix. lxxxix. cviii. clxxi.
Longfellow, Henry Wadsworth, cxvii. clxxxiv.
Lowell, James Russell, xvi. xxix. clxviii. clxix. clxxv.
    clxxxv. clxxxvi.
Lytton, Lord, x. cxix.

MacDonald, George, lxxxvi. cxxviii.
Marston, Philip Bourke, cxli. clvi. clvii.
Marzials, Theophile, lxxxiii. lxxxiv. lxxxv. ccix.
Massey, Gerald, lvi. lxxix.
Meredith, George, lix. cxlviii.
Miller, Joaquin, cxvi.
Monkhouse, W. Cosmo, ccxi.
Morris, Lewis, xix. xl. xciii. cvii. cxv.
Morris, William, xcvii. xcviii. xcix.,
Myers, Ernest, xxv. cxlvi.
Myers, Frederick, lv. lxxxviii.

Newman, Dr., xci. cxliv.
Noel, Hon. Roden, xv.

O'Shaughnessy, Arthur, xviii. xxxvii. lxiii.

Palgrave, Francis Turner, liv. lxxxvii. xc. cii.
Patmore, Coventry, xiv. xcv. cxxxii.
Paton, Sir Noel, xxxii.
Payne, John, clxxix. cciii. ccvii. ccx. ccxii. ccxiii. ccxvii.
    ccxix. ccxxii.

Pennell, H. Cholmondeley, lii.
Pfeiffer, Emily, cxcviii. ccxv.

Rhoades, James, cxliii. clxxvii.
Rossetti, Christina, xxxvi. xxxviii. xxxix. cxx. cxxxvi. clxx.
Rossetti, Dante Gabriel, xvii. xlviii. cxlvii. clviii. clix.
    clxi. clxii. clxxii.

Sawyer, William, lxviii.
Saxe, John Godfrey, clxv. clxvi.
Scott, William Bell, clxiv. clxxviii. cxcv. cxcvi. cxcvii.
    cxcix.
Simcox, George Augustus, vi.
Southesk, Earl of, liii. lxx. lxxvi.
Stedman, Edmund Clarence, ix. lxxii. cxxxviii.
Story, W. W., lxxxi.
Swinburne, Algernon Charles, xii. l.

Taylor, Sir Henry, li. (*see* Vere, Aubrey de).
Tennyson, Alfred, iii. xi. xxiii. xliii. lxxvii. lxxviii. clxiii.
Tollemache, Beatrix, cxxxix.
Townley, Mary, cxxiv.
Trench, Archbishop, xciv. cxxix. clxxvi.
Turner, Rev. Charles Tennyson, cliii. clx.

Vere, Aubrey de, xxvi. lxii. cxxi. (with Sir Henry Taylor),
    clxxx. clxxxi.

Waddington, Samuel, ccviii.
Warren, Hon. J. Leicester, iv. lxxx.
Webster, Augusta, xxx. xxxv. cxiii. cxiv. cxxvii. cxl.
Wilton, Rev. Richard, clxxxii. clxxxiii.
Woolner, Thomas, lxv. lxxi.

INDEX OF FIRST LINES.

	NO.
A genial moment oft has given	94
A lark in the mesh of the tangled vine	212
A little time for laughter	141
A momentary wish passed through my brain	187
A month or twain to live on honeycomb	12
A rose, but one, none other rose had I	23
A sigh in the morning gray !	26
A smile because the nights are short !	39
Across the glory of the evening skies	101
Ah me, dread friends of mine,—Love, Time, and Death	171
Ah, memory ! ah, ruthless memory !	179
All down the linden-alley's morning shade	41
All that I know	106
Along the shore, along the shore	28
And what is Love by Nature ?	4
Are sorrows hard to bear,—the ruin	126
As a twig trembles which a bird	29
As I sat sorrowing	213
Ask nothing more of me, sweet	50
Away ! away ! The dream was vain	10
Ay, thou art welcome, heaven's delicious breath !	189
Beating heart ! we come again	47
Behold, above the mountains there is light	221
Beneath those buttressed walls with lichen grey	178
Between the hands, between the brows	48
Blessed is he who hath not trod the ways	181
Bud and leaflet, opening slowly	45
By studying my lady's eyes	8
By the bursting of the leaves	100
Came, on a Sabbath noon, my sweet	44
Close as the stars along the sky	54
Come to green under-glooms,—and in your hair	200

	NO.
Come to the woods, Medora	53
Consider the sea's listless chime	147
Could we but know	138
Count each affliction, whether light or grave	180
Dear love, I have not ask'd you yet	33
Each hour until we meet is as a bird	158
Even in a palace, life may be led well!	190
Every day a Pilgrim, blindfold	1
Fair garden, where the man and woman dwelt	198
Fair is my Love, so fair	68
Foil'd by our fellow-men, depress'd, outworn	194
"Follow Me," Jesus said; and they uprose	199
For me no roseate garlands twine	121
From morn to evening, this day, yesterday	164
From the outskirts of the town	117
Girls, when I am gone away	135
Give her but a least excuse to love me!	49
Gray cloud, gray veil 'twixt me and youth	90
Hapless doom of woman happy in betrothing!	11
He saves the sheep, the goats he cannot save!	191
Hence, rude Winter! crabbed old fellow	105
Here, in this leafy place	133
His poisoned shafts, that fresh he dips	204
How gently, beautiful, and calm	131
I ask not for those thoughts, that sudden leap	185
I bring a garland for your head	122
I cannot kiss thee as I used to kiss	80
I grieve not that ripe Knowledge takes away	186
I have been here before	17
I have not, yet I would have loved thee, sweet	35
I hold within my hand a lute	150
I know not if a keener smart	93
I learnt a lesson from the flowers to-day	183
I made another garden, yea	18
I said: "Nay, pluck not,—let the first fruit be	172
I said to Love, "Lo one thing troubles me!	157
I saw, I saw the lovely child	88
I saw in dream where met proud rivers twain	177

NO.

I thank thee, dear, for words that fleet 55
I would not have this perfect love of ours . . . 68
I would thou might'st not vex me with thine eyes, . . 107
If but thy heart were stone 146
If by any device or knowledge 87
If ever, dear 40
If he would come to-day, to-day, to-day 38
If I could choose my paradise 58
If Love should faint, and half decline 206
If our Love may fail, Lily 15
In all my singing and speaking 37
In the long enchanted weather 63
In the time when water-lilies shake 34
It is, indeed, a little while 89
It may be that our homeward longings made . . . 176
It was in the prime 104
It was not like your great and gracious ways ! . . . 132
Kiss me, sweetheart; the Spring is here 203
Let not our lips pronounce the word Farewell . . 167
Let them go by—the heats, the doubts, the strife . . 130
Life knows no dead so beautiful 116
Life lapses by for you and me 207
Light, so low upon earth 78
Light's Love, the timorous bird, to dwell . . . 2
Like an island in a river 60
Like to the moan of buried rivers 118
Little dimples so sweet and soft 66
Long fed on boundless hopes, O race of man . . . 193
Love is come with a song and a smile 3
Love is the Minstrel; for in God's own sight . . . 154
"Love thou thy Neighbour," we are told . . . 56
Love walks with weary feet the upward way . . . 156
Love within the lover's breast 59
Man dwells apart, though not alone 110
My day and night are in my lady's hand . . . 210
My heart is freighted full of love 61
My little Son, who look'd from thoughtful eyes . . 95
My only love is always near 108
My soul is sick of nightingale and rose 211

NO.

Myriad Roses, unregretted, perish in their vernal bloom .   96
Never again.   The shivering rose, that sees   .   .   .   30
Noon—and the north-west sweeps the empty road .   .   97
Not yet, not yet, the light   139
Now Autumn's fire burns slowly along the woods .   .   188
"O bairn, when I am dead   134
O bridesmaid, ere the happy knot was tied   .   .   .   163
O fair midspring, besung so oft and oft   99
O late and sweet, too sweet, too late   124
O life, O death, O world, O time   129
O Lily, with the sun of heaven's   71
O most fair God, O Love both new and old   .   .   .   222
O Summer-time, so passing sweet   215
O wherefore ever onward, Love ! O why   .   .   .   155
Of Adam's first wife, Lilith, it is told   161
Oh ! love is like the rose   27
Oh no ! you shall not catch me in the snare   .   .   81
Oh roses for the flush of youth   120
Oh ! were I rich and mighty   19
On the tall buttress of a Minster gray   182
One so fair—none so fair   79
Only a bee made prisoner   22
Only when Summer's sun is high   74
Others abide our question—Thou art free !   .   .   .   152
Others have pleasantness and praise   6
Our love is not a fading, earthly flower .   .   .   169
Pass, falling rose !   123
Passing away, saith the World, passing away .   .   136
"Princes !—and you, most valorous   218
Prune thou thy words, the thoughts control   .   .   91
Push off the boat   137
Rose kissed me to-day   202
Round the cape of a sudden came the sea   .   .   13
Seek not the tree of silkiest bark   62
Shame upon you, Robin   43
She reached a rosebud from the tree   .   .   .   84
Slayer of the winter, art thou here again ?   .   .   98
Sleep, lady fair !   46
Sleeping, I dreamed that thou wast mine   .   .   72

NO.

Slips of a kid-skin deftly sewn 67
So, the year's done with ! 24
Somewhere or other there must surely be . . . 36
Somewhere there waiteth in this world of ours . . 7
Spring,—art thou come, O Spring! 142
Stay me no more ; the flowers have ceased to blow . . 25
Sweet dimness of her loosened hair's downfall . . 162
Sweet ! in the flow'ry garland of our love . . . 32
Sweet Love is dead 5
Sweet mouth ! O let me take 75
Sweet primrose-time ! when.thou art here . . . 102
The air is white with snow-flakes clinging . . . 217
The angry sunset fades from out the west . . . 127
The bee to the heather 51
The curtains were half drawn, the floor was swept . . 170
The little gate was reached at last 16
The mother will not turn, who thinks she hears . . 159
The moth's kiss, first ! 73
The pale sun, through the spectral wood . . . 119
The rose said, " Let but this long rain be past . . 113
The sea awoke at midnight from its sleep . . . 184
The sea is calm to-night 125
The snow upon the rose-flow'r sits 70
The wanton bee that suck'd the rose 83
The waters are rising and flowing 128
The white rose decks the breast of May 52
The world is great : the birds all fly from me . . . 145
The year's at the spring 103
There never yet was flower fair in vain 175
There's a Seer's peak on Ararat, they say . . . 197
They sat beneath the mountain fir 76
Think me not unkind and rude 149
This is a spray the Bird clung to 20
This pirate bold upon Love's sea 208
To call My Lady where she stood 65
To-day, what is there in the air 209
Too soon so fair, fair lilies 114
To think of thee ! it was thy fond request . . . 166
'Twas August, and the fierce sun overhead . . . 192

	NO.
Up to her chamber window	42
Violets, shy violets !	148
Waiting, waiting. 'Tis so far	140
Walled up in sense we know no general plan . . .	195
Warm whispering through the slender olive leaves . .	109
We have loiter'd and laugh'd in the flowery croft . .	69
Weep not for me	144
Were I a breath of summer air	57
Were life to last for ever, love	82
What do we here who with reverted eyes . . .	219
What matter—what matter—O friend, though the Sea .	31
What spirit moves the quiring nightingales . . .	160
When Fancy's exhalations rise	112
When first the rose-light creeps into my room . . .	21
When first we met we did not guess	201
When I saw you last, Rose	214
When I was by Chloe kiss'd	85
When Letty had scarce pass'd her third glad year . .	153
When man alone, or leagued in governments . . .	174
When Spring comes laughing	64
When the roads are heavy with mire and rut . . .	220
When the tumult of day is done	143
Where are last year's snows	115
Where art thou loveliest, O Nature, tell ! . . .	173
Where did you come from, baby dear ? . . .	86
Where is another sweet as my sweet	77
Who can determine the frontier of Pleasure ? . .	92
Why do I sing ? I know not why, my friend . . .	151
"Why do I love thee ?" Thus, in earnest wise . .	165
Why should I constant be ?	9
With all my will, but much against my heart . . .	14
With pipe and flute the rustic Pan	205
With what vain speculations do we slake . . .	196
Wouldst thou not be content to die	216
Yes ! in the sea of life enisled	111

PRINTED BY BALLANTYNE, HANSON AND CO.
EDINBURGH AND LONDON.

CHATTO & WINDUS'S
LIST OF BOOKS.

Imperial 8vo, with 147 fine Engravings, half-morocco, 36s.

THE EARLY TEUTONIC, ITALIAN,
AND FRENCH MASTERS.

Translated and Edited from the Dohme Series by A. H. KEANE,
M.A.I. With numerous Illustrations.

Crown 8vo, 1,200 pages, cloth extra, 12s. 6d.

THE READER'S HANDBOOK
OF ALLUSIONS, REFERENCES, PLOTS, AND STORIES.

By the Rev. E. COBHAM BREWER, LL.D.   [*In the press.*

ABSTRACT OF CONTENTS.—*Authors and Dates of Dramas, Operas, and Ora-
torios—Curiosities connected with Dates, Dynasties, Names, and Letters—Dates
of Poems, Novels, Tales—Dying Words of Historic Characters—Errors of Re-
ferences and Illustrations—Anachronisms—Historical, Legendary, Dramatic,
and other Parallels—Lists of Bogie Names, of noted Diamonds and Nuggets,
Dwarfs and Giants, Fools and Jesters, Favourites of Great Men, Improvisators,
Kings with Character Names, Knights, Literary Impostors, of Lives exceeding
100 years, of Medical Quacks, of the Oaths of Great Men, Relics, Revolutionary
Songs, Ring Posies, the Sagas, &c.—Names and Characters of Dramas, Novels,
Tales, Romances, Epic Poems, &c.—Characteristics of Noted Artists—Plots of
Plays, the Stories of Epic Poems, Ballads, and other Tales—Pseudonyms,
Eponyms, Nicknames, titular Surnames, names of Similitude—Saints who are
Patrons of Diseases, Places, and Trades—Sovereigns of England: their titles
and superscriptions, the Days of their Death—Stimulants used by Public Actors
and Orators—Striking lines of noted Authors, and Sayings of Great Men—Super-
stitions and Traditions about Animals; &c. &c.*

Crown 8vo, Coloured Frontispiece and Illustrations, cloth gilt, 7s. 6d.

Advertising, A History of.

From the Earliest Times.   Illustrated by Anecdotes, Curious Specimens, and Notes of Successful Advertisers.   By HENRY SAMPSON.

"*We have here a book to be thankful for. We recommend the present volume
which takes us through antiquity, the middle ages, and the present time, illustrating all in turn by advertisements—serious, comic, roguish, or downright rascally.
The volume is full of entertainment from the first page to the last.*"—ATHENÆUM.

Crown 8vo, cloth extra, with 639 Illustrations, 7s. 6d.

Architectural Styles, A Handbook of.

Translated from the German of A. ROSENGARTEN by W. COLLETT-SANDARS. With 639 Illustrations.

Crown 8vo, with Portrait and Facsimile, cloth extra, 7s. 6d.

Artemus Ward's Works:

The Works of CHARLES FARRER BROWNE, better known as ARTEMUS WARD. With Portrait, Facsimile of Handwriting, &c.

AFGHANISTAN AND THE RUSSIAN ADVANCE ON MERV.
Second Edition, demy 8vo, cloth extra, with Map and Illustrations, 18s.

Baker's Clouds in the East:

Travels and Adventures on the Perso-Turcoman Frontier. By VALENTINE BAKER. Second Edition, revised and corrected.

Crown 8vo, cloth extra, 6s.

Balzac.—The Comédie Humaine and its

Author. With Translations from Balzac. By H. H. WALKER.

"*Deserves the highest praise. The best compliment we can pay him is to hope that we may soon see his translation of the 'Comédie Humaine' followed by another work. Good taste, good style, and conscientious work.*"—EXAMINER.

Crown 8vo, cloth extra, 7s. 6d.

Bankers, A Handbook of London;

With some Account of their Predecessors, the Early Goldsmiths; together with Lists of Bankers from 1677 to 1876. By F. G. HILTON PRICE.

Crown 8vo, cloth extra, 7s. 6d.

Bardsley's Our English Surnames:

Their Sources and Significations. By CHARLES WAREING BARDSLEY, M.A. Second Edition, revised throughout, and considerably enlarged.

"*Mr. Bardsley has faithfully consulted the original mediæval documents and works from which the origin and development of surnames can alone be satisfactorily traced. He has furnished a valuable contribution to the literature of surnames, and we hope to hear more of him in this field.*"—TIMES.

Small 4to, green and gold, 6s. 6d.; gilt edges, 7s. 6d.

Bechstein's As Pretty as Seven,

And other German Stories. Collected by LUDWIG BECHSTEIN. Additional Tales by Brothers GRIMM, and 100 Illustrations by RICHTER.

Demy 8vo, cloth extra, with Map and Illustrations, 12s.

Beerbohm's Wanderings in Patagonia;

Or, Life among the Ostrich-Hunters. By JULIUS BEERBOHM.

"*Full of well-told and exciting incident. . . . . A ride, which at all times would have had a wild and savage attraction, was destined by the merest chance to prove unexpectedly perilous and adventurous. . . . . These stirring scenes, throughout which Mr. Beerbohm shows no slight degree of bravery and coolness, are described in a manner which is both spirited and modest. . . . . A thoroughly readable story, which well fills up a not unmanageable volume.*"—GRAPHIC.

Imperial 4to, cloth extra, gilt and gilt edges, 21s. per volume.

Beautiful Pictures by British Artists:

A Gathering of Favourites from our Picture Galleries. In Two Series.

The FIRST SERIES including Examples by WILKIE, CONSTABLE, TURNER, MULREADY, LANDSEER, MACLISE, E. M. WARD, FRITH, Sir JOHN GILBERT, LESLIE, ANSDELL, MARCUS STONE, Sir NOEL PATON, FAED, EYRE CROWE, GAVIN O'NEIL, and MADOX BROWN.

The SECOND SERIES containing Pictures by ARMITAGE, FAED, GOODALL, HEMSLEY, HORSLEY, MARKS, NICHOLLS, Sir NOEL PATON, PICKERSGILL, G. SMITH, MARCUS STONE, SOLOMON, STRAIGHT, E. M. WARD, and WARREN.

All engraved on Steel in the highest style of Art. Edited, with Notices of the Artists, by SYDNEY ARMYTAGE, M.A.

"This book is well got up, and good engravings by Jeens, Lumb Stocks, and others, bring back to us Royal Academy Exhibitions of past years."—TIMES.

One Shilling Monthly, Illustrated by ARTHUR HOPKINS.

Belgravia

For January, 1880, will contain the First Chapters of Two New Novels (each to be continued throughout the year) :—I. THE CONFIDENTIAL AGENT. By JAMES PAYN, Author of "By Proxy," &c.— II. THE LEADEN CASKET. By Mrs. A. W. HUNT, Author of "Thornicroft's Model," &c. This number will also contain the First of a Series of Twelve Articles on "Our Old Country Towns," with Five Illustrations by ALFRED RIMMER. The February Number will contain a New Story entitled BIRDS IN THE SNOW, by OUIDA.

** The THIRTY-NINTH Volume of BELGRAVIA, elegantly bound in crimson cloth, full gilt side and back, gilt edges, price 7s. 6d., is now ready.—Handsome Cases for binding volumes can be had at 2s. each.

One Shilling, with numerous Illustrations.

Belgravia Annual, The,

For Christmas, 1879. With Contributions from F. W. ROBINSON, JAMES PAYN, DUTTON COOK, J. ARBUTHNOT WILSON, CUTHBERT BEDE, JEAN MIDDLEMASS, PERCY FITZGERALD, and others.

Demy 8vo, Illustrated, uniform in size for binding.

Blackburn's Art Handbooks:

,Academy Notes, 1875. With 40 Illustrations. 1s.
Academy Notes, 1876. With 107 Illustrations. 1s.
Academy Notes, 1877. With 143 Illustrations. 1s.
Academy Notes, 1878. With 150 Illustrations. 1s.
Academy Notes, 1879. With 146 Illustrations. 1s.
Grosvenor Notes, 1878. With 68 Illustrations. 1s.
Grosvenor Notes, 1879. With 60 Illustrations. 1s.
Dudley Notes, 1878. With 64 Illustrations. 1s.
Pictures at the Paris Exhibition, 1878. 80 Illustrations. 1s.
Pictures at South Kensington. (The Raphael Cartoons, Sheepshanks Collection, &c.) With 70 Illustrations. 1s.
The English Pictures at the National Gallery. With 114 Illustrations. 1s.

ART HANDBOOKS—*continued.*

The Old Masters at the National Gallery. 128 Illusts. 1s. 6d.

Academy Notes, 1875-79. Complete in One Volume, with nearly 600 Illustrations in Facsimile. Demy 8vo, cloth limp, 6s.

A Complete Illustrated Catalogue to the National Gallery. With Notes by HENRY BLACKBURN, and 242 Illustrations. Demy 8vo, cloth limp, 3s.

UNIFORM WITH "ACADEMY NOTES."

Royal Scottish Academy Notes, 1878. 117 Illustrations. 1s.

Royal Scottish Academy Notes, 1879. 125 Illustrations. 1s.

Glasgow Institute of Fine Arts Notes, 1878. 95 Illustrations. 1s.

Glasgow Institute of Fine Arts Notes, 1879. 100 Illusts. 1s.

Walker Art Gallery Notes, Liverpool, 1878. 112 Illusts. 1s.

Walker Art Gallery Notes, Liverpool, 1879. 100 Illusts. 1s.

Royal Manchester Institution Notes, 1878. 88 Illustrations. 1s.

Royal Society of Artists Notes, Birmingham, 1878. 95 Illustrations, 1s.

Children of the Great City. By F. W. LAWSON. With Facsimile Sketches by the Artist. Demy 8vo, 1s.

Folio, half-bound boards, India Proofs, 21s.

Blake (William).

Etchings from his Works. By W. B. SCOTT. With descriptive Text.

"*The best side of Blake's work is given here, and makes a really attractive volume, which all can enjoy. . . . The etching is of the best kind, more refined and delicate than the original work.*"—SATURDAY REVIEW.

Crown 8vo, cloth extra, gilt, with Illustrations, 7s. 6d.

Boccaccio's Decameron;

or, Ten Days' Entertainment. Translated into English, with an Introduction by THOMAS WRIGHT, Esq., M.A., F.S.A. With Portrait, and STOTHARD's beautiful Copperplates.

Crown 8vo, cloth extra, gilt, 7s. 6d.

Brand's Observations on Popular Antiquities,

chiefly Illustrating the Origin of our Vulgar Customs, Ceremonies, and Superstitions. With the Additions of Sir HENRY ELLIS. An entirely New and Revised Edition, with fine full-page Illustrations.

Bowers' (Georgina) Hunting Sketches:

Canters in Crampshire. By G. BOWERS. I. Gallops from Gorseborough. II. Scrambles with Scratch Packs. III. Studies with Stag Hounds. Oblong 4to, half-bound boards, 21s.

Leaves from a Hunting Journal. By G. BOWERS. Coloured in facsimile of the originals. Oblong 4to, half-bound, 21s.

[*In preparation.*

Bret Harte, Works by:

The Select Works of Bret Harte, in Prose and Poetry. With Introductory Essay by J. M. BELLEW, Portrait of the Author, and 50 Illustrations. Crown 8vo, cloth extra, 7s. 6d.

An Heiress of Red Dog, and other Stories. By BRET HARTE. Post 8vo, illustrated boards, 2s. ; cloth limp, 2s. 6d.

"*Few modern English-writing humourists have achieved the popularity of Mr. Bret Harte. He has passed, so to speak, beyond book-fame into talk-fame. People who may never perhaps have held one of his little volumes in their hands, are perfectly familiar with some at least of their contents . . . . Pictures of Californian camp-life, unapproached in their quaint picturesqueness and deep human interest.*"—DAILY NEWS.

The Twins of Table Mountain. By BRET HARTE. Fcap. 8vo, picture cover, 1s. ; crown 8vo, cloth extra, 3s. 6d.

The Luck of Roaring Camp, and other Sketches. By BRET HARTE. Post 8vo, illustrated boards, 2s.

Jeff Briggs's Love Story. By BRET HARTE. Fcap. 8vo, picture cover, 1s. *[In the press.*

Small crown 8vo, cloth extra, gilt, with full-page Portraits, 4s. 6d.

Brewster's (Sir David) Martyrs of Science.

Small crown 8vo, cloth extra, gilt, with Astronomical Plates, 4s. 6d.

Brewster's (Sir D.) More Worlds than One,
the Creed of the Philosopher and the Hope of the Christian.

Demy 8vo, profusely Illustrated in Colours, 30s.

British Flora Medica:
A History of the Medicinal Plants of Great Britain. Illustrated by a Figure of each Plant, COLOURED BY HAND. By BENJAMIN H. BARTON, F.L.S., and THOMAS CASTLE, M.D., F.R.S. A New Edition, revised and partly re-written by JOHN R. JACKSON, A.L.S., Curator of the Museums of Economic Botany, Royal Gardens, Kew.

THE STOTHARD BUNYAN.—Crown 8vo, cloth extra, gilt, 7s. 6d.

Bunyan's Pilgrim's Progress.
Edited by Rev. T. SCOTT. With 17 beautiful Steel Plates by STOTHARD, engraved by GOODALL ; and numerous Woodcuts.

Crown 8vo, cloth extra, gilt, with Illustrations, 7s. 6d.

Byron's Letters and Journals.
With Notices of his Life. By THOMAS MOORE. A Reprint of the Original Edition newly revised, with Twelve full-page Plates.

Demy 8vo, cloth extra, 14s.

Campbell's (Sir G.) White and Black:
The Outcome of a Visit to the United States. By Sir GEORGE CAMPBELL, M.P.

Few persons are likely to take it up without finishing it."—NONCONFORMIST.

Crown 8vo. cloth extra, 1s. 6d.

Carlyle (Thomas) On the Choice of Books.
With Portrait and Memoir.

Small 4to, cloth gilt, with Coloured Illustrations, 10s. 6d.

Chaucer for Children:
A Golden Key.   By Mrs. H. R. HAWEIS.   With Eight Coloured
Pictures and numerous Woodcuts by the Author.

"*It must not only take a high place among the Christmas and New Year books
of this season, but is also of permanent value as an introduction to the study of
Chaucer, whose works, in selections of some kind or other, are now text-books in
every school that aspires to give sound instruction in English.*"—ACADEMY.

Crown 8vo, cloth limp, with Map and Illustrations, 2s. 6d.

Cleopatra's Needle:
Its Acquisition and Removal to England Described.   By Sir J. E.
ALEXANDER.

Crown 8vo, cloth extra, gilt, 7s. 6d.

Colman's Humorous Works:
"Broad Grins," "My Nightgown and Slippers," and other Humorous
Works, Prose and Poetical, of GEORGE COLMAN.   With Life by G.
B. BUCKSTONE, and Frontispiece by HOGARTH.

Two Vols. royal 8vo, with Sixty-five Illustrations, 28s.

Conway's Demonology and Devil-Lore.
By MONCURE DANIEL CONWAY, M.A., B.D. of Divinity College,
Harvard University; Member of the Anthropological Inst., London.

"*A valuable contribution to mythological literature. . . . There is much good
writing among these disquisitions, a vast fund of humanity, undeniable earnest-
ness, and a delicate sense of humour, all set forth in pure English.*"—CONTEMPO-
RARY REVIEW.

Square 8vo, cloth extra, profusely Illustrated, 6s.

Conway's A Necklace of Stories.
By MONCURE D. CONWAY.   Illustrated by W. J. HENNESSY.

Demy 8vo, cloth extra, with Coloured Illustrations and Maps, 24s.

Cope's History of the Rifle Brigade
(The Prince Consort's Own), formerly the 95th.   By Sir WILLIAM
H. COPE, formerly Lieutenant, Rifle Brigade.

Crown 8vo, cloth extra, gilt, with 13 Portraits, 7s. 6d.

Creasy's Memoirs of Eminent Etonians;
with Notices of the Early History of Eton College.   By Sir EDWARD
CREASY, Author of "The Fifteen Decisive Battles of the World."

"*A new edition of 'Creasy's Etonians' will be welcome.   The book was a
favourite a quarter of a century ago, and it has maintained its reputation.   The
value of this new edition is enhanced by the fact that Sir Edward Creasy has
added to it several memoirs of Etonians who have died since the first edition
appeared.   The work is eminently interesting.*"—SCOTSMAN.

Crown 8vo, cloth gilt, Two very thick Volumes, 7s. 6d. each.

Cruikshank's Comic Almanack.

Complete in TWO SERIES: The FIRST from 1835 to 1843; the SECOND from 1844 to 1853. A Gathering of the BEST HUMOUR of THACKERAY, HOOD, MAYHEW, ALBERT SMITH, A'BECKETT, ROBERT BROUGH, &c. With 2,000 Woodcuts and Steel Engravings by CRUIKSHANK, HINE, LANDELLS, &c.

Parts I. to XIV. now ready, 21s. each.

Cussans' History of Hertfordshire.

By JOHN E. CUSSANS. Illustrated with full-page Plates on Copper and Stone, and a profusion of small Woodcuts.

"*Mr. Cussans has, from sources not accessible to Clutterbuck, made most valuable additions to the manorial history of the county from the earliest period downwards, cleared up many doubtful points, and given original details concerning various subjects untouched or imperfectly treated by that writer. The pedigrees seem to have been constructed with great care, and are a valuable addition to the genealogical history of the county. Mr. Cussans appears to have done his work conscientiously, and to have spared neither time, labour, nor expense to render his volumes worthy of ranking in the highest class of County Histories*" —ACADEMY.

COMPLETION OF PLANCHÉ'S CYCLOPÆDIA OF COSTUME.

Now ready, in Two Volumes, demy 4to, handsomely bound in half-morocco, gilt, profusely Illustrated with Coloured and Plain Plates and Woodcuts, price £7 7s.

Cyclopædia of Costume;

or, A Dictionary of Dress—Regal, Ecclesiastical, Civil, and Military— from the Earliest Period in England to the reign of George the Third. Including Notices of Contemporaneous Fashions on the Continent, and a General History of the Costumes of the Principal Countries of Europe. By J. R. PLANCHÉ, Somerset Herald.

The Volumes may also be had *separately* (each Complete in itself) at £3 13s.6d. each:

Vol. I. THE DICTIONARY.
Vol. II. A GENERAL HISTORY OF COSTUME IN EUROPE.

Also in 25 Parts, at 5s. each. Cases for binding, 5s. each.

"*A comprehensive and highly valuable book of reference. . . . We have rarely failed to find in this book an account of an article of dress, while in most of the entries curious and instructive details are given. . . . Mr. Planché's enormous labour of love, the production of a text which, whether in its dictionary form or in that of the 'General History,' is within its intended scope immeasurably the best and richest work on Costume in English. . . . This book is not only one of the most readable works of the kind, but intrinsically attractive and amusing.*"—ATHENÆUM.

"*A most readable and interesting work—and it can scarcely be consulted in vain, whether the reader is in search for information as to military, court, ecclesiastical, legal, or professional costume. . . . All the chromo-lithographs, and most of the woodcut illustrations—the latter amounting to several thousands —are very elaborately executed; and the work forms a livre de luxe which renders it equally suited to the library and the ladies' drawing-room.*"—TIMES.

"*One of the most perfect works ever published upon the subject. The illustrations are numerous and excellent, and would, even without the letterpress, render the work an invaluable book of reference for information as to costumes for fancy balls and character quadrilles. . . Beautifully printed and superbly illustrated.*"—STANDARD.

Demy 8vo, cloth extra, with Illustrations, 24*s.*

Dodge's (Colonel) The Hunting Grounds of

the Great West : A Description of the Plains, Game, and Indians of the Great North American Desert. By RICHARD IRVING DODGE, Lieutenant-Colonel of the United States Army. With an Introduction by WILLIAM BLACKMORE ; Map, and numerous Illustrations drawn by ERNEST GRISET.

"*This magnificent volume is one of the most able and most interesting works which has ever proceeded from an American pen, while its freshness is equal to that of any similar book. Col. Dodge has chosen a subject of which he is master, and treated it with a fulness that leaves nothing to be desired, and in a style which is charming equally for its picturesqueness and purity.*"—NONCONFORMIST.

Demy 8vo, cloth extra. 12*s.* 6*d.*

Doran's Memories of our Great Towns.

With Anecdotic Gleanings concerning their Worthies and their Oddities. By Dr. JOHN DORAN, F.S.A.

"*A greater genius for writing of the anecdotic kind few men have had. As to giving any idea of the contents of the book, it is quite impossible. Those who know how Dr. Doran used to write—it is sad to have to use the past tense of one of the most cheerful of men—will understand what we mean ; and those who do not must take it on trust from us that this is a remarkably entertaining volume.*"—SPECTATOR.

Second Edition, demy 8vo, cloth gilt, with Illustrations, 18*s.*

Dunraven's The Great Divide :

A Narrative of Travels in the Upper Yellowstone in the Summer of 1874. By the EARL of DUNRAVEN. With Maps and numerous striking full-page Illustrations by VALENTINE W. BROMLEY.

"*There has not for a long time appeared a better book of travel than Lord Dunraven's 'The Great Divide.' . . . The book is full of clever observation, and both narrative and illustrations are thoroughly good.*"—ATHENÆUM.

Crown 8vo, cloth boards, 6*s.* per Volume.

Early English Poets.

Edited, with Introductions and Annotations, by Rev. A. B. GROSART.

"*Mr. Grosart has spent the most laborious and the most enthusiastic care on the perfect restoration and preservation of the text; and it is very unlikely that any other edition of the poet can ever be called for. . . From Mr. Grosart we always expect and always receive the final results of most patient and competent scholarship.*"—EXAMINER.

1. **Fletcher's (Giles, B.D.) Com-**
plete Poems : Christ's Victorie in Heaven, Christ's Victorie on Earth, Christ's Triumph over Death, and Minor Poems. With Memorial-Introduction and Notes. One Vol.

2. **Davies' (Sir John) Complete**
Poetical Works, including Psalms I. to L. in Verse, and other hitherto Unpublished MSS., for the first time Collected and Edited. Memorial-Introduction and Notes. Two Vols.

3. **Herrick's (Robert) Hesperi-**
des, Noble Numbers, and Complete Collected Poems. With Memorial-Introduction and Notes, Steel Portrait, Index of First Lines, and Glossarial Index, &c. Three Vols.

4. **Sidney's (Sir Philip) Com-**
plete Poetical Works, including all those in "Arcadia." With Portrait, Memorial-Introduction, Essay on the Poetry of Sidney, and Notes. Three Vols.

Crown 8vo, cloth extra, gilt, with Illustrations, 6s.

Emanuel On Diamonds and Precious

Stones ; their History, Value, and Properties ; with Simple Tests for ascertaining their Reality. By HARRY EMANUEL, F.R.G.S. With numerous Illustrations, Tinted and Plain.

Crown 8vo, cloth extra, with Illustrations, 7s. 6d.

Englishman's House, The :

A Practical Guide to all interested in Selecting or Building a House, with full Estimates of Cost, Quantities, &c. By C. J. RICHARDSON. Third Edition. With nearly 600 Illustrations.

Folio, cloth extra, £1 11s. 6d.

Examples of Contemporary Art.

Etchings from Representative Works by living English and Foreign Artists. Edited, with Critical Notes, by J. COMYNS CARR.

"*It would not be easy to meet with a more sumptuous, and at the same time a more tasteful and instructive drawing-room book.*"—NONCONFORMIST.

Crown 8vo, cloth extra, with Illustrations, 6s.

Fairholt's Tobacco :

Its History and Associations ; with an Account of the Plant and its Manufacture, and its Modes of Use in all Ages and Countries. By F. W. FAIRHOLT, F.S.A. With Coloured Frontispiece and upwards of 100 Illustrations by the Author.

"*A very pleasant and instructive history of tobacco and its associations, which we cordially recommend alike to the votaries and to the enemies of the much-maligned but certainly not neglected weed. . . . Full of interest and information.*"—DAILY NEWS.

Crown 8vo, cloth extra, with Illustrations, 4s. 6d.

Faraday's Chemical History of a Candle.

Lectures delivered to a Juvenile Audience. A New Edition. Edited by W. CROOKES, F.C S. With numerous Illustrations.

Crown 8vo, cloth extra, with Illustrations, 4s. 6d.

Faraday's Various Forces of Nature.

A New Edition. Edited by W. CROOKES, F.C.S. With numerous Illustrations.

Crown 8vo, cloth extra, with Illustrations, 7s. 6d.

Finger-Ring Lore :

Historical, Legendary, and Anecdotal. By WILLIAM JONES, F.S.A. With Hundreds of Illustrations of Curious Rings of all Ages and Countries.

"*One of those gossiping books which are as full of amusement as of instruction.*"—ATHENÆUM.

One Shilling Monthly, Illustrated.

Gentleman's Magazine, The,

For January, 1880, will contain the First Chapters of a New Novel entitled QUEEN COPHETUA, by R. E. FRANCILLON.

*** *Now ready, the Volume for* JULY *to* DECEMBER, 1879, *cloth extra, price 8s. 6d.; and Cases for binding, price 2s. each.*

Demy 8vo, pictorial cover, price 1s.

Gentleman's Annual, The,

for Christmas, 1879. Containing Two Complete Stories: ESTHER'S GLOVE, by R. E. FRANCILLON; and THE ROMANCE OF GIOVANNI CALVOTTI, by D. CHRISTIE MURRAY.

THE RUSKIN GRIMM.—Square 8vo, cloth extra, 6s. 6d.; gilt edges, 7s. 6d.

German Popular Stories.

Collected by the Brothers GRIMM, and Translated by EDGAR TAYLOR. Edited with an Introduction by JOHN RUSKIN. With 22 Illustrations after the inimitable designs of GEORGE CRUIKSHANK. Both Series Complete.

" *The illustrations of this volume . . . are of quite sterling and admirable art, of a class precisely parallel in elevation to the character of the tales which they illustrate; and the original etchings, as I have before said in the Appendix to my ' Elements of Drawing,' were unrivalled in masterfulness of touch since Rembrandt (in some qualities of delineation, unrivalled even by him). . . . . To make somewhat enlarged copies of them, looking at them through a magnifying glass, and never putting two lines where Cruikshank has put only one, would be an exercise in decision and severe drawing which would leave afterwards little to be learnt in schools.*"—*Extract from Introduction by* JOHN RUSKIN.

Post 8vo, cloth limp, 2s. 6d.

Glenny's A Year's Work in Garden and

Greenhouse: Practical Advice to Amateur Gardeners. By GEORGE GLENNY. *[In the press.*

A New Edition, demy 8vo, cloth extra, with Illustrations, 15s.

Greeks and Romans, The Life of the,

Described from Antique Monuments. By ERNST GUHL and W. KONER. Translated from the Third German Edition, and Edited by Dr. F. HUEFFER. With 545 Illustrations.

Crown 8vo, cloth extra, gilt, with Illustrations, 7s. 6d.

Greenwood's Low-Life Deeps:

An Account of the Strange Fish to be found there. By JAMES GREENWOOD. With Illustrations in tint by ALFRED CONCANEN.

Crown 8vo, cloth extra, gilt, with Illustrations, 7s. 6d.

Greenwood's Wilds of London:

Descriptive Sketches, from Personal Observations and Experience, of Remarkable Scenes, People, and Places in London. By JAMES GREENWOOD. With 12 Tinted Illustrations by ALFRED CONCANEN.

Square 16mo (Tauchnitz size), cloth extra, 2s. per volume.

Golden Library, The:

Ballad History of England. By W. C. BENNETT.

Bayard Taylor's Diversions of the Echo Club.

Byron's Don Juan.

Emerson's Letters and Social Aims.

Godwin's (William) Lives of the Necromancers.

Holmes's Autocrat of the Breakfast Table. With an Introduction by G. A. SALA.

Holmes's Professor at the Breakfast Table.

Hood's Whims and Oddities. Complete. With all the original Illustrations.

Irving's (Washington) Tales of a Traveller.

Irving's (Washington) Tales of the Alhambra.

Jesse's (Edward) Scenes and Occupations of Country Life.

Lamb's Essays of Elia. Both Series Complete in One Vol.

Leigh Hunt's Essays: A Tale for a Chimney Corner, and other Pieces. With Portrait, and Introduction by EDMUND OLLIER.

Mallory's (Sir Thomas) Mort d'Arthur: The Stories of King Arthur and of the Knights of the Round Table. Edited by B. MONTGOMERIE RANKING.

Pascal's Provincial Letters. A New Translation, with Historical Introduction and Notes, by T. M'CRIE, D.D.

Pope's Poetical Works. Complete.

Rochefoucauld's Maxims and Moral Reflections. With Notes, and an Introductory Essay by SAINTE-BEUVE.

St. Pierre's Paul and Virginia, and The Indian Cottage. Edited, with Life, by the Rev. E. CLARKE.

Shelley's Early Poems, and Queen Mab, with Essay by LEIGH HUNT.

Shelley's Later Poems: Laon and Cythna, &c.

Shelley's Posthumous Poems, the Shelley Papers, &c.

Shelley's Prose Works, including A Refutation of Deism, Zastrozzi, St. Irvyne, &c.

White's Natural History of Sel- borne. Edited, with additions, by THOMAS BROWN, F.L.S.

Crown 8vo, cloth gilt and gilt edges, 7s. 6d.

Golden Treasury of Thought, The:

An ENCYCLOPÆDIA OF QUOTATIONS from Writers of all Times and Countries. Selected and Edited by THEODORE TAYLOR.

Large 4to, with 14 facsimile Plates, price ONE GUINEA.

Grosvenor Gallery Illustrated Catalogue.

Winter Exhibition (1877–78) of Drawings by the Old Masters and Water-Colour Drawings by Deceased Artists of the British School. With a Critical Introduction by J. COMYNS CARR.

Crown 8vo, cloth extra, gilt, with Illustrations, 4s. 6d.

Guyot's Earth and Man;

or, Physical Geography in its Relation to the History of Mankind. With Additions by Professors AGASSIZ, PIERCE, and GRAY; 12 Maps and Engravings on Steel, some Coloured, and copious Index.

Medium 8vo, cloth extra, gilt, with Illustrations, 7s. 6d.

Hall's (Mrs. S. C.) Sketches of Irish Character.

With numerous Illustrations on Steel and Wood by MACLISE, GILBERT, HARVEY, and G. CRUIKSHANK.

"The Irish Sketches of this lady resemble Miss Mitford's beautiful English sketches in 'Our Village,' but they are far more vigorous and picturesque and bright."—BLACKWOOD'S MAGAZINE.

Post 8vo, cloth extra, 4s. 6d.; a few large-paper copies, half-Roxb., 10s. 6d.

Handwriting, The Philosophy of.

By Don FELIX DE SALAMANCA. With 134 Facsimiles of Signatures.

Small 8vo, with numerous Illustrations, illustrated cover, 1s.; cloth limp, 1s. 6d.;

Haweis's (Mrs.) The Art of Dress.

By Mrs. H. R. HAWEIS, Author of "The Art of Beauty," &c. Illustrated by the Author.

"A well-considered attempt to apply canons of good taste to the costumes of ladies of our time. . . . Mrs. Haweis writes frankly and to the point, she does not mince matters, but boldly remonstrates with her own sex on the follies they indulge in. . . . We may recommend the book to the ladies whom it concerns."—ATHENÆUM.

Square 8vo, cloth extra, gilt, gilt edges, with Coloured Frontispiece and numerous Illustrations, 10s. 6d.

Haweis's (Mrs.) The Art of Beauty.

By Mrs. H. R. HAWEIS, Author of "Chaucer for Children." With nearly One Hundred Illustrations by the Author.

"A most interesting book, full of valuable hints and suggestions. . . . . If young ladies would but lend their ears for a little to Mrs. Haweis, we are quite sure that it would result in their being at once more tasteful, more happy, and more healthy than they now often are, with their false hair, high heels, tight corsets, and ever so much else of the same sort."—NONCONFORMIST.

Fcap. 8vo, picture cover, 1s.; cloth extra, 2s. 6d.

Hawthorne.— Mrs. Gainsborough's Diamonds: A Romance. By JULIAN HAWTHORNE.

THIRTEENTH EDITION. Vols. I. and II., demy 8vo, 12s. each.

History of Our Own Times, from the Accession of Queen Victoria to the Berlin Congress. By JUSTIN McCARTHY.

"Criticism is disarmed before a composition which provokes little but approval. This is a really good book on a really interesting subject, and words piled on words could say no more for it. . . . Such is the effect of its general justice, its breadth of view, and its sparkling buoyancy, that very few of its readers will close these volumes without looking forward with interest to the two that are to follow."—SATURDAY REVIEW.

** Vols. III. and IV., completing the work, will be ready in January.

Crown 8vo, cloth extra, 6s.

Hobhouse's The Dead Hand:

Addresses on the subject of Endowments and Settlements of Property. By Sir ARTHUR HOBHOUSE, Q.C., K.C.S.I. *[In the press.*

Crown 8vo, cloth extra, gilt, 7s. 6d.

Hood's (Thomas) Choice Works,

In Prose and Verse. Including the CREAM OF THE COMIC ANNUALS. With Life of the Author, Portrait, and over Two Hundred Original Illustrations.

Square crown 8vo, cloth extra, gilt edges, 6s.

Hood's (Tom) From Nowhere to the North

Pole : A Noah's Arkæological Narrative. With 25 Illustrations by W. BRUNTON and E. C. BARNES.

" The amusing letterpress is profusely interspersed with the jingling rhymes which children love and learn so easily. Messrs. Brunton and Barnes do full justice to the writer's meaning, and a pleasanter result of the harmonious co-operation of author and artist could not be desired." -TIMES.

Crown 8vo, cloth extra, gilt, 7s. 6d.

Hook's (Theodore) Choice Humorous Works,

including his Ludicrous Adventures, Bons-mots, Puns, and Hoaxes. With a new Life of the Author, Portraits, Facsimiles, and Illustrations.

Crown 8vo, cloth extra, 7s. 6d.

Howell's Conflicts of Capital and Labour

Historically and Economically considered. Being a History and Review of the Trade Unions of Great Britain, showing their Origin, Progress, Constitution, and Objects, in their Political, Social, Economical, and Industrial Aspects. By GEORGE HOWELL.

" This book is an attempt, and on the whole a successful attempt, to place the work of trade unions in the past, and their objects in the future, fairly before the public from the working man's point of view."—PALL MALL GAZETTE.

Demy 8vo, cloth extra, 12s. 6d.

Hueffer's The Troubadours :

A History of Provencal Life and Literature in the Middle Ages. By FRANCIS HUEFFER.

" This very pleasant volume, in which a very difficult subject is handled in a light and lively manner, but at the same time with an erudition and amount of information which show him to be thoroughly master of the language and literature of Provence."—TIMES.

A NEW EDITION, Revised and partly Re-written, with several New Chapters and Illustrations, crown 8vo, cloth extra, 7s. 6d.

Jennings' The Rosicrucians :

Their Rites and Mysteries. With Chapters on the Ancient Fire and Serpent Worshippers, and Explanations of the Mystic Symbols represented in the Monuments and Talismans of the Primæval Philosophers. By HARGRAVE JENNINGS. With Five full-page Plates and upwards of 300 Illustrations.

" One of those volumes which may be taken up and dipped into at random for half-an-hour's reading, or, on the other hand, appealed to by the student as a source of valuable information on a system which has not only exercised for hundreds of years an extraordinary influence on the mental development of so shrewd a people as the Jews, but has captivated the minds of some of the greatest thinkers of Christendom in the sixteenth and seventeenth centuries."—LEEDS MERCURY.

Two Vols. 8vo, with 52 Illustrations and Maps, cloth extra, gilt, 14s.

Josephus, The Complete Works of.

Translated by WHISTON. Containing both "The Antiquities of the Jews" and "The Wars of the Jews."

Small 8vo, cloth, full gilt, gilt edges, with Illustrations, 6s.

Kavanaghs' Pearl Fountain,

And other Fairy Stories. By BRIDGET and JULIA KAVANAGH. With Thirty Illustrations by J. MOYR SMITH.

"*Genuine new fairy stories of the old type, some of them as delightful as the best of Grimm's 'German Popular Stories.' . . . . For the most part the stories are downright, thorough-going fairy stories of the most admirable kind. . . . . Mr. Moyr Smith's illustrations, too, are admirable.*"—SPECTATOR.

Crown 8vo, illustrated boards, with numerous Plates, 2s. 6d.

Lace (Old Point), and How to Copy and

Imitate it. By DAISY WATERHOUSE HAWKINS. With 17 Illustrations by the Author.

Crown 8vo, cloth extra, with numerous Illustrations, 10s. 6d.

Lamb (Mary and Charles):

Their Poems, Letters, and Remains. With Reminiscences and Notes by W. CAREW HAZLITT. With HANCOCK'S Portrait of the Essayist, Facsimiles of the Title-pages of the rare First Editions of Lamb's and Coleridge's Works, and numerous Illustrations.

"*Very many passages will delight those fond of literary trifles; hardly any portion will fail in interest for lovers of Charles Lamb and his sister.*"—STANDARD.

Small 8vo, cloth extra, 5s.

Lamb's Poetry for Children, and Prince

Dorus. Carefully Reprinted from unique copies.

"*The quaint and delightful little book, over the recovery of which all the hearts of his lovers are yet warm with rejoicing.*"—A. C. SWINBURNE.

Crown 8vo, cloth extra, gilt, with Portraits, 7s. 6d.

Lamb's Complete Works,

In Prose and Verse, reprinted from the Original Editions, with many Pieces hitherto unpublished. Edited, with Notes and Introduction, by R. H. SHEPHERD. With Two Portraits and Facsimile of a Page of the "Essay on Roast Pig."

"*A complete edition of Lamb's writings, in prose and verse, has long been wanted, and is now supplied. The editor appears to have taken great pains to bring together Lamb's scattered contributions, and his collection contains a number of pieces which are now reproduced for the first time since their original appearance in various old periodicals.*"—SATURDAY REVIEW.

Demy 8vo, cloth extra, with Maps and Illustrations, 18s.

Lamont's Yachting in the Arctic Seas;

or, Notes of Five Voyages of Sport and Discovery in the Neighbour-hood of Spitzbergen and Novaya Zemlya. By JAMES LAMONT, F.R.G.S. With numerous full-page Illustrations by Dr. LIVESAY.

"*After wading through numberless volumes of icy fiction, concocted narrative, and spurious biography of Arctic voyagers, it is pleasant to meet with a real and genuine volume. . . . He shows much tact in recounting his adventures, and they are so interspersed with anecdotes and information as to make them anything but wearisome. . . . The book, as a whole, is the most important addition made to our Arctic literature for a long time.*"—ATHENÆUM.

Crown 8vo, cloth, full gilt, 7s. 6d.

Latter-Day Lyrics:

Poems of Sentiment and Reflection by Living Writers; selected and arranged, with Notes, by W. DAVENPORT ADAMS. With a Note on some Foreign Forms of Verse, by AUSTIN DOBSON.

Crown 8vo, cloth, full gilt, 6s.

Leigh's A Town Garland.

By HENRY S. LEIGH, Author of "Carols of Cockayne."

"*If Mr. Leigh's verse survive to a future generation—and there is no reason why that honour should not be accorded productions so delicate, so finished, and so full of humour—their author will probably be remembered as the Poet of the Strand. . . . . Very whimsically does Mr. Leigh treat the subjects which commend themselves to him. His verse is always admirable in rhythm, and his rhymes are happy enough to deserve a place by the best of Barham. . . . . The entire contents of the volume are equally noteworthy for humour and for daintiness of workmanship.*"—ATHENÆUM.

SECOND EDITION.—Crown 8vo, cloth extra, with Illustrations, 10s. 6d

Leisure-Time Studies, chiefly Biological.

By ANDREW WILSON, Ph.D., Lecturer on Zoology and Comparative Anatomy in the Edinburgh Medical School.

"*It is well when we can take up the work of a really qualified investigator, who in the intervals of his more serious professional labours sets himself to impart knowledge in such a simple and elementary form as may attract and instruct, with no danger of misleading the tyro in natural science. Such a work is this little volume, made up of essays and addresses written and delivered by Dr. Andrew Wilson, lecturer and examiner in science at Edinburgh and Glasgow, at leisure intervals in a busy professional life. . . . Dr. Wilson's pages teem with matter stimulating to a healthy love of science and a reverence for the truths of nature.*"—SATURDAY REVIEW.

Crown 8vo, cloth extra, with Illustrations, 7s. 6d.

Life in London;

or, The History of Jerry Hawthorn and Corinthian Tom. With the whole of CRUIKSHANK'S Illustrations, in Colours, after the Originals.

Crown 8vo, cloth extra, 6s.

Lights on the Way:

Some Tales within a Tale. By the late J. H. ALEXANDER, B.A. Edited, with an Explanatory Note, by H. A. PAGE, Author of "Thoreau: A Study."

Crown 8vo, cloth extra, with Illustrations, 7s. 6d.

Longfellow's Complete Prose Works.

Including "Outre Mer," "Hyperion," "Kavanagh," "The Poets and Poetry of Europe," and "Driftwood." With Portrait and Illustrations by VALENTINE BROMLEY.

Crown 8vo, cloth extra, gilt, with Illustrations, 7s. 6d.

Longfellow's Poetical Works.

Carefully Reprinted from the Original Editions. With numerous fine Illustrations on Steel and Wood.

Crown 8vo, cloth extra, 5s.

Lunatic Asylum, My Experiences in a.

By a SANE PATIENT.

"*The story is clever and interesting, sad beyond measure though the subject be. There is no personal bitterness, and no violence or anger. Whatever may have been the evidence for our author's madness when he was consigned to an asylum, nothing can be clearer than his sanity when he wrote this book; it is bright, calm, and to the point.*"—SPECTATOR.

Royal 8vo, cloth extra, with 14 fine Plates, 12s. 6d.

Lusiad (The), of Camoens.

A New Translation by ROBERT FFRENCH DUFF. [*In the press.*

A NORMAN AND BRETON TOUR.

Square 8vo, cloth gilt, gilt top, profusely Illustrated, 10s. 6d.

Macquoid's Pictures and Legends from

Normandy and Brittany. By KATHARINE S. MACQUOID. With numerous Illustrations by THOMAS R. MACQUOID.

"*Mr. and Mrs. Macquoid have been strolling in Normandy and Brittany, and the result of their observations and researches in that picturesque land of romantic associations is an attractive volume, which is neither a work of travel nor a collection of stories, but a book partaking almost in equal degree of each of these characters. . . . The wanderings of the tourists, their sojournings in old inns, their explorations of ancient towns, and loiterings by rivers and other pleasant spots, are all related in a fresh and lively style. . . . The illustrations, which are numerous, are drawn, as a rule, with remarkable delicacy as well as with true artistic feeling.*"—DAILY NEWS.

Crown 8vo, cloth extra, with Illustrations, 2s. 6d.

Madre Natura v. The Moloch of Fashion.

By LUKE LIMNER. With 32 Illustrations by the Author. FOURTH EDITION, revised and enlarged.

Handsomely printed in facsimile, price 5s.

Magna Charta.

An exact Facsimile of the Original Document in the British Museum, printed on fine plate paper, nearly 3 feet long by 2 feet wide, with the Arms and Seals emblazoned in Gold and Colours.

*** A full Translation, with Notes, on a large sheet, 6d.

Mallock's Is Life Worth Living ?

By WILLIAM HURRELL MALLOCK.

"*This deeply interesting volume. . . . . It is the most powerful vindication of religion, both natural and revealed, that has appeared since Bishop Butler wrote, and is much more useful than either the Analogy or the Sermons of that great divine, as a refutation of the peculiar form assumed by the infidelity of the present day. . . . . Deeply philosophical as the book is, there is not a heavy page in it. The writer is 'possessed,' so to speak, with his great subject, has sounded its depths, surveyed it in all its extent, and brought to bear on it all the resources of a vivid, rich, and impassioned style, as well as an adequate acquaintance with the science, the philosophy, and the literature of the day.*"—IRISH DAILY NEWS.

Mark Twain's Works :

The Choice Works of Mark Twain. Revised and Corrected throughout by the Author. With Life, Portrait, and numerous Illustrations. Crown 8vo, cloth extra, 7s. 6d.

The Adventures of Tom Sawyer. By MARK TWAIN. With One Hundred Illustrations. Small 8vo, cloth extra, 7s. 6d.

*** Also a Cheap Edition, in illustrated boards, at 2s.

"*A book to be read. There is a certain freshness and novelty about it, a practically romantic character, so to speak, which will make it very attractive.*"—SPECTATOR.

A Pleasure Trip on the Continent of Europe : The Innocents Abroad, and The New Pilgrim's Progress. By MARK TWAIN. Post 8vo, illustrated boards, 2s.

An Idle Excursion, and other Sketches. By MARK TWAIN. Post 8vo, illustrated boards, 2s.

Small 8vo, cloth limp, with Illustrations, 2s. 6d.

Miller's Physiology for the Young ;

Or, The House of Life : HUMAN PHYSIOLOGY, with its Applications to the Preservation of Health. For use in Classes and Popular Reading. With numerous Illustrations. By Mrs. F. FENWICK MILLER.

"*A clear and convenient little book.*"—SATURDAY REVIEW.
"*An admirable introduction to a subject which all who value health and enjoy life should have at their fingers' ends.*"—ECHO.

Small 8vo, 1s. ; cloth extra, 1s. 6d.

Milton's The Hygiene of the Skin.

A Concise Set of Rules for the Management of the Skin ; with Directions for Diet, Wines, Soaps, Baths, &c. By J. L. MILTON, Senior Surgeon to St. John's Hospital.

Crown 8vo, cloth extra, with Frontispiece, 7s. 6d.

Moore's (Thos.) Prose and Verse—Humorous,

Satirical, and Sentimental. Including Suppressed Passages from the Memoirs of Lord Byron. Chiefly from the Author's MSS., and all hitherto Inedited and Uncollected. Edited, with Notes, by RICHARD HERNE SHEPHERD.

Post 8vo, cloth limp, 2*s.* 6*d.* per vol.

Mayfair Library, The:

The New Republic. By W. H. MALLOCK.

The New Paul and Virginia. By W. H. MALLOCK.

The True History of Joshua Davidson. By E. LYNN LINTON.

Old Stories Re-told. By WALTER THORNBURY.

Thoreau: His Life and Aims. By H. A. PAGE.

By Stream and Sea. By WILLIAM SENIOR.

Jeux d'Esprit. Edited by HENRY S. LEIGH.

Puniana. By the Hon. HUGH ROWLEY.

More Puniana. By the Hon. HUGH ROWLEY.

Puck on Pegasus. By H. CHOLMONDELEY-PENNELL.

Muses of Mayfair. Edited by H. CHOLMONDELEY-PENNELL.

Gastronomy as a Fine Art. By BRILLAT-SAVARIN.

Original Plays. By W. S. GILBERT.

*** *Other Volumes are in preparation.*

New Novels at every Library.

THE FALLEN LEAVES. By WILKIE COLLINS. Three Vols., crown 8vo.

UNDER ONE ROOF. By JAMES PAYN, Author of "By Proxy," &c. Three Vols., crown 8vo.

MAID, WIFE, OR WIDOW? By Mrs. ALEXANDER, Author of "The Wooing o't." SECOND EDITION. Crown 8vo, cloth extra, 10*s.* 6*d.*

THE CURE OF SOULS: A Novel. By MACLAREN COBBAN. Crown 8vo, cloth extra, 10*s.* 6*d.*

> "*It is long since we have seen a more promising début. . . . He has force, a certain rude pathos and realistic intensity of sentiment, and a remarkable faculty for inventing natural dialogue. It is refreshing to come upon a novel by a new hand which is neither silly, weak, nor flighty, and which shows proof of thought and care in the writer.*"—SATURDAY REVIEW.

MR. PAYN'S NEW NOVEL.

HIGH SPIRITS: Being Stories written in them. By JAMES PAYN, Author of "By Proxy," &c. Three Vols., crown 8vo.

> "*In those comic historiettes of which Mr. Payn only among living writers has the secret, there is as much occasion for good, honest, sociable laughter, as in any three volumes we remember during the last ten years to have read.*"—ATHENÆUM.

MRS. LINTON'S NEW NOVEL.

UNDER WHICH LORD? By E. LYNN LINTON, Author of "Patricia Kemball," &c. Three Vols., crown 8vo. With Twelve Illustrations by ARTHUR HOPKINS.

MR. JUSTIN McCARTHY'S NEW NOVEL.

DONNA QUIXOTE. By JUSTIN McCARTHY, Author of "Dear Lady Disdain," &c. Three Vols., crown 8vo. With Twelve Illustrations by ARTHUR HOPKINS.

NEW NOVELS—*continued.*

NEW NOVEL BY HENRY JAMES, JUN.

CONFIDENCE. By HENRY JAMES, Jun. [*Dec.* 10.

CHARLES GIBBON'S NEW NOVEL.

QUEEN OF THE MEADOW. By CHARLES GIBBON, Author of "Robin Gray," &c. Three Vols., crown 8vo. With Twelve Illustrations by ARTHUR HOPKINS. [*Dec.* 15.

OUIDA'S NEW NOVEL.

MOTHS. By OUIDA, Author of "Puck," "Ariadne," &c. Three Vols., crown 8vo. [*January.*

NEW AND CHEAPER EDITION.

THORNICROFT'S MODEL. By Mrs. A. W. HUNT. Crown 8vo, cloth extra, 6s.

UNIFORM EDITION OF CHARLES GIBBON'S WORKS.

In the press, crown 8vo, cloth extra, 6s. each.

IN LOVE AND WAR. By CHARLES GIBBON.

WHAT WILL THE WORLD SAY? By CHARLES GIBBON.

FOR THE KING. By CHARLES GIBBON.

IN HONOUR BOUND. By CHARLES GIBBON.

Square 8vo, cloth extra, with numerous Illustrations, 9s.

North Italian Folk.

By Mrs. COMYNS CARR. Illustrations by RANDOLPH CALDECOTT.

"*A delightful book, of a kind which is far too rare. If anyone wants to really know the North Italian folk, we can honestly advise him to omit the journey, and sit down to read Mrs. Carr's pages instead. . . . Description with Mrs. Carr is a real gift. . . . It is rarely that a book is so happily illustrated.*"—CONTEMPORARY REVIEW.

Crown 8vo, cloth extra, with Vignette Portraits, price 6s. per Vol.

Old Dramatists, The:

Ben Jonson's Works.
With Notes, Critical and Explanatory, and a Biographical Memoir by WILLIAM GIFFORD. Edited by Colonel CUNNINGHAM. Three Vols.

Chapman's Works.
Now First Collected. Complete in Three Vols. Vol. I. contains the Plays complete, including the doubtful ones; Vol. II. the Poems and Minor Translations, with an Introductory Essay by ALGERNON CHARLES SWINBURNE; Vol. III. the Translations of the Iliad and Odyssey.

Marlowe's Works.
Including his Translations. Edited, with Notes and Introduction, by Col. CUNNINGHAM. One Vol.

Massinger's Plays.
From the Text of WILLIAM GIFFORD. With the addition of the Tragedy of "Believe as you List." Edited by Col. CUNNINGHAM. One Vol.

Crown 8vo, red cloth extra, 5s. each.

Ouida's Novels.—Library Edition.

Held in Bondage.	By OUIDA.	Folle Farine.	By OUIDA.
Strathmore.	By OUIDA.	Dog of Flanders.	By OUIDA.
Chandos.	By OUIDA.	Pascarel.	By OUIDA.
Under Two Flags.	By OUIDA.	Two Wooden Shoes.	By OUIDA.
Idalia.	By OUIDA.	Signa.	By OUIDA.
Cecil Castlemaine.	By OUIDA.	In a Winter City.	By OUIDA.
Tricotrin.	By OUIDA.	Ariadne.	By OUIDA.
Puck.	By OUIDA.	Friendship.	By OUIDA.

CHEAP EDITION OF OUIDA'S NOVELS.

Post 8vo, illustrated boards, 2s. each.

Held in Bondage.	By OUIDA.	Idalia.	By OUIDA.
Strathmore.	By OUIDA.	Cecil Castlemaine.	By OUIDA.
Chandos.	By OUIDA.	Tricotrin.	By OUIDA.
Under Two Flags.	By OUIDA.	Puck.	By OUIDA.

The other Novels will follow in Monthly Volumes.

Two Vols. 8vo, cloth extra, with Illustrations, 10s. 6d.

Plutarch's Lives of Illustrious Men.

Translated from the Greek, with Notes, Critical and Historical, and a Life of Plutarch, by JOHN and WILLIAM LANGHORNE. New Edition, with Medallion Portraits.

Crown 8vo, cloth extra, with Portrait and Illustrations, 7s. 6d.

Poe's Choice Prose and Poetical Works.

With BAUDELAIRE'S "Essay."

Crown 8vo, cloth extra, Illustrated, 7s. 6d.

Poe, The Life of Edgar Allan.

By W. F. GILL. With numerous Illustrations and Facsimiles.

Crown 8vo, cloth extra, 7s. 6d.

Primitive Manners and Customs.

By JAMES A. FARRER.

"*A book which is really both instructive and amusing, and which will open a new field of thought to many readers.*"—ATHENÆUM.

"*An admirable example of the application of the scientific method and the working of the truly scientific spirit.*"—SATURDAY REVIEW.

Small 8vo, cloth extra, with Illustrations, 3s. 6d.

Prince of Argolis, The:

A Story of the Old Greek Fairy Time. By J. MOYR SMITH. With 130 Illustrations by the Author.

Crown 8vo, carefully printed on creamy paper, and tastefully bound
in cloth for the Library, price 6s. each.

Piccadilly Novels, The.

Popular Stories by the Best Authors.

READY-MONEY MORTIBOY. By W. BESANT and JAMES RICE.

MY LITTLE GIRL. By W. BESANT and JAMES RICE.

THE CASE OF MR. LUCRAFT. By W. BESANT and JAMES RICE.

THIS SON OF VULCAN. By W. BESANT and JAMES RICE.

WITH HARP AND CROWN. By W. BESANT and JAMES RICE.

THE GOLDEN BUTTERFLY. By W. BESANT and JAMES RICE.
With a Frontispiece by F. S. WALKER.

BY CELIA'S ARBOUR. By W. BESANT and JAMES RICE.

THE MONKS OF THELEMA. By W. BESANT and JAMES RICE.

'TWAS IN TRAFALGAR'S BAY. By W. BESANT & JAMES RICE.

ANTONINA. By WILKIE COLLINS. Illustrated by Sir J. GILBERT
and ALFRED CONCANEN.

BASIL. By WILKIE COLLINS. Illustrated by Sir JOHN GILBERT
and J. MAHONEY.

HIDE AND SEEK. By WILKIE COLLINS. Illustrated by Sir
JOHN GILBERT and J. MAHONEY.

THE DEAD SECRET. By WILKIE COLLINS. Illustrated by Sir
JOHN GILBERT and H. FURNISS.

QUEEN OF HEARTS. By WILKIE COLLINS. Illustrated by Sir
JOHN GILBERT and A. CONCANEN.

MY MISCELLANIES. By WILKIE COLLINS. With Steel Portrait, and Illustrations by A. CONCANEN.

THE WOMAN IN WHITE. By WILKIE COLLINS. Illustrated
by Sir J. GILBERT and F. A. FRASER.

THE MOONSTONE. By WILKIE COLLINS. Illustrated by G.
DU MAURIER and F. A. FRASER.

MAN AND WIFE. By WILKIE COLLINS. Illust. by WM. SMALL.

POOR MISS FINCH. By WILKIE COLLINS. Illustrated by G.
DU MAURIER and EDWARD HUGHES.

MISS OR MRS. ? By WILKIE COLLINS. Illustrated by S. L.
FILDES and HENRY WOODS.

THE NEW MAGDALEN. By WILKIE COLLINS. Illustrated by
G. DU MAURIER and C. S. RANDS.

THE FROZEN DEEP. By WILKIE COLLINS. Illustrated by G.
DU MAURIER and J. MAHONEY.

THE LAW AND THE LADY. By WILKIE COLLINS. Illustrated by S. L. FILDES and SYDNEY HALL.

PICCADILLY NOVELS—*continued.*

THE TWO DESTINIES. By WILKIE COLLINS.

THE HAUNTED HOTEL. By WILKIE COLLINS. Illustrated by ARTHUR HOPKINS.

DECEIVERS EVER. By Mrs. H. LOVETT CAMERON.

JULIET'S GUARDIAN. By Mrs. H. LOVETT CAMERON. Illustrated by VALENTINE BROMLEY.

FELICIA. By M. BETHAM-EDWARDS. Frontispiece by W. BOWLES.

OLYMPIA. By R. E. FRANCILLON.

UNDER THE GREENWOOD TREE. By THOMAS HARDY.

THORNICROFT'S MODEL. By Mrs. A. W. HUNT.

FATED TO BE FREE. By JEAN INGELOW.

THE QUEEN OF CONNAUGHT. By HARRIETT JAY.

THE DARK COLLEEN. By HARRIETT JAY.

NUMBER SEVENTEEN. By HENRY KINGSLEY.

OAKSHOTT CASTLE. By HENRY KINGSLEY. With a Frontispiece by SHIRLEY HODSON.

THE WORLD WELL LOST. By E. LYNN LINTON. Illustrated by J. LAWSON and HENRY FRENCH.

THE ATONEMENT OF LEAM DUNDAS. By E. LYNN LINTON. With a Frontispiece by HENRY WOODS.

PATRICIA KEMBALL. By E. LYNN LINTON. With a Frontispiece by G. DU MAURIER.

THE WATERDALE NEIGHBOURS. By JUSTIN MCCARTHY.

MY ENEMY'S DAUGHTER. By JUSTIN MCCARTHY.

LINLEY ROCHFORD. By JUSTIN MCCARTHY.

A FAIR SAXON. By JUSTIN MCCARTHY.

DEAR LADY DISDAIN. By JUSTIN MCCARTHY.

MISS MISANTHROPE. By JUSTIN MCCARTHY. Illustrated by ARTHUR HOPKINS.

LOST ROSE. By KATHARINE S. MACQUOID.

THE EVIL EYE, and other Stories. By KATHARINE S. MACQUOID. Illustrated by THOMAS R. MACQUOID and PERCY MACQUOID.

OPEN! SESAME! By FLORENCE MARRYAT. Illustrated by F. A. FRASER.

TOUCH AND GO. By JEAN MIDDLEMASS.

WHITELADIES. By Mrs. OLIPHANT. With Illustrations by A. HOPKINS and H. WOODS.

THE BEST OF HUSBANDS. By JAMES PAYN. Illustrated by J. MOYR SMITH.

PICCADILLY NOVELS—*continued.*

FALLEN FORTUNES. By JAMES PAYN.

HALVES. By JAMES PAYN. With a Frontispiece by J. MAHONEY.

WALTER'S WORD. By JAMES PAYN. Illust. by J. MOYR SMITH.

WHAT HE COST HER. By JAMES PAYN.

LESS BLACK THAN WE'RE PAINTED. By JAMES PAYN.

BY PROXY. By JAMES PAYN. Illustrated by ARTHUR HOPKINS.

HER MOTHER'S DARLING. By Mrs. J. H. RIDDELL.

BOUND TO THE WHEEL. By JOHN SAUNDERS.

GUY WATERMAN. By JOHN SAUNDERS.

ONE AGAINST THE WORLD. By JOHN SAUNDERS.

THE LION IN THE PATH. By JOHN SAUNDERS.

THE WAY WE LIVE NOW. By ANTHONY TROLLOPE. Illust.

THE AMERICAN SENATOR. By ANTHONY TROLLOPE.

DIAMOND CUT DIAMOND. By T. A. TROLLOPE.

Post 8vo, illustrated boards, 2s. each.

Popular Novels, Cheap Editions of.

[WILKIE COLLINS' NOVELS and BESANT and RICE'S NOVELS may also be had in cloth limp at 2s. 6d. *See, too, the* PICCADILLY NOVELS, *for Library Editions.*]

Ready-Money Mortiboy. By WALTER BESANT and JAMES RICE.

The Golden Butterfly. By Authors of "Ready-Money Mortiboy."

This Son of Vulcan. By the same.

My Little Girl. By the same.

The Case of Mr. Lucraft. By Authors of "Ready-Money Mortiboy."

With Harp and Crown. By Authors of "Ready-Money Mortiboy."

Surly Tim. By F. H. BURNETT.

The Woman in White. By WILKIE COLLINS.

Antonina. By WILKIE COLLINS.

Basil. By WILKIE COLLINS.

Hide and Seek. By the same.

The Dead Secret. By the same.

The Queen of Hearts. By WILKIE COLLINS.

My Miscellanies. By the same.

The Moonstone. By the same.

Man and Wife. By WILKIE COLLINS.

Poor Miss Finch. By the same.

Miss or Mrs. ? By the same.

The New Magdalen. By WILKIE COLLINS.

The Frozen Deep. By the same.

The Law and the Lady. By WILKIE COLLINS.

The Two Destinies. By WILKIE COLLINS.

Roxy. By EDWARD EGGLESTON.

Felicia. M. BETHAM-EDWARDS.

Filthy Lucre. By ALBANY DE FONBLANQUE.

Olympia. By R. E. FRANCILLON.

Dick Temple. By JAMES GREENWOOD.

Under the Greenwood Tree. By THOMAS HARDY.

An Heiress of Red Dog. By BRET HARTE.

POPULAR NOVELS—*continued.*

The Luck of Roaring Camp. By BRET HARTE.

Fated to be Free. By JEAN INGELOW.

The Queen of Connaught. By HARRIETT JAY.

The Dark Colleen. By HARRIETT JAY.

Number Seventeen. By HENRY KINGSLEY.

Oakshott Castle. By the same.

The Waterdale Neighbours. By JUSTIN McCARTHY.

My Enemy's Daughter. By JUSTIN McCARTHY.

Linley Rochford. By the same.

A Fair Saxon. By the same.

Dear Lady Disdain. By the same.

The Evil Eye. By KATHARINE S. MACQUOID.

Open! Sesame! By FLORENCE MARRYAT.

Whiteladies. Mrs. OLIPHANT.

Held in Bondage. By OUIDA.

Strathmore. By OUIDA.

Chandos. By OUIDA.

Under Two Flags. By OUIDA.

Idalia. By OUIDA.

Cecil Castlemaine. By OUIDA.

Tricotrin. By OUIDA.

Puck. By OUIDA.

The Best of Husbands. By JAMES PAYN.

Walter's Word. By J. PAYN.

The Mystery of Marie Roget. By EDGAR A. POE.

Her Mother's Darling. By Mrs. J. H. RIDDELL.

Gaslight and Daylight. By GEORGE AUGUSTUS SALA.

Bound to the Wheel. By JOHN SAUNDERS.

Guy Waterman. J. SAUNDERS.

One Against the World. By JOHN SAUNDERS.

The Lion in the Path. By JOHN and KATHERINE SAUNDERS.

Tales for the Marines. By WALTER THORNBURY.

The Way we Live Now. By ANTHONY TROLLOPE.

The American Senator. By ANTHONY TROLLOPE.

Diamond Cut Diamond. By T. A. TROLLOPE.

An Idle Excursion. By MARK TWAIN.

Adventures of Tom Sawyer. By MARK TWAIN.

A Pleasure Trip on the Continent of Europe. By MARK TWAIN.

Fcap. 8vo, picture covers, 1*s.* each.

Jeff Briggs's Love Story. By BRET HARTE.

The Twins of Table Mountain. By BRET HARTE.

Mrs. Gainsborough's Diamonds. By JULIAN HAWTHORNE.

Kathleen Mavourneen. By the Author of "That Lass o' Lowrie's."

Lindsay's Luck. By the Author of "That Lass o' Lowrie's."

Pretty Polly Pemberton. By Author of "That Lass o' Lowrie's."

Crown 8vo, cloth extra, with Portrait and Facsimile, 7*s.* 6*d.*

Prout (Father), The Final Reliques of.

Collected and Edited, from MSS. supplied by the family of the Rev. FRANCIS MAHONY, by BLANCHARD JERROLD.

Proctor's (R. A.) Works :

Myths and Marvels of Astronomy. By RICH. A. PROCTOR, Author of "Other Worlds than Ours," &c. Demy 8vo, cloth extra, 12s. 6d.

Pleasant Ways in Science. By RICHARD A. PROCTOR. Crown 8vo, cloth extra, 10s. 6d.

" When scientific problems of an abstruse and difficult character are presented to the unscientific mind, something more than mere knowledge is necessary in order to achieve success. The ability to trace such problems through the several stages of observation and experiment to their successful solution, without once suffering the reader's attention to flag, or his interest in the issue of the investigation to abate, argues the possession by the writer, not only of a thorough acquaintance with his subject, but also of that rare gift, the power of readily imparting his knowledge to those who have not the aptitude to acquire it, undivested of scientific formulæ. Now, such a writer is Mr. R. A. Proctor."—SCOTSMAN.

Rough Ways made Smooth : A Series of Familiar Essays on Scientific Subjects. By RICHARD A. PROCTOR. Crown 8vo, cloth extra, 10s. 6d.

Our Place Among Infinities : A Series of Essays contrasting our Little Abode in Space and Time with the Infinities Around us. By RICHARD A. PROCTOR. Crown 8vo, cloth extra, 6s.

The Expanse of Heaven : A Series of Essays on the Wonders of the Firmament. By RICHARD A. PROCTOR. Crown 8vo, cloth extra, 6s.

Wages and Wants of Science Workers. By RICHARD A. PROCTOR. Second Edition, crown 8vo, 1s. 6d.

Crown 8vo, cloth extra, gilt, 7s. 6d.

Pursuivant of Arms, The ;

or, Heraldry founded upon Facts. A Popular Guide to the Science of Heraldry. By J. R. PLANCHE, Esq., Somerset Herald. With Coloured Frontispiece, Plates, and 200 Illustrations.

Crown 8vo, cloth extra, with Illustrations, 7s. 6d.

Rabelais' Works.

Faithfully Translated from the French, with variorum Notes, and numerous characteristic Illustrations by GUSTAVE DORE.

" His buffoonery was not merely Brutus's rough skin, which contained a rod of gold : it was necessary as an amulet against the monks and legates ; and he must be classed with the greatest creative minds in the world—with Shakespeare, with Dante, and with Cervantes."—S. T. COLERIDGE.

Crown 8vo, cloth gilt, with numerous Illustrations, and a beautifully executed Chart of the various Spectra, 7s. 6d.

Rambosson's Astronomy.

By J. RAMBOSSON, Laureate of the Institute of France. Translated by C. B. PITMAN. Profusely Illustrated.

Crown 8vo, cloth extra, with Illustrations, 7s. 6d.

Regalia: Crowns, Coronations, and Inaugurations, in various Ages and Countries. By W. JONES, F.S.A., Author of "Finger-Ring Lore," &c. With very numerous Illustrations. *[In preparation.*

Crown 8vo, cloth extra, 10s. 6d,

Richardson's (Dr.) A Ministry of Health,

and other Papers. By BENJAMIN WARD RICHARDSON, M.D., &c.

*" This highly interesting volume contains upwards of nine addresses, written in the author's well-known style, and full of great and good thoughts. . . . The work is, like all those of the author, that of a man of genius, of great power, of experience, and noble independence of thought."—*POPULAR SCIENCE REVIEW.

Handsomely printed, price 5s.

Roll of Battle Abbey, The;

or, A List of the Principal Warriors who came over from Normandy with William the Conqueror, and Settled in this Country, A.D. 1066-7. Printed on fine plate paper, nearly three feet by two, with the principal Arms emblazoned in Gold and Colours.

Two Vols., large 4to, profusely Illustrated, half-morocco, £2 16s.

Rowlandson, the Caricaturist.

A Selection from his Works, with Anecdotal Descriptions of his Famous Caricatures, and a Sketch of his Life, Times, and Contemporaries. With nearly 400 Illustrations, mostly in Facsimile of the Originals. By JOSEPH GREGO, Author of " James Gillray, the Caricaturist; his Life, Works, and Times."

Crown 8vo, cloth extra, profusely Illustrated, 4s. 6d. each.

"Secret Out" Series, The.

The Pyrotechnist's Treasury; or, Complete Art of Making Fireworks. By THOMAS KENTISH. With numerous Illustrations.

The Art of Amusing: A Collection of Graceful Arts, Games, Tricks, Puzzles, and Charades. By FRANK BELLEW. 300 Illustrations.

Hanky-Panky: Very Easy Tricks, Very Difficult Tricks, White Magic, Sleight of Hand. Edited by W. H. CREMER. 200 Illustrations.

The Merry Circle: A Book of New Intellectual Games and Amusements. By CLARA BELLEW. Many Illustrations.

Magician's Own Book: Performances with Cups and Balls, Eggs, Hats, Handkerchiefs, &c. All from Actual Experience. Edited by W. H. CREMER. 200 Illustrations.

Magic No Mystery: Tricks with Cards, Dice, Balls, &c., with fully descriptive Directions; the Art of Secret Writing; Training of Performing Animals, &c. Coloured Frontispiece and many Illustrations.

The Secret Out: One Thousand Tricks with Cards, and other Recreations; with Entertaining Experiments in Drawing-room or "White Magic.' By W. H. CREMER. 300 Engravings.

Crown 8vo, cloth extra, 7s. 6d.

Sanson Family, Memoirs of the:

Seven Generations of Executioners. By HENRI SANSON. Translated from the French, with Introduction, by CAMILLE BARRÈRE.

*" A faithful translation of this curious work, which will certainly repay perusal —not on the ground of its being full of horrors, for the original author seems to be rather ashamed of the technical aspect of his profession, and is commendably reticent as to its details, but because it contains a lucid account of the most notable causes célèbres from the time of Louis XIV. to a period within the memory of persons still living. . . . Extremely entertaining."—*DAILY TELEGRAPH.

Crown 8vo, cloth extra, 6s.

Senior's Travel and Trout in the Antipodes.

An Angler's Sketches in Tasmania and New Zealand. By WILLIAM
SENIOR ("Red Spinner"), Author of "Stream and Sea."

Shakespeare and Shakespeareana :

Shakespeare, The First Folio. Mr. WILLIAM SHAKESPEARE'S
Comedies, Histories, and Tragedies. Published according to the true
Originall Copies. London, Printed by ISAAC IAGGARD and ED. BLOUNT,
1623.—A Reproduction of the extremely rare original, in reduced facsimile
by a photographic process—ensuring the strictest accuracy in every detail.
Small 8vo, half-Roxburghe, 10s. 6d.

*" To Messrs. Chatto and Windus belongs the merit of having done more
to facilitate the critical study of the text of our great dramatist than all the
Shakespeare clubs and societies put together. A complete facsimile of the
celebrated First Folio edition of 1623 for half-a-guinea is at once a miracle of
cheapness and enterprise. Being in a reduced form, the type is necessarily
rather diminutive, but it is as distinct as in a genuine copy of the original,
and will be found to be as useful and far more handy to the student than the
latter."—ATHENÆUM.*

Shakespeare, The Lansdowne. Beautifully printed in red
and black, in small but very clear type. With engraved facsimile of
DROESHOUT's Portrait. Post 8vo, cloth extra, 7s. 6d.

Shakspere's Dramatic Works, Poems, Doubtful Plays, and
Biography.—CHARLES KNIGHT'S PICTORIAL EDITION, with many hundred
beautiful Engravings on Wood of Views, Costumes, Old Buildings, Antiquities, Portraits, &c. Eight Vols., royal 8vo, cloth extra, £3 12s.

Shakespeare for Children: Tales from Shakespeare. By
CHARLES and MARY LAMB. With numerous Illustrations, coloured and
plain, by J. MOYR SMITH. Crown 4to, cloth gilt, 10s. 6d.

Shakspere, The School of. Including "The Life and Death
of Captain Thomas Stukeley," "Nobody and Somebody," "Histriomastix,"
"The Prodigal Son," "Jack Drum's Entertainment," "A Warning for Fair
Women," and "Fair Em." Edited, with Notes, by RICHARD SIMPSON.
Introduction by F. J. FURNIVALL. Two Vols., crown 8vo, cloth extra, 18s.

Shakespeare Music, The Handbook of. Being an Account of
Three Hundred and Fifty Pieces of Music, set to Words taken from the
Plays and Poems of Shakespeare, the compositions ranging from the Eliza-
bethan Age to the Present Time. By ALFRED ROFFE. 4to, half-Roxburghe, 7s.

Shakespeare, A Study of. By ALGERNON CHARLES SWIN-
BURNE. Crown 8vo, cloth extra, 8s. 						*[In the press.*

Crown 8vo, cloth extra, gilt, with 10 full-page Tinted Illustrations, 7s. 6d.

Sheridan's Complete Works,

with Life and Anecdotes. Including his Dramatic Writings, printed
from the Original Editions, his Works in Prose and Poetry, Translations, Speeches, Jokes, Puns, &c. ; with a Collection of Sheridaniana.

*" The editor has brought together within a manageable compass not only the
seven plays by which Sheridan is best known, but a collection also of his poetical
pieces which are less familiar to the public, sketches of unfinished dramas, selections
from his reported witticisms, and extracts from his principal speeches. To these
is prefixed a short but well-written memoir, giving the chief facts in Sheridan's
literary and political career ; so that, with this volume in his hand, the student
may consider himself tolerably well furnished with all that is necessary for a
general comprehension of the subject of it."—PALL MALL GAZETTE.*

Crown 8vo, cloth extra, with Illustrations, 7s. 6d.

Signboards:

Their History. With Anecdotes of Famous Taverns and Remarkable Characters. By JACOB LARWOOD and JOHN CAMDEN HOTTEN. With nearly 100 Illustrations.

"*Even if we were ever so maliciously inclined, we could not pick out all Messrs. Larwood and Hotten's plums, because the good things are so numerous as to defy the most wholesale depredation.*"—TIMES.

Crown 8vo, cloth extra, gilt, 6s. 6d.

Slang Dictionary, The:

Etymological, Historical, and Anecdotal. An ENTIRELY NEW EDITION, revised throughout, and considerably Enlarged.

"*We are glad to see the Slang Dictionary reprinted and enlarged. From a high scientific point of view this book is not to be despised. Of course it cannot fail to be amusing also. It contains the very vocabulary of unrestrained humour, and oddity, and grotesqueness. In a word, it provides valuable material both for the student of language and the student of human nature.*"—ACADEMY.

Exquisitely printed in miniature, cloth extra, gilt edges, 2s. 6d.

Smoker's Text-Book, The.

By J. HAMER, F.R.S.L.

Crown 8vo, cloth extra, 5s.

Spalding's Elizabethan Demonology:

An Essay in Illustration of the Belief in the Existence of Devils, and the Powers possessed by them, as it was generally held during the period of the Reformation, and the times immediately succeeding; with Special Reference to Shakspere and his Works. By T. ALFRED SPALDING, LL.B.

Crown 4to, uniform with "Chaucer for Children," with Coloured Illustrations, cloth gilt, 10s. 6d.

Spenser for Children.

By M. H. TOWRY. With Illustrations in Colours by WALTER J. MORGAN.

"*Spenser has simply been transferred into plain prose, with here and there a line or stanza quoted, where the meaning and the diction are within a child's comprehension, and additional point is thus given to the narrative without the cost of obscurity. . . . Altogether the work has been well and carefully done.*"—THE TIMES.

Crown 8vo, cloth extra, 9s.

Stedman's Victorian Poets:

Critical Essays. By EDMUND CLARENCE STEDMAN.

"*We ought to be thankful to those who do critical work with competent skill and understanding, with honesty of purpose, and with diligence and thoroughness of execution. And Mr. Stedman, having chosen to work in this line, deserves the thanks of English scholars by these qualities and by something more; . . . he is faithful, studious, and discerning.*"—SATURDAY REVIEW.

Crown 8vo, cloth extra, with Illustrations, 7s. 6d.

Strutt's Sports and Pastimes of the People

of England; including the Rural and Domestic Recreations, May Games, Mummeries, Shows, Processions, Pageants, and Pompous Spectacles, from the Earliest Period to the Present Time. With 140 Illustrations. Edited by WILLIAM HONE.

Crown 8vo, cloth extra, with Illustrations, 7s. 6d.

Swift's Choice Works,

In Prose and Verse. With Memoir, Portrait, and Facsimiles of the Maps in the Original Edition of "Gulliver's Travels."

"If he had never written either the 'Tale of a Tub' or 'Gulliver's Travels,' his name merely as a poet would have come down to us, and have gone down to posterity, with well-earned honours."—HAZLITT.

Swinburne's Works:

The Queen Mother and Rosamond. Fcap. 8vo, 5s.

Atalanta in Calydon.
A New Edition. Crown 8vo, 6s.

Chastelard.
A Tragedy. Crown 8vo, 7s.

Poems and Ballads.
FIRST SERIES. Fcap. 8vo, 9s. Also in crown 8vo, at same price.

Poems and Ballads.
SECOND SERIES. Fcap. 8vo, 9s. Also in crown 8vo, at same price.

Notes on "Poems and Ballads." 8vo, 1s.

William Blake:
A Critical Essay. With Facsimile Paintings. Demy 8vo, 16s.

Songs before Sunrise.
Crown 8vo, 10s. 6d.

Bothwell:
A Tragedy. Crown 8vo, 12s. 6d.

George Chapman:
An Essay. Crown 8vo, 7s.

Songs of Two Nations.
Crown 8vo, 6s.

Essays and Studies.
Crown 8vo, 12s.

Erechtheus:
A Tragedy. Crown 8vo, 6s.

Note of an English Republican
on the Muscovite Crusade. 8vo, 1s.

A Note on Charlotte Brontë.
Crown 8vo, 6s.

A Study of Shakespeare.
Crown 8vo, 8s. [*In the press.*

Medium 8vo, cloth extra, with Illustrations, 7s. 6d.

Syntax's (Dr.) Three Tours,

in Search of the Picturesque, in Search of Consolation, and in Search of a Wife. With the whole of ROWLANDSON's droll page Illustrations, in Colours, and Life of the Author by J. C. HOTTEN.

Four Vols. small 8vo, cloth boards, 30s.

Taine's History of English Literature.

Translated by HENRY VAN LAUN.

*** Also a POPULAR EDITION, in Two Vols. crown 8vo, cloth extra, 15s.

Crown 8vo, cloth gilt, profusely Illustrated, 6s.

Tales of Old Thule.

Collected and Illustrated by J. MOYR SMITH.

"It is not often that we meet with a volume of fairy tales possessing more fully the double recommendation of absorbing interest and purity of tone than does the one before us containing a collection of "Tales of Old Thule." These come, to say the least, near fulfilling the idea of perfect works of the kind; and the illustrations with which the volume is embellished are equally excellent. . . . We commend the book to parents and teachers as an admirable gift to their children and pupils."—LITERARY WORLD.

One Vol. crown 8vo, cloth extra, 7s. 6d.

Taylor's (Tom) Historical Dramas:

"Clancarty," "Jeanne Darc," "'Twixt Axe and Crown," "The Fool's Revenge," "Arkwright's Wife," "Anne Boleyn," "Plot and Passion."

** The Plays may also be had separately, at 1s. each.

Crown 8vo, cloth extra, with Coloured Frontispiece and numerous Illustrations, 7s. 6d.

Thackerayana :

Notes and Anecdotes. Illustrated by a profusion of Sketches by WILLIAM MAKEPEACE THACKERAY, depicting Humorous Incidents in his School-life, and Favourite Characters in the books of his everyday reading. With Hundreds of Wood Engravings, facsimiled from Mr. Thackeray's Original Drawings.

"It would have been a real loss to bibliographical literature had copyright difficulties deprived the general public of this very amusing collection. One of Thackeray's habits, from his schoolboy days, was to ornament the margins and blank pages of the books he had in use with caricature illustrations of their contents. This gave special value to the sale of his library, and is almost cause for regret that it could not have been preserved in its integrity. Thackeray's place in literature is eminent enough to have made this an interest to future generations. The anonymous editor has done the best that he could to compensate for the lack of this. It is an admirable addendum, not only to his collected works, but also to any memoir of him that has been, or that is likely to be, written."—BRITISH QUARTERLY REVIEW.

Crown 8vo, cloth extra, gilt edges, with Illustrations, 7s. 6d.

Thomson's Seasons and Castle of Indolence.

With a Biographical and Critical Introduction by ALLAN CUNNINGHAM, and over 50 fine Illustrations on Steel and Wood.

Crown 8vo, cloth extra, with numerous Illustrations, 7s. 6d.

Thornbury's (Walter) Haunted London.

A New Edition, edited by EDWARD WALFORD, M.A., with numerous Illustrations by F. W. FAIRHOLT, F.S.A.

Crown 8vo, cloth extra, with Illustrations, 7s. 6d.

Timbs' Clubs and Club Life in London.

With Anecdotes of its famous Coffee-houses, Hostelries, and Taverns. By JOHN TIMBS, F.S.A. With numerous Illustrations.

Crown 8vo, cloth extra, with Illustrations, 7s. 6d.

Timbs' English Eccentrics and Eccentrici-
ties: Stories of Wealth and Fashion, Delusions, Impostures, and Fanatic Missions, Strange Sights and Sporting Scenes, Eccentric Artists, Theatrical Folks, Men of Letters, &c. By JOHN TIMBS, F.S.A. With nearly 50 Illustrations.

Demy 8vo, cloth extra, 14s.

Torrens' The Marquess Wellesley,
Architect of Empire. An Historic Portrait. *Forming Vol. I. of* PROCONSUL and TRIBUNE: WELLESLEY and O'CONNELL: Historic Portraits. By W. M. TORRENS, M.P. In Two Vols.

Crown 8vo, cloth extra, with Coloured Illustrations, 7s. 6d.

Turner's (J. M. W.) Life and Correspondence.
Founded upon Letters and Papers furnished by his Friends and fellow-Academicians. By WALTER THORNBURY. A New Edition, considerably Enlarged. With numerous Illustrations in Colours, facsimiled from Turner's original Drawings.

Two Vols., crown 8vo, cloth extra, with Map and Ground-Plans, 14s.

Walcott's Church Work and Life in English
Minsters; and the English Student's Monasticon. By the Rev. MACKENZIE E. C. WALCOTT, B.D.

The 20th Annual Edition, for 1880, elegantly bound, cloth, full gilt, price 50s.

Walford's County Families of the United
Kingdom. A Royal Manual of the Titled and Untitled Aristocracy of Great Britain and Ireland. By EDWARD WALFORD, M.A., late Scholar of Balliol College, Oxford. Containing Notices of the Descent, Birth, Marriage, Education, &c., of more than 12,000 distinguished Heads of Families in the United Kingdom, their Heirs Apparent or Presumptive, together with a Record of the Patronage at their disposal, the Offices which they hold or have held, their Town Addresses, Country Residences, Clubs, &c. *[In the press.*

*" What would the gossips of old have given for a book which opened to them the recesses of every County Family in the Three Kingdoms? . . This work, however, will serve other purposes besides those of mere curiosity, envy, or malice. It is just the book for the lady of the house to have at hand when making up the County dinner, as it gives exactly that information which punctilious and particular people are so desirous of obtaining—the exact standing of every person in the county. To the business man, 'The County Families' stands in the place of directory and biographical dictionary. The fund of information it affords respecting the Upper Ten Thousand must give it a place in the lawyer's library; and to the money-lender, who is so interested in finding out the difference between a gentleman and a 'gent,' between heirs-at-law and younger sons, Mr. Walford has been a real bene-factor. In this splendid volume he has managed to meet a universal want—one which cannot fail to be felt by the lady in her drawing-room, the peer in his library, the tradesman in his counting-house, and the gentleman in his club."—*TIMES.

Large crown 8vo, cloth antique, with Illustrations, 7s. 6d.

Walton and Cotton's Complete Angler;

or, The Contemplative Man's Recreation ; being a Discourse of Rivers, Fishponds, Fish and Fishing, written by IZAAK WALTON ; and Instructions how to Angle for a Trout or Grayling in a clear Stream, by CHARLES COTTON. With Original Memoirs and Notes by Sir HARRIS NICOLAS, and 61 Copperplate Illustrations.

Carefully printed on paper to imitate the Original, 22 in. by 14 in., 2s.

Warrant to Execute Charles I.

An exact Facsimile of this important Document, with the Fifty-nine Signatures of the Regicides, and corresponding Seals.

Beautifully printed on paper to imitate the Original MS., price 2s.

Warrant to Execute Mary Queen of Scots.

An exact Facsimile, including the Signature of Queen Elizabeth, and a Facsimile of the Great Seal.

Crown 8vo, cloth limp, with numerous Illustrations, 4s. 6d.

Westropp's Handbook of Pottery and Porce-

lain ; or, History of those Arts from the Earliest Period. By HODDER M. WESTROPP, Author of "Handbook of Archæology," &c. With numerous beautiful Illustrations, and a List of Marks.   [*In the press.*

SEVENTH EDITION.   Square 8vo, 1s.

Whistler v. Ruskin: Art and Art Critics.

By J. A. MACNEILL WHISTLER.

Crown 8vo, cloth extra, with Illustrations, 7s. 6d.

Wright's Caricature History of the Georges.

(The House of Hanover.) With 400 Pictures, Caricatures, Squibs, Broadsides, Window Pictures, &c. By THOMAS WRIGHT, Esq., M.A., F.S.A.

Large post 8vo, cloth extra, gilt, with Illustrations, 7s. 6d.

Wright's History of Caricature and of the

Grotesque in Art, Literature, Sculpture, and Painting, from the Earliest Times to the Present Day. By THOMAS WRIGHT, M.A., F.S.A. Profusely Illustrated by F. W. FAIRHOLT, F.S.A.

J. OGDEN AND CO., PRINTERS, 172, ST. JOHN STREET, E.C.